Selected Tales

To David,
with all my
Love
from the last 50p bohemian
Paula
xp

Selected Tales from Conrad

Edited with an
Introduction and Commentary by

NIGEL STEWART

FABER AND FABER
3 Queen Square
London

*First published in 1977
by Faber and Faber Limited
3 Queen Square London WC1
Printed in Great Britain by
Latimer Trend & Company Ltd Plymouth*

All rights reserved

ISBN 0 571 10763 X

© *Nigel Stewart 1977*

CONDITIONS OF SALE
This book is sold subject to the condition that it shall not, by way of trade or otherwise, be lent, re-sold, hired out or otherwise circulated without the publisher's prior consent in any form of binding or cover other that than in which it is published and without a similar condition including this condition being imposed on the subsequent purchaser

Contents

Introduction	*page* 7
An Outpost of Progress	14
Commentary on 'An Outpost of Progress'	43
Karain: A Memory	46
Commentary on 'Karain: A Memory'	92
The Secret Sharer	96
Commentary on 'The Secret Sharer'	143
The Planter of Malata	147
Commentary on 'The Planter of Malata'	221

Introduction

Jósef Teodor Konrad was born in Poland in 1857, the only son of Apollo and Evelina Nalecz Korzeniowski. Poland at this time was partitioned and Joseph's father played a leading role in the revolutionary movement against Russia, the dominant partitioning power. As a result of these activities he was exiled to Siberia, which broke his health and led to his early death in 1869. Evelina, who had voluntarily joined him in exile, had died four years previously. Apollo was also a literary scholar who had translated Shakespeare and Victor Hugo into Polish, so Joseph's earliest years were spent in a house full of books and he was reading Dickens, Scott and Thackeray in French or Polish translations by the time he was ten. After his father's death, Joseph came under the guardianship of Thaddeus Bobrowski, his mother's brother. This uncle appointed a tutor, and it was on a walking tour with this young man in Switzerland in 1873 that Joseph, now aged fifteen, declared his determination to go to sea. In *A Personal Record* Conrad describes how a chance meeting with a Scots engineer working on the St. Gothard tunnel confirmed him in his determination. He goes on, 'Eleven years later I stood on the steps of St. Katherine's Dockhouse, a Master in the British Merchant Service.'

Only a complete biography can do full justice to those eleven years. They started in Marseilles with casual sea-

Introduction

going jobs along the coast and a voyage to the West Indies during which Conrad, now seventeen, met Dominic Cervoni, a Corsican adventurer and model for the heroes of three of his novels. Together they were involved in gun-running in Spain, and Conrad had a brief but passionate affair with a wealthy Spanish beauty, Doña Rita, who was actively supporting the Carlist Pretender to the throne. She broke off the affair and Conrad in a fit of depression attempted suicide by shooting himself in the chest. A contributory factor may have been the loss of a considerable sum of money gambling at Monte Carlo and some stern rebukes from his uncle Thaddeus who had been keeping him in funds from Poland. Fortunately the bullet just missed the heart and the wound was later explained away as the result of a duel. On 24 April 1878 Conrad embarked on an English steamer, the *Mavis*, which brought him to Lowestoft via Constantinople; he had taken a momentous step almost without noticing it.

Conrad's first introduction to the British Merchant Service, and his first full introduction to the English language, were six brief voyages up to Newcastle in a small coaster. These were followed by a return trip to Sydney as an ordinary seaman of a wool clipper, the *Duke of Sutherland*; he celebrated his twenty-first birthday on the outward leg. Despite thoughts about returning to the Mediterranean, or even leaving the sea altogether, Conrad passed his Second Mate's exam in June 1880 and two months later made his first voyage as an officer. This was also to Australia on a wool clipper, the *Loch Etive*, and in an essay entitled 'Initiation' in *The Mirror of the Sea* Conrad recalls the impact of this voyage during which the ship helped to rescue a Danish crew in mid Atlantic. The principal events of the next three years were: the experience so vividly recalled in his story *Youth* of shipwreck at sea and the first sight of the East from an open boat; a second voyage to India returning in the *Narcissus*, an experience which was to result in his

Introduction

third novel, *The Nigger of the Narcissus*; and finally, the passing of his First Mate's exam at the end of 1884.

After a further voyage to Singapore and India in 1885, during which he wrote his first recorded letter in English, Conrad became a naturalized British subject in August 1886 and gained his Master's Certificate in November. The next two years were to be vital in his Eastern experience. A voyage, still as First Mate, to Java early in 1887 was followed by a three-month illness in Singapore and then a fascinating five months as Mate of a small steamship, the *Vidar*, making several brief voyages in the Malay Archipelago. During this time he became familiar with such romantic-sounding places as Banjermassim, Bulungan and Cotic Berouw, and in the last met Olmeijer who was to become the hero of his first novel, *Almayer's Folly*. His second novel, *An Outcast of the Islands*, and several of his tales, including *Karain* (1897) and *The Planter of Malata* (1914), illustrate the lasting appeal this area had for Conrad. 'I have known,' he wrote, 'its fascination since. I have seen the mysterious shores, the still water, the lands of brown nations, where a stealthy Nemesis lies in wait, pursues, overtakes so many of the conquering race, who are proud of their wisdom, of their knowledge, of their strength.' Many of Conrad's heroes fall victim to this stealthy Goddess of Retribution that lies in wait to destroy those who are so dependent on Western social structures and morality that they cannot survive in isolation.

The circumstances in which Conrad got his first command were highly dramatic; he inherited the barque *Otago* and her ailing crew from a dead Captain at Bangkok in January 1888. The first harrowing weeks of this experience are recalled in *The Shadow Line*, and the third tale in this collection, *The Secret Sharer*, draws on this same experience of being 'a stranger to the ship and somewhat a stranger to myself.' Conrad's habitual interest in the predicament of man's loneliness and isolation is here combined with a return to

Introduction

the theme of fidelity and betrayal which had formed the central conflict in *Karain*. Most critics agree that *The Secret Sharer* is the greatest of all Conrad's tales, but they do not all agree on its interpretation. He took the *Otago* to Sydney, Mauritius and back to Australia again before resigning the command early in 1889. A few months after resigning his command Conrad started to write *Almayer's Folly* but the novel was not to be finished for six years. Work on it was to be interrupted, almost before he had started, by his harrowing experiences in the Congo.

At the end of April 1890, some months after first enquiring in Brussels about a job with the *Société Anonyme pour le Commerce du Haut-Congo*, Conrad was offered command of one of the Company's river-steamers. The previous Captain had been killed by natives; Conrad's second command was to begin as inauspiciously as his first. In *Heart of Darkness*, a story that powerfully conveys the debilitating effects, both physical and psychological, of the Congo expedition, Conrad describes how sailing down the coast of Africa they passed a French warship. 'It appears the French had one of their wars going on thereabouts. Her ensign dropped limp like a rag; the muzzles of the long six-inch guns stuck out all over the low hull; the greasy, slimy swell swung her up lazily and let her down, swaying her thin masts. In the empty immensity of earth, sky and water, there she was, incomprehensible, firing into a continent.' Conrad was to find much else that was incomprehensible in the next four months. At Matadi, forty miles up the Congo, and the highest navigable point, he saw the full effect of 'the vilest scramble for loot that ever disfigured the history of human conscience and geographical exploration', as he watched the exhausted remnants of an African chain-gang crawl away to die. On the two-hundred-mile trek to the Company's outpost at Kinshasa, Conrad kept a diary and noted: 'Met an officer of the State inspecting. A few minutes afterwards saw at a camping place the dead

Introduction

body of a Backongo. Shot? Horrid smell.' Like the longer *Heart of Darkness*, the first story in this selection, *An Outpost of Progress*, reveals the results of the human degradation Conrad witnessed here. It also ironically exposes the gulf between the ideals man so often preaches and the selfishness he too frequently practises. The steamer Conrad was to command turned out to have been badly damaged and was undergoing repair, and after journeying with the Assistant-Director of the Company to an up-river outpost to collect a dying agent, Conrad quarrelled with the Company, fell ill and hastened back to England.

After returning to England, during the first half of 1891 Conrad had several periods of illness and depression which can be directly attributed to his Congo experiences. By the autumn he was sufficiently recovered to accept his last real job in the Merchant Marine; he signed as First Mate on the *Torrens*, one of the most celebrated of the old clippers, and made a return journey to Australia during which he worked on the manuscript of *Almayer's Folly* and possibly discussed it with a passenger called John Galsworthy. But it was another two years before it was submitted to Edward Garnett, a young publisher's reader who, like Galsworthy, was to become a lifelong friend and supporter. It was finally published in 1895 and in the following year Conrad married Jessie George, the daughter of a London bookseller, and published his second novel, *An Outcast of the Islands*. By the turn of the century, having also published *The Nigger of the Narcissus*, *Lord Jim*, *Heart of Darkness*, and six other tales, Conrad was winning a wide circle of literary friends which included H. G. Wells, R. B. Cunninghame Graham, Henry James and Stephen Crane. Unfortunately it took the general reading public some time to realize that Joseph Conrad deserved to rank with such men; his books sold slowly and the writing of them became more and more burdensome as they became longer and more ambitious. The peculiar

Introduction

problems Conrad had to face in writing in a language that was not his own are perhaps too frequently forgotten or too easily overlooked. At the time of writing his first novel he can have had little opportunity to develop his English through conversation with educated people. Edward Garnett wrote in a letter: 'When he read aloud to me some new written MS pages of *An Outcast of the Islands* he mispronounced so many words that I followed him with difficulty. I found then that he had never once heard these English words spoken, but had learned them all from books!' *Nostromo*, his greatest novel, received little critical notice when published in 1904, and despite the publication of his two masterly political novels, *The Secret Agent* (1906) and *Under Western Eyes* (1910), he had to wait until 1913 and the publication of a slighter novel, *Chance*, before he became a best seller. *Victory*, perhaps his second most impressive novel, was published in the following year and his literary fame grew rapidly at last. By 1923, the year in which his last full novel, *The Rover*, was published, he had achieved such eminence that his manuscripts fetched £4,000 in a New York sale.

Joseph Conrad died on 3 August 1924 and the lines from Spenser which he had chosen as epigraph to *The Rover* were inscribed on his tomb:

Sleep after toyle, port after stormie seas,
Ease after warre, death after life, does greatly please.

The blend of nautical and literary is particularly appropriate; so too is the suggestion of calm after the violent conflicts of life. Just after writing the first two tales in this collection, Conrad wrote the *Preface to The Nigger of the Narcissus* in which he said: 'My task which I am trying to achieve is by the power of the written word to make you hear, to make you feel—it is, before all, to make you *see*. . . . When it is accomplished—behold!—all the truth of life is there: a

Introduction

moment of vision, a sigh, a smile—and the return to an eternal rest.' Conrad accomplished his task by creating vivid and dramatic settings and then introducing into them complex characters at a point of crisis in their lives. In this way he formulated some of the questions to which we all want to know the answers. In what can we believe? Is man a free agent? What qualities do we require to survive loneliness and isolation? We move towards some possible answers in these tales as we see that human solidarity and fidelity to a code of conduct can give some protection against isolation; betrayal and guilt inevitably provoke retribution; some illusions save rather than destroy. 'Those who read me,' Conrad wrote in *A Personal Record*, 'know my conviction that the world, the temporal world, rests on a few very simple ideas; so simple that they must be as old as the hills. It rests notably, among others, on the idea of Fidelity.'

The four tales printed here have been chosen as outstanding in themselves and as constituting a good introduction to the settings, themes and techniques used in the major novels. *An Outpost of Progress* and *Karain* come from Conrad's first published collection, *Tales of Unrest* (1898), and were written while the impact of his experiences in the East and the Congo was still fresh. *The Secret Sharer* was written in 1909 when his literary powers were at their peak. *The Planter of Malata* comes from the last collection published in Conrad's lifetime, *Within the Tides* (1915), and reveals a late return to the East and to one of his most familiar themes: the dangers of solitude and isolation.

An Outpost of Progress

I

There were two white men in charge of the trading station. Kayerts, the chief, was short and fat; Carlier, the assistant, was tall, with a large head and a very broad trunk perched upon a long pair of thin legs. The third man on the staff was a Sierra Leone Nigger, who maintained that his name was Henry Price. However, for some reason or other, the natives down the river had given him the name of Makola, and it stuck to him through all his wanderings about the country. He spoke English and French with a warbling accent, wrote a beautiful hand, understood bookkeeping, and cherished in his innermost heart the worship of evil spirits. His wife was a Negress from Loanda, very large and very noisy. Three children rolled about in sunshine before the door of his low, shed-like dwelling. Makola, taciturn and impenetrable, despised the two white men. He had charge of a small clay storehouse with a dried-grass roof, and pretended to keep a correct account of beads, cotton cloth, red kerchiefs, brass wire, and other trade goods it contained. Besides the storehouse and Makola's hut, there was only one large building in the cleared ground of the station. It was built neatly of reeds, with a verandah on all the four sides. There were three rooms in it. The one in the middle was the living-room, and had two rough tables and a few stools in it. The other two were the bedrooms for the white men. Each had a bedstead and a mosquito net for all furniture. The plank floor was

An Outpost of Progress

littered with the belongings of the white men; open half-empty boxes, town wearing apparel, old boots; all the things dirty, and all the things broken, that accumulate mysteriously round untidy men. There was also another dwelling-place some distance away from the buildings. In it, under a tall cross much out of the perpendicular, slept the man who had seen the beginning of all this; who had planned and had watched the construction of this outpost of progress. He had been, at home, an unsuccessful painter who, weary of pursuing fame on an empty stomach, had gone out there through high protections. He had been the first chief of that station. Makola had watched the energetic artist die of fever in the just finished house with his usual kind of "I told you so" indifference. Then, for a time, he dwelt alone with his family, his account books, and the Evil Spirit that rules the lands under the equator. He got on very well with his god. Perhaps he had propitiated him by a promise of more white men to play with, by and by. At any rate the director of the Great Trading Company, coming up in a steamer that resembled an enormous sardine box with a flat-roofed shed erected on it, found the station in good order, and Makola as usual quietly diligent. The director had the cross put up over the first agent's grave, and appointed Kayerts to the post. Carlier was told off as second in charge. The director was a man ruthless and efficient, who at times, but very imperceptibly, indulged in grim humour. He made a speech to Kayerts and Carlier, pointing out to them the promising aspect of their station. The nearest trading-post was about three hundred miles away. It was an exceptional opportunity for them to distinguish themselves and to earn percentages on the trade. This appointment was a favour done to beginners. Kayerts was moved almost to tears by his director's kindness. He would, he said, by doing his best, try to justify the flattering confidence, etc., etc. Kayerts had been in the Administration of the Telegraphs, and knew how

An Outpost of Progress

to express himself correctly. Carlier, an ex-non-commissioned officer of cavalry in an army guaranteed from harm by several European Powers, was less impressed. If there were commissions to get, so much the better; and, trailing a sulky glance over the river, the forests, the impenetrable bush that seemed to cut off the station from the rest of the world, he muttered between his teeth, "We shall see, very soon."

Next day, some bales of cotton goods and a few cases of provisions having been thrown on shore, the sardine-box steamer went off, not to return for another six months. On the deck the director touched his cap to the two agents, who stood on the bank waving their hats, and turning to an old servant of the Company on his passage to headquarters, said, "Look at those two imbeciles. They must be mad at home to send me such specimens. I told those fellows to plant a vegetable garden, build new storehouses and fences, and construct a landing-stage. I bet nothing will be done! They won't know how to begin. I always thought the station on this river useless, and they just fit the station!"

"They will form themselves there," said the old stager with a quiet smile.

"At any rate, I am rid of them for six months," retorted the director.

The two men watched the steamer round the bend, then, ascending arm in arm the slope of the bank, returned to the station. They had been in this vast and dark country only a very short time, and as yet always in the midst of other white men, under the eye and guidance of their superiors. And now dull as they were to the subtle influences of surroundings, they felt themselves very much alone, when suddenly left unassisted to face the wilderness; a wilderness rendered more strange, more incomprehensible by the mysterious glimpses of the vigorous life it contained. They were two perfectly insignificant and incapable individuals,

An Outpost of Progress

whose existence is only rendered possible through the high organization of civilized crowds. Few men realize that their life, the very essence of their character, their capabilities and their audacities, are only the expression of their belief in the safety of their surroundings. The courage, the composure, the confidence; the emotions and principles; every great and every insignificant thought belongs not to the individual but to the crowd: to the crowd that believes blindly in the irresistible force of its institutions and of its morals, in the power of its police and of its opinion. But the contact with pure unmitigated savagery, with primitive nature and primitive man, brings sudden and profound trouble into the heart. To the sentiment of being alone of one's kind, to the clear perception of the loneliness of one's thoughts, of one's sensations—to the negation of the habitual, which is safe, there is added the affirmation of the unusual, which is dangerous; a suggestion of things vague, uncontrollable and repulsive, whose discomposing intrusion excites the imagination and tries the civilized nerves of the foolish and the wise alike.

Kayerts and Carlier walked arm in arm, drawing close to one another as children do in the dark; and they had the same, not altogether unpleasant, sense of danger which one half suspects to be imaginary. They chatted persistently in familiar tones. "Our station is prettily situated," said one. The other assented with enthusiasm, enlarging volubly on the beauties of the situation. Then they passed near the grave. "Poor devil!" said Kayerts. "He died of fever, didn't he?" muttered Carlier, stopping short. "Why," retorted Kayerts, with indignation, "I've been told that the fellow exposed himself recklessly to the sun. The climate here, everybody says, is not at all worse than at home, as long as you keep out of the sun. Do you hear that, Carlier? I am chief here, and my orders are that you should not expose yourself to the sun!" He assumed his superiority jocularly, but his meaning was serious. The idea that he would, per-

An Outpost of Progress

haps, have to bury Carlier and remain alone, gave him an inward shiver. He felt suddenly that this Carlier was more precious to him here, in the centre of Africa, than a brother could be anywhere else. Carlier, entering into the spirit of the thing, made a military salute and answered in a brisk tone, "Your orders shall be attended to, chief!" Then he burst out laughing, slapped Kayerts on the back and shouted, "We shall let life run easily here! Just sit still and gather in the ivory those savages will bring. This country has its good points, after all!" They both laughed loudly while Carlier thought: That poor Kayerts; he is so fat and unhealthy. It would be awful if I had to bury him here. He is a man I respect. . . . Before they reached the verandah of their house they called one another "my dear fellow".

The first day they were very active, pottering about with hammers and nails and red calico, to put up curtains, make their house habitable and pretty; resolved to settle down comfortably to their new life. For them an impossible task. To grapple effectually with even purely material problems requires more serenity of mind and more lofty courage than people generally imagine. No two beings could have been more unfitted for such a struggle. Society, not from any tenderness, but because of its strange needs, had taken care of those two men, forbidding them all independent thought, all initiative, all departure from routine; and forbidding it under pain of death. They could only live on condition of being machines. And now, released from the fostering care of men with pens behind the ears, or of men with gold lace on the sleeves, they were like those lifelong prisoners who, liberated after many years, do not know what use to make of their freedom. They did not know what use to make of their faculties, being both, through want of practice, incapable of independent thought.

At the end of two months Kayerts often would say, "If it was not for my Melie, you wouldn't catch me here." Melie

An Outpost of Progress

was his daughter. He had thrown up his post in the Administration of the Telegraphs, though he had been for seventeen years perfectly happy there, to earn a dowry for his girl. His wife was dead, and the child was being brought up by his sisters. He regretted the streets, the pavements, the cafés, his friends of many years; all the things he used to see, day after day; all the thoughts suggested by familiar things—the thoughts effortless, monotonous, and soothing of a Government clerk; he regretted all the gossip, the small enmities, the mild venom, and the little jokes of Government offices. "If I had had a decent brother-in-law," Carlier would remark, "a fellow with a heart, I would not be here." He had left the army and had made himself so obnoxious to his family by his laziness and impudence, that an exasperated brother-in-law had made superhuman efforts to procure him an appointment in the Company as a second-class agent. Having not a penny in the world he was compelled to accept this means of livelihood as soon as it became quite clear to him that there was nothing more to squeeze out of his relations. He, like Kayerts, regretted his old life. He regretted the clink of sabre and spurs on a fine afternoon, the barrack-room witticisms, the girls of garrison towns; but, besides, he had also a sense of grievance. He was evidently a much ill-used man. This made him moody at times. But the two men got on well together in the fellowship of their stupidity and laziness. Together they did nothing, absolutely nothing and enjoyed the sense of idleness for which they were paid. And in time they came to feel something resembling affection for one another.

They lived like blind men in a large room, aware only of what came in contact with them (and of that only imperfectly), but unable to see the general aspect of things. The river, the forest, all the great land throbbing with life, were like a great emptiness. Even the brilliant sunshine disclosed nothing intelligible. Things appeared and disappeared before

An Outpost of Progress

their eyes in an unconnected and aimless kind of way. The river seemed to come from nowhere and flow nowhither. It flowed through a void. Out of that void, at times, came canoes, and men with spears in their hands would suddenly crowd the yard of the station. They were naked, glossy black, ornamented with snowy shells and glistening brass wire, perfect of limb. They made an uncouth babbling noise when they spoke, moved in a stately manner, and sent quick, wild glances out of their startled, never-resting eyes. Those warriors would squat in long rows, four or more deep, before the verandah, while their chiefs bargained for hours with Makola over an elephant tusk. Kayerts sat on his chair and looked down on the proceedings, understanding nothing. He stared at them with his round blue eyes, called out to Carlier, "Here, look! look at that fellow there—and that other one, to the left. Did you ever see such a face? Oh, the funny brute!"

Carlier, smoking native tobacco in a short wooden pipe, would swagger up twirling his moustaches, and surveying the warriors with haughty indulgence, would say—

"Fine animals. Brought any bone? Yes? It's not any too soon. Look at the muscles of that fellow—third from the end. I wouldn't care to get a punch on the nose from him. Fine arms, but legs no good below the knee. Couldn't make cavalry men of them." And after glancing down complacently at his own shanks, he always concluded: "Pah! Don't they stink! You, Makola! Take that herd over to the fetish" (the storehouse was in every station called the fetish, perhaps because of the spirit of civilization it contained) "and give them up some of the rubbish you keep there. I'd rather see it full of bone than full of rags."

Kayerts approved.

"Yes, yes! Go and finish that palaver over there, Mr. Makola. I will come round when you are ready, to weigh the tusk. We must be careful." Then turning to his com-

An Outpost of Progress

panion: "This is the tribe that lives down the river; they are rather aromatic. I remember, they had been once before here. D'ye hear that row? What a fellow has got to put up with in this dog of a country! My head is split."

Such profitable visits were rare. For days the two pioneers of trade and progress would look on their empty courtyard in the vibrating brilliance of vertical sunshine. Below the high bank, the silent river flowed on glittering and steady. On the sands in the middle of the stream, hippos and alligators sunned themselves side by side. And stretching away in all directions, surrounding the insignificant cleared spot of the trading post, immense forests, hiding fateful complications of fantastic life, lay in the eloquent silence of mute greatness. The two men understood nothing, cared for nothing but for the passage of days that separated them from the steamer's return. Their predecessor had left some torn books. They took up these wrecks of novels, and, as they had never read anything of the kind before, they were surprised and amused. Then during long days there were interminable and silly discussions about plots and personages. In the centre of Africa they made acquaintance of Richelieu and of d'Artagnan, of Hawk's Eye and of Father Goriot, and of many other people. All these imaginary personages became subjects for gossip as if they had been living friends. They discounted their virtues, suspected their motives, decried their successes; were scandalized at their duplicity or were doubtful about their courage. The accounts of crimes filled them with indignation, while tender or pathetic passages moved them deeply. Carlier cleared his throat and said in a soldierly voice, "What nonsense!" Kayerts, his round eyes suffused with tears, his fat cheeks quivering, rubbed his bald head, and declared, "This is a splendid book. I had no idea there were such clever fellows in the world." They also found some old copies of a home paper. That print discussed what it was pleased to call "Our

An Outpost of Progress

Colonial Expansion" in high-flown language. It spoke much of the rights and duties of civilization, of the sacredness of the civilizing work, and extolled the merits of those who went about bringing light, and faith and commerce to the dark places of the earth. Carlier and Kayerts read, wondered, and began to think better of themselves. Carlier said one evening, waving his hand about, "In a hundred years, there will be perhaps a town here. Quays, and warehouses, and barracks, and—and—billiard-rooms. Civilization, my boy, and virtue—and all. And then, chaps will read that two good fellows, Kayerts and Carlier, were the first civilized men to live in this very spot!" Kayerts nodded, "Yes, it is a consolation to think of that." They seemed to forget their dead predecessor; but, early one day, Carlier went out and replanted the cross firmly. "It used to make me squint whenever I walked that way," he explained to Kayerts over the morning coffee. "It made me squint, leaning over so much. So I just planted it upright. And solid, I promise you! I suspended myself with both hands to the cross-piece. Not a move. Oh, I did that properly."

At times Gobila came to see them. Gobila was the chief of the neighbouring villages. He was a gray-headed savage, thin and black, with a white cloth round his loins and a mangy panther skin hanging over his back. He came up with long strides of his skeleton legs, swinging a staff as tall as himself, and, entering the common room of the station, would squat on his heels to the left of the door. There he sat, watching Kayerts, and now and then making a speech which the other did not understand. Kayerts, without interrupting his occupation, would from time to time say in a friendly manner: "How goes it, you old image?" and they would smile at one another. The two whites had a liking for that old and incomprehensible creature, and called him Father Gobila. Gobila's manner was paternal, and he seemed really to love all white men. They all appeared to him very young,

An Outpost of Progress

indistinguishably alike (except for stature), and he knew that they were all brothers, and also immortal. The death of the artist, who was the first white man whom he knew intimately, did not disturb this belief, because he was firmly convinced that the white stranger had pretended to die and got himself buried for some mysterious purpose of his own, into which it was useless to inquire. Perhaps it was his way of going home to his own country? At any rate, these were his brothers, and he transferred his absurd affection to them. They returned it in a way. Carlier slapped him on the back, and recklessly struck off matches for his amusement. Kayerts was always ready to let him have a sniff at the ammonia bottle. In short, they behaved just like that other white creature that had hidden itself in a hole in the ground. Gobila considered them attentively. Perhaps they were the same being with the other —or one of them was. He couldn't decide—clear up that mystery; but he remained always very friendly. In consequence of that friendship the women of Gobila's village walked in single file through the reedy grass, bringing every morning to the station, fowls, and sweet potatoes, and palm wine, and sometimes a goat. The Company never provisions the stations fully, and the agents required those local supplies to live. They had them through the good-will of Gobila, and lived well. Now and then one of them had a bout of fever, and the other nursed him with gentle devotion. They did not think much of it. It left them weaker, and their appearance changed for the worse. Carlier was hollow-eyed and irritable. Kayerts showed a drawn, flabby face above the rotundity of his stomach, which gave him a weird aspect. But being constantly together, they did not notice the change that took place gradually in their appearance, and also in their dispositions.

Five months passed in that way.

Then, one morning, as Kayerts and Carlier, lounging in their chairs under the verandah, talked about the approach-

An Outpost of Progress

ing visit of the steamer, a knot of armed men came out of the forest and advanced towards the station. They were strangers to that part of the country. They were tall, slight, draped classically from neck to heel in blue fringed cloths, and carried percussion muskets over their bare right shoulders. Makola showed signs of excitement, and ran out of the storehouse (where he spent all his days) to meet these visitors. They came into the courtyard and looked about them with steady, scornful glances. Their leader, a powerful and determined-looking negro with bloodshot eyes, stood in front of the verandah and made a long speech. He gesticulated much, and ceased very suddenly.

There was something in his intonation, in the sounds of the long sentences he used, that startled the two whites. It was like a reminiscence of something not exactly familiar, and yet resembling the speech of civilized men. It sounded like one of those impossible languages which sometimes we hear in our dreams.

"What lingo is that?" said the amazed Carlier. "In the first moment I fancied the fellow was going to speak French. Anyway, it is a different kind of gibberish to what we ever heard."

"Yes," replied Kayerts. "Hey, Makola, what does he say? Where do they come from? Who are they?"

But Makola, who seemed to be standing on hot bricks, answered hurriedly, "I don't know. They come from very far. Perhaps Mrs. Price will understand. They are perhaps bad men."

The leader, after waiting for a while, said something sharply to Makola, who shook his head. Then the man, after looking round, noticed Makola's hut and walked over there. The next moment Mrs. Makola was heard speaking with great volubility. The other strangers—they were six in all—strolled about with an air of ease, put their heads through the door of the storeroom, congregated round the

An Outpost of Progress

grave, pointed understandingly at the cross, and generally made themselves at home.

"I don't like those chaps—and, I say, Kayerts, they must be from the coast; they've got firearms," observed the sagacious Carlier.

Kayerts also did not like those chaps. They both, for the first time, became aware that they lived in conditions where the unusual may be dangerous, and that there was no power on earth outside of themselves to stand between them and the unusual. They became uneasy, went in and loaded their revolvers. Kayerts said, "We must order Makola to tell them to go away before dark."

The strangers left in the afternoon, after eating a meal prepared for them by Mrs. Makola. The immense woman was excited, and talked much with the visitors. She rattled away shrilly, pointing here and there at the forests and at the river. Makola sat apart and watched. At times he got up and whispered to his wife. He accompanied the strangers across the ravine at the back of the station-ground, and returned slowly looking very thoughtful. When questioned by the white men he was very strange, seemed not to understand, seemed to have forgotten French—seemed to have forgotten how to speak altogether. Kayerts and Carlier agreed that the nigger had had too much palm wine.

There was some talk about keeping a watch in turn, but in the evening everything seemed so quiet and peaceful that they retired as usual. All night they were disturbed by a lot of drumming in the villages. A deep, rapid roll near by would be followed by another far off—then all ceased. Soon short appeals would rattle out here and there, then all mingle together, increase, become vigorous and sustained, would spread out over the forest, roll through the night, unbroken and ceaseless, near and far, as if the whole land had been one immense drum booming out steadily an appeal to heaven. And through the deep and tremendous noise sudden yells that resembled snatches of songs from a madhouse darted shrill and high in discordant jets of sound which seemed to rush far above the earth and drive all peace from under the stars.

Carlier and Kayerts slept badly. They both thought they had heard shots fired during the night—but they could not agree as to the direction. In the morning Makola was gone somewhere. He returned about noon with one of yesterday's strangers, and eluded all Kayerts' attempts to close with him: had become deaf apparently. Kayerts wondered. Carlier, who had been fishing off the bank, came back and remarked while he showed his catch, "The niggers seem to be in a deuce of a stir; I wonder what's up. I saw about fifteen canoes cross the river during the two hours I was there fishing." Kayerts, worried, said, "Isn't this Makola very queer today?" Carlier advised, "Keep all our men together in case of some trouble."

II

There were ten station men who had been left by the Director. Those fellows, having engaged themselves to the Company for six months (without having any idea of a month in particular and only a very faint notion of time in general), had been serving the cause of progress for upwards of two years. Belonging to a tribe from a very distant part of the land of darkness and sorrow, they did not run away, naturally supposing that as wandering strangers they would be killed by the inhabitants of the country; in which they were right. They lived in straw huts on the slope of a ravine overgrown with reedy grass, just behind the station buildings. They were not happy, regretting the festive incantations, the sorceries, the human sacrifices of their own land; where they also had parents, brothers, sisters, admired chiefs, respected magicians, loved friends, and other ties supposed generally

An Outpost of Progress

to be human. Besides, the rice rations served out by the Company did not agree with them, being a food unknown to their land, and to which they could not get used. Consequently they were unhealthy and miserable. Had they been of any other tribe they would have made up their minds to die—for nothing is easier to certain savages than suicide—and so have escaped from the puzzling difficulties of existence. But belonging, as they did, to a warlike tribe with filed teeth, they had more grit, and went on stupidly living through disease and sorrow. They did very little work, and had lost their splendid physique. Carlier and Kayerts doctored them assiduously without being able to bring them back into condition again. They were mustered every morning and told off to different tasks—grass-cutting, fence-building, tree-felling, etc., etc., which no power on earth could induce them to execute efficiently. The two whites had practically very little control over them.

In the afternoon Makola came over to the big house and found Kayerts watching three heavy columns of smoke rising above the forests. "What is that?" asked Kayerts. "Some villages burn." answered Makola, who seemed to have regained his wits. Then he said abruptly: "We have got very little ivory; bad six months' trading. Do you like get a little more ivory?"

"Yes," said Kayerts, eagerly. He thought of percentages which were low.

"Those men who came yesterday are traders from Loanda who have got more ivory than they can carry home. Shall I buy? I know their camp."

"Certainly," said Kayerts. "What are those traders?"

"Bad fellows," said Makola, indifferently. "They fight with people, and catch women and children. They are bad men, and got guns. There is a great disturbance in the country. Do you want ivory?"

"Yes," said Kayerts. Makola said nothing for a while.

An Outpost of Progress

Then: "Those workmen of ours are no good at all," he muttered, looking round. "Station in very bad order, sir. Director will growl. Better get a fine lot of ivory, then he say nothing."

"I can't help it; the men won't work," said Kayerts. "When will you get that ivory?"

"Very soon," said Makola. "Perhaps tonight. You leave it to me, and keep indoors, sir. I think you had better give some palm wine to our men to make a dance this evening. Enjoy themselves. Work better tomorrow. There's plenty palm wine—gone a little sour."

Kayerts said yes, and Makola, with his own hands, carried big calabashes to the door of his hut. They stood there till the evening, and Mrs. Makola looked into every one. The men got them at sunset. When Kayerts and Carlier retired, a big bonfire was flaring before the men's huts. They could hear their shouts and drumming. Some men from Gobila's village had joined the station hands, and the entertainment was a great success.

In the middle of the night, Carlier waking suddenly, heard a man shout loudly; then a shot was fired. Only one. Carlier ran out and met Kayerts on the verandah. They were both startled. As they went across the yard to call Makola, they saw shadows moving in the night. One of them cried, "Don't shoot! It's me, Price." Then Makola appeared close to them. "Go back, go back, please," he urged, "you spoil all." "There are strange men about," said Carlier. "Never mind; I know," said Makola. Then he whispered, "All right. Bring ivory. Say nothing! I know my business." The two white men reluctantly went back to the house, but did not sleep. They heard footsteps, whispers, some groans. It seemed as if a lot of men came in, dumped heavy things on the ground, squabbled a long time, then went away. They lay on their hard beds and thought: "This Makola is invaluable." In the morning Carlier came out, very sleepy, and pulled at the

An Outpost of Progress

cord of the big bell. The station hands mustered every morning to the sound of the bell. That morning nobody came. Kayerts turned out also, yawning. Across the yard they saw Makola come out of his hut, a tin basin of soapy water in his hand. Makola, a civilized nigger, was very neat in his person. He threw the soapsuds skilfully over a wretched little yellow cur he had, then turning his face to the agent's house, he shouted from the distance, "All the men gone last night!"

They heard him plainly, but in their surprise they both yelled out together: "What!" Then they stared at one another. "We are in a proper fix now," growled Carlier. "It's incredible!" muttered Kayerts. "I will go to the huts and see," said Carlier, striding off. Makola coming up found Kayerts standing alone.

"I can hardly believe it," said Kayerts, tearfully. "We took care of them as if they had been our children."

"They went with the coast people," said Makola after a moment of hesitation.

"What do I care with whom they went—the ungrateful brutes!" exlaimed the other. Then with sudden suspicion, and looking hard at Makola, he added: "What do you know about it?"

Makola moved his shoulders, looking down on the ground. "What do I know? I think only. Will you come and look at the ivory I've got there? It is a fine lot. You never saw such."

He moved towards the store. Kayerts followed him mechanically, thinking about the incredible desertion of the men. On the ground before the door of the fetish lay six splendid tusks.

"What did you give for it?" asked Kayerts, after surveying the lot with satisfaction.

"No regular trade," said Makola. "They brought the ivory and gave it to me. I told them to take what they most wanted in the station. It is a beautiful lot. No station can show such tusks. Those traders wanted carriers badly, and

An Outpost of Progress

our men were no good here. No trade, no entry in books; all correct."

Kayerts nearly burst with indignation. "Why!" he shouted, "I believe you have sold our men for these tusks!" Makola stood impassive and silent. "I—I—will—I," stuttered Kayerts. "You fiend!" he yelled out.

"I did the best for you and the Company," said Makola, imperturbably. "Why you shout so much? Look at this tusk."

"I dismiss you! I will report you—I won't look at the tusk. I forbid you to touch them. I order you to throw them into the river. You—you!"

"You very red, Mr. Kayerts. If you are so irritable in the sun, you will get fever and die—like the first chief!" pronounced Makola impressively.

They stood still, contemplating one another with intense eyes, as if they had been looking with effort across immense distances. Kayerts shivered. Makola had meant no more than he said, but his words seemed to Kayerts full of ominous menace! He turned sharply and went away to the house. Makola retired into the bosom of his family; and the tusks, left lying before the store, looked very large and valuable in the sunshine.

Carlier came back on the verandah. "They're all gone, hey?" asked Kayerts from the far end of the common room in a muffled voice. "You did not find anybody?"

"Oh, yes," said Carlier, "I found one of Gobila's people lying dead before the huts—shot through the body. We heard that shot last night."

Kayerts came out quickly. He found his companion staring grimly over the yard at the tusks, away by the store. They both sat in silence for a while. Then Kayerts related his conversation with Makola. Carlier said nothing. At the midday meal they ate very little. They hardly exchanged a word that day. A great silence seemed to lie heavily over the station and press on their lips. Makola did not open the

An Outpost of Progress

store; he spent the day playing with his children. He lay full-length on the mat outside his door, and the youngsters sat on his chest and clambered all over him. It was a touching picture. Mrs. Makola was busy cooking all day as usual. The white men made a somewhat better meal in the evening. Afterwards, Carlier smoking his pipe strolled over to the store; he stood for a long time over the tusks, touched one or two with his foot, even tried to lift the largest one by its small end. He came back to his chief, who had not stirred from the verandah, threw himself in the chair and said—

"I can see it! They were pounced upon while they slept heavily after drinking all that palm wine you've allowed Makola to give them. A put-up job! See? The worst is, some of Gobila's people were there, and got carried off too, no doubt. The least drunk woke up, and got shot for his sobriety. This is a funny country. What will you do now?"

"We can't touch it, of course," said Kayerts.

"Of course not," assented Carlier.

"Slavery is an awful thing," stammered out Kayerts in an unsteady voice.

"Frightful—the sufferings," grunted Carlier with conviction.

They believed their words. Everybody shows a respectful deference to certain sounds that he and his fellows can make. But about feelings people really know nothing. We talk with indignation or enthusiasm; we talk about oppression, cruelty, crime, devotion, self-sacrifice, virtue, and we know nothing real beyond the words. Nobody knows what suffering or sacrifice mean—except, perhaps, the victims of the mysterious purpose of these illusions.

Next morning they saw Makola very busy setting up in the yard the big scales used for weighing ivory. By and by Carlier said: "What's that filthy scoundrel up to?" and lounged out into the yard. Kayerts followed. They stood watching. Makola took no notice. When the balance was

An Outpost of Progress

swung true, he tried to lift a tusk into the scale. It was too heavy. He looked up helplessly without a word, and for a minute they stood round that balance as mute and still as three statues. Suddenly Carlier said: "Catch hold of the other end, Makola—you beast!" and together they swung the tusk up. Kayerts trembled in every limb. He muttered, "I say! O! I say!" and putting his hand in his pocket found there a dirty bit of paper and the stump of a pencil. He turned his back on the others, as if about to do something tricky, and noted stealthily the weights which Carlier shouted out to him with unnecessary loudness. When all was over Makola whispered to himself: "The sun's very strong here for the tusks." Carlier said to Kayerts in a careless tone: "I say, chief, I might just as well give him a lift with this lot into the store."

As they were going back to the house Kayerts observed with a sigh: "It had to be done." And Carlier said: "It's deplorable, but, the men being Company's men the ivory is Company's ivory. We must look after it." "I will report to the Director, of course," said Kayerts. "Of course; let him decide," approved Carlier.

At midday they made a hearty meal. Kayerts sighed from time to time. Whenever they mentioned Makola's name they always added to it an opprobrious epithet. It eased their conscience. Makola gave himself a half-holiday, and bathed his children in the river. No one from Gobila's villages came near the station that day. No one came the next day, and the next, nor for a whole week. Gobila's people might have been dead and buried for any sign of life they gave. But they were only mourning for those they had lost by the witchcraft of white men, who had brought wicked people into their country. The wicked people were gone, but fear remained. Fear always remains. A man may destroy everything within himself, love and hate and belief, and even doubt; but as long as he clings to life he cannot destroy fear: the fear, subtle, indestructible, and terrible, that pervades his being; that

An Outpost of Progress

tinges his thoughts; that lurks in his heart; that watches on his lips the struggle of his last breath. In his fear, the mild old Gobila offered extra human sacrifices to all the Evil Spirits that had taken possession of his white friends. His heart was heavy. Some warriors spoke about burning and killing, but the cautious old savage dissuaded them. Who could foresee the woe those mysterious creatures, if irritated, might bring? They should be left alone. Perhaps in time they would disappear into the earth as the first one had disappeared. His people must keep away from them, and hope for the best.

Kayerts and Carlier did not disappear, but remained above on this earth, that, somehow, they fancied had become bigger and very empty. It was not the absolute and dumb solitude of the post that impressed them so much as an inarticulate feeling that something from within them was gone, something that worked for their safety, and had kept the wilderness from interfering with their hearts. The images of home; the memory of people like them, of men that thought and felt as they used to think and feel, receded into distances made indistinct by the glare of unclouded sunshine. And out of the great silence of the surrounding wilderness, its very hopelessness and savagery seemed to approach them nearer, to draw them gently, to look upon them, to envelop them with a solicitude irresistible, familiar, and disgusting.

Days lengthened into weeks, then into months. Gobila's people drummed and yelled to every new moon, as of yore, but kept away from the station. Makola and Carlier tried once in a canoe to open communications, but were received with a shower of arrows, and had to fly back to the station for dear life. That attempt set the country up and down the river into an uproar that could be very distinctly heard for days. The steamer was late. At first they spoke of delay jauntily, then anxiously, then gloomily. The matter was becoming serious. Stores were running short. Carlier cast his lines

An Outpost of Progress

off the bank, but the river was low, and the fish kept out in the stream. They dared not stroll far away from the station to shoot. Moreover, there was no game in the impenetrable forest. Once Carlier shot a hippo in the river. They had no boat to secure it, and it sank. When it floated up it drifted away, and Gobila's people secured the carcase. It was the occasion for a national holiday, but Carlier had a fit of rage over it and talked about the necessity of exterminating all the niggers before the country could be made habitable. Kayerts mooned about silently; spent hours looking at the portrait of his Melie. It represented a little girl with long bleached tresses and a rather sour face. His legs were much swollen, and he could hardly walk. Carlier, undermined by fever, could not swagger any more, but kept tottering about, still with a devil-may-care air, as became a man who remembered his crack regiment. He had become hoarse, sarcastic, and inclined to say unpleasant things. He called it "being frank with you". They had long ago reckoned their percentages on trade, including in them that last deal of "this infamous Makola". They had also concluded not to say anything about it. Kayerts hesitated at first—was afraid of the Director.

"He has seen worse things done on the quiet," maintained Carlier, with a hoarse laugh. "Trust him! He won't thank you if you blab. He is no better than you or me. Who will talk if we hold our tongues? There is nobody here."

That was the root of the trouble! There was nobody there; and being left there alone with their weakness, they became daily more like a pair of accomplices than like a couple of devoted friends. They had heard nothing from home for eight months. Every evening they said, "Tomorrow we shall see the steamer." But one of the Company's steamers had been wrecked and the Director was busy with the other, relieving very distant and important stations on the main river. He thought that the useless station, and the useless men, could

An Outpost of Progress

wait. Meantime Kayerts and Carlier lived on rice boiled without salt, and cursed the Company, all Africa, and the day they were born. One must have lived on such diet to discover what ghastly trouble the necessity of swallowing one's food may become. There was literally nothing else in the station but rice and coffee; they drank the coffee without sugar. The last fifteen lumps Kayerts had solemnly locked away in his box, together with a half-bottle of Cognac, "in case of sickness", he explained. Carlier approved. "When one is sick," he said, "any little extra like that is cheering."

They waited. Rank grass began to sprout over the courtyard. The bell never rang now. Days passed, silent, exasperating, and slow. When the two men spoke, they snarled; and their silences were bitter, as if tinged by the bitterness of their thoughts.

One day after a lunch of boiled rice, Carlier put down his cup untasted, and said: "Hang it all! Let's have a decent cup of coffee for once. Bring out that sugar, Kayerts!"

"For the sick," muttered Kayerts, without looking up.

"For the sick," mocked Carlier. "Bosh! . . . Well! I am sick."

"You are no more sick than I am, and I go without," said Kayerts in a peaceful tone.

"Come! out with that sugar, you stingy old slave-dealer."

Kayerts looked up quickly. Carlier was smiling with marked insolence. And suddenly it seemed to Kayerts that he had never seen that man before. Who was he? He knew nothing about him. What was he capable of? There was a surprising flash of violent emotion within him, as if in the presence of something undreamt-of, dangerous and final. But he managed to pronounce with composure—

"That joke is in very bad taste. Don't repeat it."

"Joke!" said Carlier, hitching himself forward on his seat. "I am hungry—I am sick—I don't joke! I hate hypocrites. You are a hypocrite. You are a slave-dealer. I am a slave-

An Outpost of Progress

dealer. There's nothing but slave-dealers in this cursed country. I mean to have sugar in my coffee today, anyhow!"

"I forbid you to speak to me in that way," said Kayerts with a fair show of resolution.

"You!—What?" shouted Carlier, jumping up.

Kayerts stood up also. "I am your chief," he began, trying to master the shakiness of his voice.

"What?" yelled the other. "Who's chief? There's no chief here. There's nothing here: there's nothing but you and I. Fetch the sugar—you pot-bellied ass."

"Hold your tongue. Go out of this room," screamed Kayerts. "I dismiss you—you scoundrel!"

Carlier swung a stool. All at once he looked dangerously in earnest. "You flabby, good-for-nothing civilian—take that!" he howled.

Kayerts dropped under the table, and the stool struck the grass inner wall of the room. Then, as Carlier was trying to upset the table, Kayerts in desperation made a blind rush, head low, like a cornered pig would do, and over-turning his friend, bolted along the verandah, and into his room. He locked the door, snatched his revolver, and stood panting. In less than a minute Carlier was kicking at the door furiously, howling, "If you don't bring out that sugar, I will shoot you at sight, like a dog. Now then—one—two—three. You won't? I will show you who's the master."

Kayerts thought the door would fall in, and scrambled through the square hole that served for a window in his room. There was then the whole breadth of the house between them. But the other was apparently not strong enough to break in the door, and Kayerts heard him running round. Then he also began to run laboriously on his swollen legs. He ran as quickly as he could, grasping the revolver, and unable yet to understand what was happening to him. He saw in succession Makola's house, the store, the river, the ravine, and the low bushes; and he saw all those things again as

An Outpost of Progress

he ran for the second time round the house. Then again they flashed past him. That morning he could not have walked a yard without a groan.

And now he ran. He ran fast enough to keep out of sight of the other man.

Then as, weak and desperate, he thought, "Before I finish the next round I shall die," he heard the other man stumble heavily, then stop. He stopped also. He had the back and Carlier the front of the house, as before. He heard him drop into a chair cursing, and suddenly his own legs gave way, and he slid down into a sitting posture with his back to the wall. His mouth was as dry as a cinder, and his face was wet with perspiration—and tears. What was it all about? He thought it must be a horrible illusion; he thought he was dreaming; he thought he was going mad! After a while he collected his senses. What did they quarrel about? That sugar! How absurd! He would give it to him—didn't want it himself. And he began scrambling to his feet with a sudden feeling of security. But before he had fairly stood upright, a common-sense reflection occurred to him and drove him back into despair. He thought: If I give way now to that brute of a soldier, he will begin this horror again tomorrow—and the day after—every day—raise other pretensions, trample on me, torture me, make me his slave—and I will be lost! Lost! The steamer may not come for days—may never come. He shook so that he had to sit down on the floor again. He shivered forlornly. He felt he could not, would not move any more. He was completely distracted by the sudden perception that the position was without issue—that death and life had in a moment become equally difficult and terrible.

All at once he heard the other push his chair back; and he leaped to his feet with extreme facility. He listened and got confused. Must run again! Right or left? He heard footsteps. He darted to the left, grasping his revolver, and at the very same instant, as it seemed to him, they came into violent

An Outpost of Progress

collision. Both shouted with surprise. A loud explosion took place between them; a roar of red fire, thick smoke; and Kayerts, deafened and blinded, rushed back thinking: I am hit—it's all over. He expected the other to come round—to gloat over his agony. He caught hold of an upright of the roof—"All over!" Then he heard a crashing fall on the other side of the house, as if somebody had tumbled headlong over a chair—then silence. Nothing more happened. He did not die. Only his shoulder felt as if it had been badly wrenched, and he had lost his revolver. He was disarmed and helpless! He waited for his fate. The other man made no sound. It was a stratagem. He was stalking him now! Along what side? Perhaps he was taking aim this very minute!

After a few moments of an agony frightful and absurd, he decided to go and meet his doom. He was prepared for every surrender. He turned the corner, steadying himself with one hand on the wall; made a few paces, and nearly swooned. He had seen on the floor, protruding past the other corner, a pair of turned-up feet. A pair of white naked feet in red slippers. He felt deadly sick, and stood for a time in profound darkness. Then Makola appeared before him, saying quietly: "Come along, Mr. Kayerts. He is dead." He burst into tears of gratitude; a loud, sobbing fit of crying. After a time he found himself sitting in a chair and looking at Carlier, who lay stretched on his back. Makola was kneeling over the body.

"Is this your revolver?" asked Makola, getting up.

"Yes," said Kayerts; then he added very quickly, "He ran after me to shoot me—you saw!"

"Yes, I saw," said Makola. "There is only one revolver; where's his?"

"Don't know," whispered Kayerts in a voice that had become suddenly very faint.

"I will go and look for it," said the other, gently. He made the round along the verandah, while Kayerts sat still and

An Outpost of Progress

looked at the corpse. Makola came back empty-handed, stood in deep thought, then stepped quietly into the dead man's room, and came out directly with a revolver, which he held up before Kayerts. Kayerts shut his eyes. Everything was going round. He found life more terrible and difficult than death. He had shot an unarmed man.

After meditating for a while, Makola said softly, pointing at the dead man who lay there with his right eye blown out—

"He died of fever." Kayerts looked at him with a stony stare. "Yes," repeated Makola, thoughtfully, stepping over the corpse, "I think he died of fever. Bury him to-morrow." And he went away slowly to his expectant wife, leaving the two white men alone on the verandah.

Night came, and Kayerts sat unmoving on his chair. He sat quiet as if he had taken a dose of opium. The violence of the emotions he had passed through produced a feeling of exhausted serenity. He had plumbed in one short afternoon the depths of horror and despair, and now found repose in the conviction that life had no more secrets for him: neither had death! He sat by the corpse thinking; thinking very actively, thinking very new thoughts. He seemed to have broken loose from himself altogether. His old thoughts, convictions, likes and dislikes, things he respected and things he abhorred, appeared in their true light at last! Appeared contemptible and childish, false and ridiculous. He revelled in his new wisdom while he sat by the man he had killed. He argued with himself about all things under heaven with that kind of wrong-headed lucidity which may be observed in some lunatics. Incidentally he reflected that the fellow dead there had been a noxious beast anyway; that men died every day in thousands; perhaps in hundreds of thousands—who could tell?—and that in the number, that one death could not possibly make any difference; couldn't have any importance, at least to a thinking creature. He, Kayerts, was a thinking creature. He had been all his life, till that moment, a

An Outpost of Progress

believer in a lot of nonsense like the rest of mankind— who are fools; but now he thought! He knew! He was at peace; he was familiar with the highest wisdom! Then he tried to imagine himself dead, and Carlier sitting in his chair watching him; and his attempt met with such unexpected success, that in a very few moments he became not at all sure who was dead and who was alive. This extraordinary achievement of his fancy startled him, however, and by a clever and timely effort of mind he saved himself just in time from becoming Carlier. His heart thumped, and he felt hot all over at the thought of that danger. Carlier! What a beastly thing! To compose his now disturbed nerves—and no wonder!—he tried to whistle a little. Then, suddenly, he fell asleep, or thought he had slept; but at any rate there was a fog, and somebody had whistled in the fog.

He stood up. The day had come, and a heavy mist had descended upon the land: the mist penetrating, enveloping, and silent; the morning mist of tropical lands; the mist that clings and kills; the mist white and deadly, immaculate and poisonous. He stood up, saw the body, and threw his arms above his head with a cry like that of a man who, waking from a trance, finds himself immured forever in a tomb. "*Help!* . . . *My God!*"

A shriek inhuman, vibrating and sudden, pierced like a sharp dart the white shroud of that land of sorrow. Three short, impatient screeches followed, and then, for a time, the fog-wreaths rolled on, undisturbed, through a formidable silence. Then many more shrieks, rapid and piercing, like the yells of some exasperated and ruthless creature, rent the air. Progress was calling to Kayerts from the river. Progress and civilization and all the virtues. Society was calling to its accomplished child to come, to be taken care of, to be instructed, to be judged, to be condemned; it called him to return to that rubbish heap from which he had wandered away, so that justice could be done.

An Outpost of Progress

Kayerts heard and understood. He stumbled out of the verandah, leaving the other man quite alone for the first time since they had been thrown there together. He groped his way through the fog, calling in his ignorance upon the invisible heaven to undo its work. Makola flitted by in the mist, shouting as he ran—

"Steamer! Steamer! They can't see. They whistle for the station. I go ring the bell. Go down to the landing, sir. I ring."

He disappeared. Kayerts stood still. He looked upwards; the fog rolled low over his head. He looked round like a man who has lost his way; and he saw a dark smudge, a cross-shaped stain, upon the shifting purity of the mist. As he began to stumble towards it, the station bell rang in a tumultuous peal its answer to the impatient clamour of the steamer.

The Managing Director of the Great Civilizing Company (since we know that civilization follows trade) landed first, and incontinently lost sight of the steamer. The fog down by the river was exceedingly dense; above, at the station, the bell rang unceasing and brazen.

The Director shouted loudly to the steamer:

"There is nobody down to meet us; there may be something wrong, though they are ringing. You had better come, too!"

And he began to toil up the steep bank. The captain and the engine-driver of the boat followed behind. As they scrambled up the fog thinned, and they could see their Director a good way ahead. Suddenly they saw him start forward, calling to them over his shoulders—"Run! Run to the house! I've found one of them. Run, look for the other!"

He had found one of them! And even he, the man of varied and startling experience, was somewhat discomposed by the manner of this finding. He stood and fumbled in his

An Outpost of Progress

pockets (for a knife) while he faced Kayerts, who was hanging by a leather strap from the cross. He had evidently climbed the grave, which was high and narrow, and after tying the end of the strap to the arm, had swung himself off. His toes were only a couple of inches above the ground; his arms hung stiffly down; he seemed to be standing rigidly at attention, but with one purple cheek playfully posed on the shoulder. And, irreverently, he was putting out a swollen tongue at his Managing Director.

Commentary on 'An Outpost of Progress'

Conrad's feeling about this story is touched on in a letter to his publisher. After referring to his harrowing experiences in the Congo, he went on: 'All the bitterness of those days, all my puzzled wonder as to the meaning of what I saw—all my indignation at masquerading philanthropy have been with me again while I wrote. The story is simple—there is hardly any description . . . I have divested myself of everything but pity—and some scorn—while putting down the insignificant events that bring on the catastrophe.' His theme is clearly the rapid disintegration of two simple human beings unprepared by civilization for the corroding power of solitude, and incapable of recognizing and resisting the inhuman exploitation that masquerades as philanthropy. To estimate the success with which he conveys this theme we can look more closely at the ways in which he develops the plot, reveals the characters, and evokes the atmosphere of the setting. And first we must study the style to discover who is telling the story and in what tone of voice.

We need look no further than the long first paragraph to discover that the story is being told by an anonymous, omniscient narrator whose tone is decidedly ironic. The main role of irony will always be to highlight the contrast between what might be, and what is; the ideal and the actual. The ruthless director makes a speech to Carlier and Kayerts 'pointing out to them the promising aspects of their station . . . It was an

Commentary on 'An Outpost of Progress'

exceptional opportunity for them to distinguish themselves and to earn percentages on the trade.' Kayerts is then 'moved almost to tears by his director's kindness', and in the next paragraph we hear the director say, 'Look at those two imbeciles... I always thought the station on this river useless, and they just fit the station!' We can find further examples of irony in the introduction of Makola, and in the description of their predecessor's grave. By the time we reach the end of the first paragraph, we can have no doubt that the title of the story is heavily ironical. In general the style is unusually terse and direct for Conrad, but there are several passages of disturbingly abstract reflection in which points already made through action or irony are repeated. An example is the paragraph that links the two men's comments on how 'awful' slavery is with the description of their active participation in Makola's callously casual practice of that trade as they help weigh and store the ivory:

'Slavery is an awful thing,' stammered out Kayerts in an unsteady voice.

'Frightful—the sufferings,' grunted Carlier with conviction.

They believed their words. Everybody shows a respectful deference to certain sounds that he and his fellows can make. But about feelings people really know nothing. We talk with indignation or enthusiasm; we talk about oppression, cruelty, crime, devotion, self-sacrifice, virtue, and we know nothing real beyond the words. Nobody knows what suffering or sacrifice mean—except, perhaps, the victims of the mysterious purpose of these illusions.

Conrad's friend Edward Garnett complained that in this tale human interest is forfeited from the beginning. If this is so, such negative criticism conveyed through the narrator's tone of voice must be partly responsible. Conrad has here succumbed to a technical problem that we shall see him

Commentary on 'An Outpost of Progress'

start to solve in the next story, *Karain*. He needed a narrator who was also an individual actor in the drama.

Carlier and Kayerts live, we are told, 'incapable of independent thought . . . like blind men in a large room.' Their mental and spiritual poverty is further indicated by the desolation of the setting in which we find them. 'The plank floor was littered with the belongings of the white men; open half-empty boxes, town wearing apparel, old boots; all the things dirty, and all the things broken, that accumulate mysteriously round untidy men.' The contrast of the natural African family scene—Makola's large, noisy wife, and his three children happily rolling about in the sunshine—helps to stress how out of place the white men are. But the interest of the story, surely, lies not in the characters, but in the force of the narrator's attack on what they represent. This attack is sustained with unrelenting irony. With this in mind it is interesting to consider their responses to the novels they find and read, or to the group of armed strangers: 'They both, for the first time, became aware that they lived in conditions where the unusual may be dangerous . . .'. The two main characters may indeed have been too shallow and obtuse; it is interesting to see what changes Conrad made when he returned to this theme and setting in *Heart of Darkness*—Kurtz is very much an individual and an intellectual.

SUGGESTIONS FOR FURTHER READING

Heart of Darkness—published in 1899, two years after *An Outpost of Progress*

Joseph Conrad—a critical biography by Jocelyn Baines. Chapter 4, 'Congo Episode', is particularly relevant

The Man Who Would Be King—a short story by Rudyard Kipling with interesting affinities to *An Outpost of Progress*

Karain: A Memory

We knew him in those unprotected days when we were content to hold in our hands our lives and our property. None of us, I believe, has any property now, and I hear that many, negligently, have lost their lives; but I am sure that the few who survive are not yet so dim-eyed as to miss in the befogged respectability of their newspapers the intelligence of various native risings in the Eastern Archipelago. Sunshine gleams between the lines of those short paragraphs—sunshine and the glitter of the sea. A strange name wakes up memories; the printed words scent the smoky atmosphere of today faintly, with the subtle and penetrating perfume as of land breezes breathing through the starlight of bygone nights; a signal fire gleams like a jewel on the high brow of a sombre cliff; great trees, the advanced sentries of immense forests, stand watchful and still over sleeping stretches of open water; a line of white surf thunders on an empty beach, the shallow water foams on the reefs; and green islets scattered through the calm of noonday lie upon the level of a polished sea, like a handful of emeralds on a buckler of steel.

There are faces too—faces dark, truculent, and smiling; the frank audacious faces of men barefooted, well armed and noiseless. They thronged the narrow length of our schooner's decks with their ornamented and barbarous crowd, with the variegated colours of checkered sarongs, red turbans, white jackets, embroideries; with the gleam of scabbards, gold

Karain: A Memory

rings, charms, armlets, lance blades, and jewelled handles of their weapons. They had an independent bearing, resolute eyes, a restrained manner; and we seem yet to hear their soft voices speaking of battles, travels, and escapes; boasting with composure, joking quietly; sometimes in well-bred murmurs extolling their own valour, our generosity; or celebrating with loyal enthusiasm the virtues of their ruler. We remember the faces, the eyes, the voices, we see again the gleam of silk and metal; the murmuring stir of that crowd, brilliant, festive, and martial; and we seem to feel the touch of friendly brown hands that, after one short grasp, return to rest on a chased hilt. They were Karain's people—a devoted following. Their movements hung on his lips; they read their thoughts in his eyes; he murmured to them nonchalantly of life and death, and they accepted his words humbly, like gifts of fate. They were all free men, and when speaking to him said, "Your slave." On his passage voices died out as though he had walked guarded by silence; awed whispers followed him. They called him their warchief. He was the ruler of three villages on a narrow plain; the master of an insignificant foothold on the earth—of a conquered foothold that, shaped like a young moon, lay ignored between the hills and the sea.

From the deck of our schooner, anchored in the middle of the bay, he indicated by a theatrical sweep of his arm along the jagged outline of the hills the whole of his domain; and the ample movement seemed to drive back its limits, augmenting it suddenly into something so immense and vague that for a moment it appeared to be bounded only by the sky. And really, looking at that place, landlocked from the sea and shut off from the land by the precipitous slopes of mountains, it was difficult to believe in the existence of any neighbourhood. It was still, complete, unknown, and full of a life that went on stealthily with a troubling effect of solitude; of a life that seemed unaccountably empty of anything that

Karain: A Memory

would stir the thought, touch the heart, give a hint of the ominous sequence of days. It appeared to us a land without memories, regrets, and hopes; a land where nothing could survive the coming of the night, and where each sunrise, like a dazzling act of special creation, was disconnected from the eve and the morrow.

Karain swept his hand over it. "All mine!" He struck the deck with his long staff; the gold head flashed like a falling star; very close behind him a silent old fellow in a richly embroidered black jacket alone of all the Malays around did not follow the masterful gesture with a look. He did not even lift his eyelids. He bowed his head behind his master, and without stirring held hilt up over his right shoulder a long blade in a silver scabbard. He was there on duty, but without curiosity, and seemed weary, not with age, but with the possession of a burdensome secret of existence. Karain, heavy and proud, had a lofty pose and breathed calmly. It was our first visit, and we looked about curiously.

The bay was like a bottomless pit of intense light. The circular sheet of water reflected a luminous sky, and the shores enclosing it made an opaque ring of earth floating in an emptiness of transparent blue. The hills, purple and arid, stood out heavily on the sky: their summits seemed to fade into a coloured tremble as of ascending vapour; their steep sides were streaked with the green of narrow ravines; at their foot lay rice-fields, plantain-patches, yellow sands. A torrent wound about like a dropped thread. Clumps of fruit-trees marked the villages; slim palms put their nodding heads together above the low houses; dried palm-leaf roofs shone afar, like roofs of gold, behind the dark colonnades of tree-trunks; figures passed vivid and vanishing; the smoke of fires stood upright above the masses of flowering bushes; bamboo fences glittered, running away in broken lines between the fields. A sudden cry on the shore sounded plaintive in the distance and ceased abruptly, as if stifled in the

Karain: A Memory

downpour of sunshine. A puff of breeze made a flash of darkness on the smooth water, touched our faces, and became forgotten. Nothing moved. The sun blazed down into a shadowless hollow of colours and stillness.

It was the stage where, dressed splendidly for his part, he strutted, incomparably dignified, made important by the power he had to awaken an absurd expectation of something heroic going to take place—a burst of action or song—upon the vibrating tone of a wonderful sunshine. He was ornate and disturbing, for one could not imagine what depth of horrible void such an elaborate front could be worthy to hide. He was not masked—there was too much life in him and a mask is only a lifeless thing; but he presented himself essentially as an actor, as a human being aggressively disguised. His smallest acts were prepared and unexpected, his speeches grave, his sentences ominous like hints and complicated like arabesques. He was treated with a solemn respect accorded in the irreverent West only to the monarchs of the stage, and he accepted the profound homage with a sustained dignity seen nowhere else but behind the footlights and in the condensed falseness of some grossly tragic situation. It was almost impossible to remember who he was—only a petty chief of a conveniently isolated corner of Mindanao, where we could in comparative safety break the law against the traffic in firearms and ammunition with the natives. What would happen should one of the moribund Spanish gun-boats be suddenly galvanized into a flicker of active life did not trouble us, once we were inside the bay—so completely did it appear out of the reach of a meddling world; and besides, in those days we were imaginative enough to look with a kind of joyous equanimity on any chance there was of being quietly hanged somewhere out of the way of diplomatic remonstrance. As to Karain, nothing could happen to him unless what happens to all—failure and death; but his quality was to appear clothed in

Karain: A Memory

the illusion of unavoidable success. He seemed too effective, too necessary there, too much of an essential condition for the existence of his land and his people, to be destroyed by anything short of an earthquake. He summed up his race, his country, the elemental force of ardent life, of tropical nature. He had its luxuriant strength, its fascination; and, like it, he carried the seed of peril within.

In many successive visits we came to know his stage well—the purple semicircle of hills, the slim trees leaning over houses, the yellow sands, the streaming green of ravines. All that had the crude and blended colouring, the appropriateness almost excessive, the suspicious immobility of a painted scene; and it enclosed so perfectly the accomplished acting of his amazing pretences that the rest of the world seemed shut out forever from the gorgeous spectacle. There could be nothing outside. It was as if the earth had gone on spinning, and had left that crumb of its surface alone in space. He appeared utterly cut off from everything but the sunshine, and that even seemed to be made for him alone. Once when asked what was on the other side of the hills, he said, with a meaning smile, "Friends and enemies—many enemies; else why should I buy your rifles and powder?" He was always like this—word-perfect in his part, playing up faithfully to the mysteries and certitudes of his surroundings. "Friends and enemies"—nothing else. It was impalpable and vast. The earth had indeed rolled away from under his land, and he, with his handful of people, stood surrounded by a silent tumult as of contending shades. Certainly no sound came from outside. "Friends and enemies!" He might have added, "and memories," at least as far as he himself was concerned; but he neglected to make that point then. It made itself later on, though; but it was after the daily performance—in the wings, so to speak, and with the lights out. Meantime he filled the stage with barbarous dignity. Some ten years ago he had led his people—a scratch lot of wandering Bugis—to

Karain: A Memory

the conquest of the bay, and now in his august care they had forgotten all the past, and had lost all concern for the future. He gave them wisdom, advice, reward, punishment, life or death, with the same serenity of attitude and voice. He understood irrigation and the art of war—the qualities of weapons and the craft of boat-building. He could conceal his heart; had more endurance; he could swim longer, and steer a canoe better than any of his people; he could shoot straighter, and negotiate more tortuously than any man of his race I knew. He was an adventurer of the sea, an outcast, a ruler—and my very good friend. I wish him a quick death in a stand-up fight, a death in sunshine; for he had known remorse and power, and no man can demand more from life. Day after day he appeared before us incomparably faithful to the illusions of the stage, and at sunset the night descended upon him quickly, like a falling curtain. The seamed hills became black shadows towering high upon a clear sky; above them the glittering confusion of stars resembled a mad turmoil stilled by a gesture; sounds ceased, men slept, forms vanished —and the reality of the universe alone remained—a marvellous thing of darkness and glimmers.

II

But it was at night that he talked openly, forgetting the exactions of his stage. In the daytime there were affairs to be discussed in state. There were at first between him and me his own splendour, my shabby suspicions, and the scenic landscape that intruded upon the reality of our lives by its motionless fantasy of outline and colour. His followers thronged round him; above his head the broad blades of their spears made a spiked halo of iron points, and they hedged him from humanity by the shimmer of silks, the gleam of weapons, the excited and respectful hum of eager voices. Before sunset he would take leave with ceremony,

Karain: A Memory

and go off sitting under a red umbrella, and escorted by a score of boats. All the paddles flashed and struck together with a mighty splash that reverberated loudly in the monumental amphitheatre of hills. A broad stream of dazzling foam trailed behind the flotilla. The canoes appeared very black on the white hiss of water; turbaned heads swayed back and forth; a multitude of arms in crimson and yellow rose and fell with one movement; the spearmen upright in the bows of canoes had variegated sarongs and gleaming shoulders like bronze statues; the muttered strophes of the paddlers' song ended periodically in a plaintive shout. They diminished in the distance; the song ceased; they swarmed on the beach in the long shadows of the western hills. The sunlight lingered on the purple crests, and we could see him leading the way to his stockade, a burly bareheaded figure walking far in advance of a straggling *cortège*, and swinging regularly an ebony staff taller than himself. The darkness deepened fast; torches gleamed fitfully, passing behind bushes; a long hail or two trailed in the silence of the evening; and at last the night stretched its smooth veil over the shore, the lights, and the voices.

Then, just as we were thinking of repose, the watchmen of the schooner would hail a splash of paddles away in the starlit gloom of the bay; a voice would respond in cautious tones, and our serang, putting his head down the open skylight, would inform us without surprise, "That Rajah, he coming. He here now." Karain appeared noiselessly in the doorway of the little cabin. He was simplicity itself then; all in white; muffled about his head; for arms only a kriss with a plain buffalo-horn handle, which he would politely conceal within a fold of his sarong before stepping over the threshold. The old sword-bearer's face, the worn-out and mournful face so covered with wrinkles that it seemed to look out through the meshes of a fine dark net, could be seen close above his shoulders. Karain never moved without that attendant, who

Karain: A Memory

stood or squatted close at his back. He had a dislike of an open space behind him. It was more than a dislike—it resembled fear, a nervous preoccupation of what went where he could not see. This, in view of the evident and fierce loyalty that surrounded him, was inexplicable. He was there alone in the midst of devoted men; he was safe from neighbourly ambushes, from fraternal ambitions; and yet more than one of our visitors had assured us that their ruler could not bear to be alone. They said, "Even when he eats and sleeps there is always one on the watch near him who has strength and weapons." There was indeed always one near him, though our informants had no conception of that watcher's strength and weapons, which were both shadowy and terrible. We knew, but only later on, when we had heard the story. Meantime we noticed that, even during the most important interviews, Karain would often give a start, and interrupting his discourse, would sweep his arm back with a sudden movement, to feel whether the old fellow was there. The old fellow, impenetrable and weary, was always there. He shared his food, his repose, and his thoughts; he knew his plans, guarded his secrets; and, impassive behind his master's agitation, without stirring the least bit, murmured above his head in a soothing tone some words difficult to catch.

It was only on board the schooner, when surrounded by white faces, by unfamiliar sights and sounds, that Karain seemed to forget the strange obsession that wound like a black thread through the gorgeous pomp of his public life. At night we treated him in a free and easy manner, which just stopped short of slapping him on the back, for there are liberties one must not take with a Malay. He said himself that on such occasions he was only a private gentleman coming to see other gentlemen whom he supposed as well born as himself. I fancy that to the last he believed us to be emissaries of Government, darkly official persons furthering by our illegal traffic some dark scheme of high statecraft.

Karain: A Memory

Our denials and protestations were unavailing. He only smiled with discreet politeness and inquired about the Queen. Every visit began with that inquiry; he was insatiable of details; he was fascinated by the holder of a sceptre the shadow of which, stretching from the westward over the earth and over the seas, passed far beyond his own hand's-breadth of conquered land. He multiplied questions; he could never know enough of the Monarch of whom he spoke with wonder and chivalrous respect—with a kind of affectionate awe! Afterwards, when we had learned that he was the son of a woman who had many years ago ruled a small Bugis state, we came to suspect that the memory of his mother (of whom he spoke with enthusiasm) mingled somehow in his mind with the image he tried to form for himself of the far-off Queen whom he called Great, Invincible, Pious, and Fortunate. We had to invent details at last to satisfy his craving curiosity; and our loyalty must be pardoned, for we tried to make them fit for his august and resplendent ideal. We talked. The night slipped over us, over the still schooner, over the sleeping land, and over the sleepless sea that thundered amongst the reefs outside the bay. His paddlers, two trustworthy men, slept in the canoe at the foot of our side-ladder. The old confidant, relieved from duty, dozed on his heels, with his back against the companion-doorway; and Karain sat squarely in the ship's wooden armchair, under the slight sway of the cabin lamp, a cheroot between his dark fingers, and a glass of lemonade before him. He was amused by the fizz of the thing, but after a sip or two would let it get flat, and with a courteous wave of his hand ask for a fresh bottle. He decimated our slender stock; but we did not begrudge it to him, for, when he began, he talked well. He must have been a great Bugis dandy in his time, for even then (and when we knew him he was no longer young) his splendour was spotlessly neat, and he dyed his hair a light shade of brown. The quiet dignity of his bearing transformed

Karain: A Memory

the dim-lit cuddy of the schooner into an audience-hall. He talked of inter-island politics with an ironic and melancholy shrewdness. He had travelled much, suffered not a little, intrigued, fought. He knew native Courts, European Settlements, the forest, the sea, and, as he said himself, had spoken in his time to many great men. He liked to talk with me because I had known some of these men: he seemed to think that I could understand him, and, with a fine confidence, assumed that I, at least, could appreciate how much greater he was himself. But he preferred to talk of his native country —a small Bugis state on the island of Celebes. I had visited it some time before, and he asked eagerly for news. As men's names came up in conversation he would say, "We swam against one another when we were boys"; or, "We had hunted the deer together—he could use the noose and the spear as well as I." Now and then his big dreamy eyes would roll restlessly; he frowned or smiled, or he would become pensive and, staring in silence, would nod slightly for a time at some regretted vision of the past.

His mother had been the ruler of a small semi-independent state on the sea-coast at the head of the Gulf of Boni. He spoke of her with pride. She had been a woman resolute in affairs of state and of her own heart. After the death of her first husband, undismayed by the turbulent opposition of the chiefs, she married a rich trader, a Korinchi man of no family. Karain was her son by that second marriage, but his unfortunate descent had apparently nothing to do with his exile. He said nothing as to its cause, though once he let slip with a sigh, "Ha! my land will not feel any more the weight of my body." But he related willingly the story of his wanderings, and told us all about the conquest of the bay. Alluding to the people beyond the hills, he would murmur gently, with a careless wave of the hand, "They came over the hills once to fight us, but those who got away never came again." He thought for a while, smiling to himself. "Very few got away,"

Karain: A Memory

he added, with proud serenity. He cherished the recollections of his successes; he had an exulting eagerness for endeavour; when he talked, his aspect was warlike, chivalrous, and uplifting. No wonder his people admired him. We saw him once walking in daylight amongst the houses of the settlement. At the doors of huts groups of women turned to look after him, warbling softly, and with gleaming eyes; armed men stood out of the way, submissive and erect; others approached from the side, bending their backs to address him humbly; an old woman stretched out a draped lean arm—"Blessings on thy head!" she cried from a dark doorway; a fiery-eyed man showed above the low fence of a plantain-patch a streaming face, a bare breast scarred in two places, and bellowed out pantingly after him, "God give victory to our master!" Karain walked fast, and with firm long strides; he answered greetings right and left by quick piercing glances. Children ran forward between the houses, peeped fearfully round corners; young boys kept up with him, gliding between bushes: their eyes gleamed through the dark leaves. The old sword-bearer, shouldering the silver scabbard, shuffled hastily at his heels with bowed head, and his eyes on the ground. And in the midst of a great stir they passed swift and absorbed, like two men hurrying through a great solitude.

In his council hall he was surrounded by the gravity of armed chiefs, while two long rows of old headmen dressed in cotton stuffs squatted on their heels, with idle arms hanging over their knees. Under the thatch roof supported by smooth columns, of which each one had cost the life of a straight-stemmed young palm, the scent of flowering hedges drifted in warm waves. The sun was sinking. In the open courtyard suppliants walked through the gate, raising, when yet far off, their joined hands above bowed heads, and bending low in the bright stream of sunlight. Young girls, with flowers in their laps, sat under the wide-spreading boughs of

Karain: A Memory

a big tree. The blue smoke of wood fires spread in a thin mist above the high-pitched roofs of houses that had glistening walls of woven reeds and all round them rough wooden pillars under the sloping eaves. He dispensed justice in the shade; from a high seat he gave orders, advice, reproof. Now and then the hum of approbation rose louder, and idle spearmen that lounged listlessly against the posts, looking at the girls, would turn their heads slowly. To no man had been given the shelter of so much respect, confidence, and awe. Yet at times he would lean forward and appear to listen as for a far-off note of discord, as if expecting to hear some faint voice, the sound of light footsteps; or he would start half up in his seat, as though he had been familiarly touched on the shoulder. He glanced back with apprehension; his aged follower whispered inaudibly at his ear; the chiefs turned their eyes away in silence, for the old wizard, the man who could command ghosts and send evil spirits against enemies, was speaking low to their ruler. Around the short stillness of the open place the trees rustled faintly, the soft laughter of girls playing with the flowers rose in clear bursts of joyous sound. At the end of upright spear-shafts the long tufts of dyed horse-hair waved crimson and filmy in the gust of wind; and beyond the blaze of hedges the brook of limpid quick water ran invisible and loud under the drooping grass of the bank, with a great murmur, passionate and gentle.

After sunset, far across the fields and over the bay, clusters of torches could be seen burning under the high roofs of the council shed. Smoky red flames swayed on high poles, and the fiery blaze flickered over faces, clung to the smooth trunks of palm-trees kindled bright sparks on the rims of metal dishes standing on fine floor-mats. That obscure adventurer feasted like a king. Small groups of men crouched in tight circles round the wooden platters; brown hands hovered over snowy heaps of rice. Sitting upon a rough couch apart from the others, he leaned on his elbow with inclined head;

Karain: A Memory

and near him a youth improvised in a high tone a song that celebrated his valour and wisdom. The singer rocked himself to and fro, rolling frenzied eyes; old women hobbled about with dishes and men, squatting low, lifted their heads to listen gravely without ceasing to eat. The song of triumph vibrated in the night, and the stanzas rolled out mournful and fiery like the thoughts of a hermit. He silenced it with a sign, "Enough!" An owl hooted far away, exulting in the delight of deep gloom in dense foliage; overhead lizards ran in the attap thatch, calling softly; the dry leaves of the roof rustled; the rumour of mingled voices grew louder suddenly. After a circular and startled glance, as of a man waking up abruptly to the sense of danger, he would throw himself back, and under the downward gaze of the old sorcerer take up, wide-eyed, the slender thread of his dream. They watched his moods; the swelling rumour of animated talk subsided like a wave on a sloping beach. The chief is pensive. And above the spreading whisper of lowered voices only a light rattle of weapons would be heard, a single louder word distinct and alone, or the grave ring of a big brass tray.

III

For two years at short intervals we visited him. We came to like him, to trust him, almost to admire him. He was plotting and preparing a war with patience, with foresight—with a fidelity to his purpose and with a steadfastness of which I would have thought him racially incapable. He seemed fearless of the future, and in his plans displayed a sagacity that was only limited by his profound ignorance of the rest of the world. We tried to enlighten him, but our attempts to make clear the irresistible nature of the forces which he desired to arrest failed to discourage his eagerness to strike a blow for his own primitive ideas. He did not understand us, and replied by arguments that almost drove one to

Karain: A Memory

desperation by their childish shrewdness. He was absurd and unanswerable. Sometimes we caught glimpses of a sombre, glowing fury within him—a brooding and vague sense of wrong, and a concentrated lust of violence which is dangerous in a native. He raved like one inspired. On one occasion after we had been talking to him late in his campong, he jumped up. A great, clear fire blazed in the grove; lights and shadows danced together between the trees; in the still night bats flitted in and out of the boughs like fluttering flakes of denser darkness. He snatched the sword from the old man, whizzed it out of the scabbard, and thrust the point into the earth. Upon the thin, upright blade the silver hilt, released, swayed before him like something alive. He stepped back a pace, and in a deadened tone spoke fiercely to the vibrating steel: "If there is virtue in the fire, in the iron, in the hand that forged thee, in the words spoken over thee, in the desire of my heart, and in the wisdom of thy makers,—then we shall be victorious together!" He drew it out, looked along the edge. "Take," he said over his shoulder to the old sword-bearer. The other, unmoved on his hams, wiped the point with a corner of his sarong, and returning the weapon to its scabbard, sat nursing it on his knees without a single look upwards. Karain, suddenly very calm, reseated himself with dignity. We gave up remonstrating after this, and let him go his way to an honourable disaster. All we could do for him was to see to it that the powder was good for the money and the rifles serviceable, if old.

But the game was becoming at last too dangerous; and if we, who had faced it pretty often, thought little of the danger, it was decided for us by some very respectable people sitting safely in counting-houses that the risks were too great, and that only one more trip could be made. After giving in the usual way many misleading hints as to our destination, we slipped away quietly, and after a very quick passage entered the bay. It was early morning, and even before the anchor

Karain: A Memory

went to the bottom the schooner was surrounded by boats.

The first thing we heard was that Karain's mysterious sword-bearer had died a few days ago. We did not attach much importance to the news. It was certainly difficult to imagine Karain without his inseparable follower; but the fellow was old, he had never spoken to one of us, we hardly ever had heard the sound of his voice; and we had come to look upon him as upon something inanimate, as a part of our friend's trappings of state—like that sword he had carried, or the fringed red umbrella displayed during an official progress. Karain did not visit us in the afternoon as usual. A message of greeting and a present of fruit and vegetables came off for us before sunset. Our friend paid us like a banker, but treated us like a prince. We sat up for him till midnight. Under the stern awning bearded Jackson jingled an old guitar and sang, with an execrable accent, Spanish love-songs; while young Hollis and I, sprawling on the deck, had a game of chess by the light of a cargo lantern. Karain did not appear. Next day we were busy unloading, and heard that the Rajah was unwell. The expected invitation to visit him ashore did not come. We sent friendly messages, but, fearing to intrude upon some secret council, remained on board. Early on the third day we had landed all the powder and rifles, and also a six-pounder brass gun with its carriage which we had subscribed together for a present for our friend. The afternoon was sultry. Ragged edges of black clouds peeped over the hills, and invisible thunderstorms circled outside, growling like wild beasts. We got the schooner ready for sea, intending to leave next morning at daylight. All day a merciless sun blazed down into the bay, fierce and pale, as if at white heat. Nothing moved on the land. The beach was empty, the villages seemed deserted; the trees far off stood in unstirring clumps, as if painted; the white smoke of some invisible bush-fire spread itself low over the shores of the bay like a settling fog. Late in the day three of Karain's

Karain: A Memory

chief men, dressed in their best and armed to the teeth, came off in a canoe, bringing a case of dollars. They were gloomy and languid, and told us they had not seen their Rajah for five days. No one had seen him! We settled all accounts, and after shaking hands in turn and in profound silence, they descended one after another into their boat, and were paddled to the shore, sitting close together, clad in vivid colours, with hanging heads: the gold embroideries of their jackets flashed dazzlingly as they went away gliding on the smooth water, and not one of them looked back once. Before sunset the growling clouds carried with a rush the ridge of hills, and came tumbling down the inner slopes. Everything disappeared; black whirling vapours filled the bay, and in the midst of them the schooner swung here and there in the shifting gusts of wind. A single clap of thunder detonated in the hollow with a violence that seemed capable of bursting into small pieces the ring of high land, and a warm deluge descended. The wind died out. We panted in the close cabin; our faces streamed; the bay outside hissed as if boiling; the water fell in perpendicular shafts as heavy as lead; it swished about the deck, poured off the spars, gurgled, sobbed, splashed, murmured in the blind night. Our lamp burned low. Hollis, stripped to the waist, lay stretched out on the lockers, with closed eyes and motionless like a despoiled corpse; at his head Jackson twanged the guitar, and gasped out in sighs a mournful dirge about hopeless love and eyes like stars. Then we heard startled voices on deck crying in the rain, hurried footsteps overhead, and suddenly Karain appeared in the doorway of the cabin. His bare breast and his face glistened in the light; his sarong, soaked, clung about his legs; he had his sheathed kriss in his left hand; and wisps of wet hair, escaping from under his red kerchief, stuck over his eyes and down his cheeks. He stepped in with a headlong stride and looking over his shoulder like a man pursued. Hollis turned on his side quickly and opened his eyes. Jackson

Karain: A Memory

clapped his big hand over the strings and the jingling vibration died suddenly. I stood up.

"We did not hear your boat's hail!" I exclaimed.

"Boat! The man's swum off," drawled out Hollis from the locker. "Look at him!"

He breathed heavily, wild-eyed, while we looked at him in silence. Water dripped from him, made a dark pool, and ran crookedly across the cabin floor. We could hear Jackson, who had gone out to drive away our Malay seamen from the doorway of the companion; he swore menacingly in the patter of a heavy shower, and there was a great commotion on deck. The watchmen, scared out of their wits by the glimpse of a shadowy figure leaping over the rail, straight out of the night as it were, had alarmed all hands.

Then Jackson, with glittering drops of water on his hair and beard, came back looking angry, and Hollis, who, being the youngest of us, assumed an indolent superiority, said without stirring, "Give him a dry sarong—give him mine; it's hanging up in the bathroom." Karain laid the kriss on the table, hilt inwards, and murmured a few words in a strangled voice.

"What's that?" asked Hollis, who had not heard.

"He apologizes for coming in with a weapon in his hand," I said, dazedly.

"Ceremonious beggar. Tell him we forgive a friend . . . on such a night," drawled out Hollis. "What's wrong?"

Karain slipped the dry sarong over his head, dropped the wet one at his feet, and stepped out of it. I pointed to the wooden armchair—his armchair. He sat down very straight, said "Ha!" in a strong voice; a short shiver shook his broad frame. He looked over his shoulder uneasily, turned as if to speak to us, but only stared in a curious blind manner, and again looked back. Jackson bellowed out, "Watch well on deck there!" heard a faint answer from above, and reaching out with his foot slammed-to the cabin door.

Karain: A Memory

"All right now," he said.

Karain's lips moved slightly. A vivid flash of lightning made the two round sternports facing him glimmer like a pair of cruel and phosphorescent eyes. The flame of the lamp seemed to wither into brown dust for an instant, and the looking-glass over the little sideboard leaped out behind his back in a smooth sheet of livid light. The roll of thunder came near, crashed over us; the schooner trembled, and the great voice went on, threatening terribly, into the distance. For less than a minute a furious shower rattled on the decks. Karain looked slowly from face to face, and then the silence became so profound that we all could hear distinctly the two chronometers in my cabin ticking along with unflagging speed against one another.

And we three, strangely moved, could not take our eyes from him. He had become enigmatical and touching, in virtue of that mysterious cause that had driven him through the night and through the thunderstorm to the shelter of the schooner's cuddy. Not one of us doubted that we were looking at a fugitive, incredible as it appeared to us. He was haggard, as though he had not slept for weeks; he had become lean, as though he had not eaten for days. His cheeks were hollow, his eyes sunk, the muscles of his chest and arms twitched slightly as if after an exhausting contest. Of course it had been a long swim off to the schooner; but his face showed another kind of fatigue, the tormented weariness, the anger and the fear of a struggle against a thought, an idea—against something that cannot be grappled, that never rests—a shadow, a nothing, unconquerable and immortal, that preys upon life. We knew it as though he had shouted it at us. His chest expanded time after time, as if it could not contain the beating of his heart. For a moment he had the power of the possessed—the power to awaken in the beholders wonder, pain, pity, and a fearful near sense of things invisible, of things dark and mute, that surround the loneliness of man-

Karain: A Memory

kind. His eyes roamed about aimlessly for a moment, then became still. He said with effort—

"I came here . . . I leaped out of my stockade as after a defeat. I ran in the night. The water was black. I left him calling on the edge of black water. . . . I left him standing alone on the beach. I swam . . . he called out after me . . . I swam . . ."

He trembled from head to foot, sitting very upright and gazing straight before him. Left whom? Who called? We did not know. We could not understand. I said at all hazards—

"Be firm."

The sound of my voice seemed to steady him into a sudden rigidity, but otherwise he took no notice. He seemed to listen, to expect something for a moment, then went on—

"He cannot come here—therefore I sought you. You men with white faces who despise the invisible voices. He cannot abide your unbelief and your strength."

He was silent for a while, then exclaimed softly—

"Oh! the strength of unbelievers!"

"There's no one here but you—and we three," said Hollis, quietly. He reclined with his head supported on elbow and did not budge.

"I know," said Karain. "He has never followed me here. Was not the wise man ever by my side? But since the old wise man, who knew of my trouble, has died, I have heard the voice every night. I shut myself up—for many days—in the dark. I can hear the sorrowful murmurs of women, the whisper of the wind, of the running waters; the clash of weapons in the hands of faithful men, their footsteps—and his voice! . . . Near . . . So! In my ear! I felt him near . . . His breath passed over my neck. I leaped out without a cry. All about me men slept quietly. I ran to the sea. He ran by my side without footsteps, whispering, whispering old words—whispering into my ear in his old voice. I ran into the sea; I swam off to you, with my kriss between my teeth. I, armed,

Karain: A Memory

I fled before a breath—to you. Take me away to your land. The wise old man has died, and with him is gone the power of his words and charms. And I can tell no one. No one. There is no one here faithful enough and wise enough to know. It is only near you, unbelievers, that my trouble fades like a mist under the eye of day."

He turned to me.

"With you I go!" he cried in a contained voice. "With you, who know so many of us. I want to leave this land—my people . . . and him—there!"

He pointed a shaking finger at random over his shoulder. It was hard for us to bear the intensity of that undisclosed distress. Hollis stared at him hard. I asked gently—

"Where is the danger?"

"Everywhere outside this place," he answered, mournfully. "In every place where I am. He waits for me on the paths, under the trees, in the place where I sleep—everywhere but here."

He looked round the little cabin, at the painted beams, at the tarnished varnish of bulkheads; he looked round as if appealing to all its shabby strangeness, to the disorderly jumble of unfamiliar things that belong to an inconceivable life of stress, of power, of endeavour, of unbelief—to the strong life of white men, which rolls on irresistible and hard on the edge of outer darkness. He stretched out his arms as if to embrace it and us. We waited. The wind and rain had ceased, and the stillness of the night round the schooner was as dumb and complete as if a dead world had been laid to rest in a grave of clouds. We expected him to speak. The necessity within him tore at his lips. There are those who say that a native will not speak to a white man. Error. No man will speak to his master; but to a wanderer and a friend, to him who does not come to teach or to rule, to him who asks for nothing and accepts all things, words are spoken by the camp-fires, in the shared solitude of the sea, in riverside

Karain: A Memory

villages, in resting-places surrounded by forests—words are spoken that take no account of race or colour. One heart speaks—another one listens; and the earth, the sea, the sky, the passing wind and the stirring leaf, hear also the futile tale of the burden of life.

He spoke at last. It is impossible to convey the effect of his story. It is undying, it is but a memory, and its vividness cannot be made clear to another mind, any more than the vivid emotions of a dream. One must have seen his innate splendour, one must have known him before—looked at him then. The wavering gloom of the little cabin; the breathless stillness outside, through which only the lapping of water against the schooner's sides could be heard; Hollis's pale face, with steady dark eyes; the energetic head of Jackson held up between two big palms, and with the long yellow hair of his beard flowing over the strings of the guitar lying on the table; Karain's upright and motionless pose, his tone—all this made an impression that cannot be forgotten. He faced us across the table. His dark head and bronze torso appeared above the tarnished slab of wood, gleaming and still as if cast in metal. Only his lips moved, and his eyes glowed, went out, blazed again, or stared mournfully. His expressions came straight from his tormented heart. His words sounded low, in a sad murmur as of running water; at times they rang loud like the clash of a war-gong—or trailed slowly like weary travellers—or rushed forward with the speed of fear.

IV

This is, imperfectly, what he said—

"It was after the great trouble that broke the alliance of the four states of Wajo. We fought amongst ourselves, and the Dutch watched from afar till we were weary. Then the smoke of their fire-ships was seen at the mouth of our rivers, and their great men came in boats full of soldiers to talk to us of protection and peace. We answered with caution and wisdom, for our villages were burnt, our stockades weak, the people weary, and the weapons blunt. They came and went; there had been much talk, but after they went away everything seemed to be as before, only their ships remained in sight from our coast, and very soon their traders came amongst us under a promise of safety. My brother was a Ruler, and one of those who had given the promise. I was young then, and had fought in the war, and Pata Matara had fought by my side. We had shared hunger, danger, fatigue, and victory. His eyes saw my danger quickly, and twice my arm had preserved his life. It was his destiny. He was my friend. And he was great amongst us—one of those who were near my brother, the Ruler. He spoke in council, his courage was great, he was the chief of many villages round the great lake that is in the middle of our country as the heart is in the middle of a man's body. When his sword was carried into a campong in advance of his coming, the maidens whispered wonderingly under the fruit-trees, the rich men consulted together in the shade, and a feast was made ready with rejoicing and songs. He had the favour of the Ruler and the affection of the poor. He loved war, deer hunts, and the charms of women. He was the possessor of jewels, of lucky weapons, and of men's devotion. He was a fierce man; and I had no other friend.

"I was the chief of a stockade at the mouth of the river, and collected tolls for my brother from the passing boats. One day I saw a Dutch trader go up the river. He went up with three boats, and no toll was demanded from him, because the smoke of Dutch war-ships stood out from the open sea, and we were too weak to forget treaties. He went up under the promise of safety, and my brother gave him protection. He said he came to trade. He listened to our voices, for we are men who speak openly and without fear; he counted the number of our spears, he examined the trees, the running waters, the grasses of the bank, the slopes of our hills. He

Karain: A Memory

went up to Matara's country and obtained permission to build a house. He traded and planted. He despised our joys, our thoughts, and our sorrows. His face was red, his hair like flame, and his eyes pale, like a river mist; he moved heavily, and spoke with a deep voice; he laughed aloud like a fool, and knew no courtesy in his speech. He was a big, scornful man, who looked into women's faces and put his hand on the shoulders of free men as though he had been a noble-born chief. We bore with him. Time passed.

"Then Pata Matara's sister fled from the campong and went to live in the Dutchman's house. She was a great and wilful lady: I had seen her once carried high on slaves' shoulders amongst the people, with uncovered face, and I had heard all men say that her beauty was extreme, silencing the reason and ravishing the heart of the beholders. The people were dismayed; Matara's face was blackened with that disgrace, for she knew she had been promised to another man. Matara went to the Dutchman's house, and said, 'Give her up to die —she is the daughter of chiefs.' The white man refused and shut himself up, while his servants kept guard night and day with loaded guns. Matara raged. My brother called a council. But the Dutch ships were near, and watched our coast greedily. My brother said, 'If he dies now our land will pay for his blood. Leave him alone till we grow stronger and the ships are gone.' Matara was wise; he waited and watched. But the white man feared for her life and went away.

"He left his house, his plantations, and his goods! He departed, armed and menacing, and left all—for her! She had ravished his heart! From my stockade I saw him put out to sea in a big boat. Matara and I watched him from the fighting platform behind the pointed stakes. He sat cross-legged, with his gun in his hands, on the roof at the stern of his prau. The barrel of his rifle glinted aslant before his big red face. The broad river was stretched under him—level, smooth, shining like a plain of silver; and his prau, looking very

68

Karain: A Memory

short and black from the shore, glided along the silver plain and over into the blue of the sea.

"Thrice Matara, standing by my side, called aloud her name with grief and imprecations. He stirred my heart. It leaped three times; and three times with the eye of my mind I saw in the gloom within the enclosed space of the prau a woman with streaming hair going away from her land and her people. I was angry—and sorry. Why? And then I also cried out insults and threats. Matara said, 'Now they have left our land their lives are mine. I shall follow and strike—and, alone, pay the price of blood.' A great wind was sweeping towards the setting sun over the empty river. I cried, 'By your side I will go!' He lowered his head in sign of assent. It was his destiny. The sun had set, and the trees swayed their boughs with a great noise above our heads.

"On the third night we two left our land together in a trading prau.

"The sea met us—the sea, wide, pathless, and without voice. A sailing prau leaves no track. We went south. The moon was full; and looking up, we said to one another, 'When the next moon shines as this one, we shall return and they will be dead.' It was fifteen years ago. Many moons have grown full and withered and I have not seen my land since. We sailed south; we overtook many praus; we examined the creeks and the bays; we saw the end of our coast, of our island—a steep cape over a disturbed strait, where drift the shadows of shipwrecked praus and drowned men clamour in the night. The wide sea was all round us now. We saw a great mountain burning in the midst of water; we saw thousands of islets scattered like bits of iron fired from a big gun; we saw a long coast of mountain and lowlands stretching away in sunshine from west to east. It was Java. We said, 'They are there; their time is near, and we shall return or die cleansed from dishonour.'

"We landed. Is there anything good in that country? The

69

Karain: A Memory

paths run straight and hard and dusty. Stone campongs, full of white faces, are surrounded by fertile fields, but every man you meet is a slave. The rulers live under the edge of a foreign sword. We ascended mountains, we traversed valleys; at sunset we entered villages. We asked everyone, 'Have you seen such a white man?' Some stared; others laughed; women gave us food, sometimes, with fear and respect, as though we had been distracted by the visitation of God; but some did not understand our language, and some cursed us, or, yawning, asked with contempt the reason of our quest. Once, as we were going away, an old man called after us, 'Desist!'

"We went on. Concealing our weapons, we stood humbly aside before the horsemen on the road; we bowed low in the courtyards of chiefs who were no better than slaves. We lost ourselves in the fields, in the jungle; and one night, in a tangled forest, we came upon a place where crumbling old walls had fallen amongst the trees, and where strange stone idols—carved images of devils with many arms and legs, with snakes twined round their bodies, with twenty heads and holding a hundred swords—seemed to live and threaten in the light of our camp fire. Nothing dismayed us. And on the road, by every fire, in resting-places, we always talked of her and of him. Their time was near. We spoke of nothing else. No! not of hunger, thirst, weariness, and faltering hearts. No! we spoke of him and her? Of her! And we thought of them—of her! Matara brooded by the fire. I sat and thought and thought, till suddenly I could see again the image of a woman, beautiful, and young, and great and proud, and tender, going away from her land and her people. Matara said, 'When we find them we shall kill her first to cleanse the dishonour—then the man must die.' I would say, 'It shall be so; it is your vengeance.' He stared long at me with his big sunken eyes.

"We came back to the coast. Our feet were bleeding, our

Karain: A Memory

bodies thin. We slept in rags under the shadow of stone enclosures; we prowled, soiled and lean, about the gateways of white men's courtyards. Their hairy dogs barked at us, and their servants shouted from afar, 'Begone!' Low-born wretches, that keep watch over the streets of stone campongs, asked us who we were. We lied, we cringed, we smiled with hate in our hearts, and we kept looking here, looking there for them—for the white man with hair like flame, and for her, for the woman who had broken faith, and therefore must die. We looked. At last in every woman's face I thought I could see hers. We ran swiftly. No! Sometimes Matara would whisper, 'Here is the man,' and we waited, crouching. He came near. It was not the man—those Dutchmen are all alike. We suffered the anguish of deception. In my sleep I saw her face, and was both joyful and sorry.... Why?... I seemed to hear a whisper near me. I turned swiftly. She was not there! And as we trudged wearily from stone city to stone city I seemed to hear a light footstep near me. A time came when I heard it always, and I was glad. I thought, walking dizzy and weary in sunshine on the hard paths of white men—I thought, She is there—with us!... Matara was sombre. We were often hungry.

"We sold the carved sheaths of our krisses—the ivory sheaths with golden ferrules. We sold the jewelled hilts. But we kept the blades—for them. The blades that never touch but kill—we kept the blades for her.... Why? She was always by our side.... We starved. We begged. We left Java at last.

"We went West, we went East. We saw many lands, crowds of strange faces, men that live in trees and men who eat their old people. We cut rattans in the forest for a handful of rice, and for a living swept the decks of big ships and heard curses heaped upon our heads. We toiled in villages; we wandered upon the seas with the Bajow people, who have no country. We fought for pay; we hired ourselves

Karain: A Memory

to work for Goram men, and were cheated, and under the orders of rough white faces we dived for pearls in barren bays, dotted with black rocks, upon a coast of sand and desolation. And everywhere we watched, we listened, we asked. We asked traders, robbers, white men. We heard jeers, mockery, threats—words of wonder and words of contempt. We never knew rest; we never thought of home, for our work was not done. A year passed, then another. I ceased to count the number of nights, of moons, of years. I watched over Matara. He had my last handful of rice; if there was water enough for one he drank it; I covered him up when he shivered with cold; and when the hot sickness came upon him I sat sleepless through many nights and fanned his face. He was a fierce man, and my friend. He spoke of her with fury in the daytime, with sorrow in the dark; he remembered her in health, in sickness. I said nothing; but I saw her every day—always! At first I saw only her head, as of a woman walking in the low mist on a river bank. Then she sat by our fire. I saw her! I looked at her! She had tender eyes and a ravishing face. I murmured to her in the night. Matara said sleepily sometimes, 'To whom are you talking? Who is there?' I answered quickly, 'No one' . . . It was a lie! She never left me. She shared the warmth of our fire, she sat on my couch of leaves, she swam on the sea to follow me. . . . I saw her! . . . I tell you I saw her long black hair spread behind her upon the moonlit water as she struck out with bare arms by the side of a swift prau. She was beautiful, she was faithful, and in the silence of foreign countries she spoke to me very low in the language of my people. No one saw her; no one heard her; she was mine only! In daylight she moved with a swaying walk before me upon the weary paths; her figure was straight and flexible like the stem of a slender tree; the heels of her feet were round and polished like shells of eggs; with her round arm she made signs. At night she looked into my face. And she was sad! Her eyes were tender and frightened;

Karain: A Memory

her voice soft and pleading. Once I murmured to her, 'You shall not die,' and she smiled . . . ever after she smiled! . . . She gave me courage to bear weariness and hardships. Those were times of pain, and she soothed me. We wandered patient in our search. We knew deception, false hopes; we knew captivity, sickness, thirst, misery, despair. . . . Enough! We found them! . . ."

He cried out the last words and paused. His face was impassive, and he kept still like a man in a trance. Hollis sat up quickly, and spread his elbows on the table. Jackson made a brusque movement, and accidentally touched the guitar. A plaintive resonance filled the cabin with confused vibrations and died out slowly. Then Karain began to speak again. The restrained fierceness of his tone seemed to rise like a voice from outside, like a thing unspoken but heard; it filled the cabin and enveloped in its intense and deadened murmur the motionless figure in the chair.

"We were on our way to Atjeh, where there was war; but the vessel ran on a sandbank, and we had to land in Delli. We had earned a little money, and had bought a gun from some Selangore traders; only one gun, which was fired by the spark of a stone: Matara carried it. We landed. Many white men lived there, planting tobacco on conquered plains, and Matara . . . But no matter. He saw him! . . . The Dutchman! . . . At last! . . . We crept and watched. Two nights and a day we watched. He had a house—a big house in a clearing in the midst of his fields; flowers and bushes grew around; there were narrow paths of yellow earth between the cut grass, and thick hedges to keep people out. The third night we came armed, and lay behind a hedge.

"A heavy dew seemed to soak through our flesh and made our very entrails cold. The grass, the twigs, the leaves, covered with drops of water, were gray in the moonlight. Matara, curled up in the grass, shivered in his sleep. My teeth rattled in my head so loud that I was afraid the noise

73

Karain: A Memory

would wake up all the land. Afar, the watchmen of white men's houses struck wooden clappers and hooted in the darkness. And, as every night, I saw her by my side. She smiled no more! ... The fire of anguish burned in my breast, and she whispered to me with compassion, with pity, softly—as women will; she soothed the pain of my mind; she bent her face over me—the face of a woman who ravishes the hearts and silences the reason of men. She was all mine, and no one could see her—no one of living mankind! Stars shone through her bosom, through her floating hair. I was overcome with regret, with tenderness, with sorrow. Matara slept . . . Had I slept? Matara was shaking me by the shoulder, and the fire of the sun was drying the grass, the bushes, the leaves. I was day. Shreds of white mist hung between the branches of trees.

"Was it night or day? I saw nothing again till I heard Matara breathe quickly where he lay, and then outside the house I saw her. I saw them both. They had come out. She sat on a bench under the wall, and twigs laden with flowers crept high above her head, hung over her hair. She had a box on her lap, and gazed into it, counting the increase of her pearls. The Dutchman stood by looking on; he smiled down at her; his white teeth flashed; the hair on his lip was like two twisted flames. He was big and fat, and joyous, and without fear. Matara tipped fresh priming from the hollow of his palm, scraped the flint with his thumb-nail, and gave the gun to me. To me! I took it . . . O fate!

"He whispered into my ear, lying on his stomach, 'I shall creep close and then amok . . . let her die by my hand. You take aim at the fat swine there. Let him see me strike my shame off the face of the earth—and then . . . you are my friend—kill with a sure shot.' I said nothing; there was no air in my chest—there was no air in the world. Matara had gone suddenly from my side. The grass nodded. Then a bush rustled. She lifted her head.

74

Karain: A Memory

"I saw her! The consoler of sleepless nights, of weary days; the companion of troubled years! I saw her! She looked straight at the place where I crouched. She was there as I had seen her for years—a faithful wanderer by my side. She looked with sad eyes and had smiling lips; she looked at me . . . Smiling lips! Had I not promised that she should not die!

"She was far off and I felt her near. Her touch caressed me, and her voice murmured, whispered above me, around me, 'Who shall be thy companion, who shall console thee if I die?' I saw a flowering thicket to the left of her stir a little . . . Matara was ready . . . I cried aloud—'Return!'

"She leaped up; the box fell; the pearls streamed at her feet. The big Dutchman by her side rolled menacing eyes through the still sunshine. The gun went up to my shoulder. I was kneeling and I was firm—firmer than the trees, the rocks, the mountains. But in front of the steady long barrel the fields, the house, the earth, the sky swayed to and fro like shadows in a forest on a windy day. Matara burst out of the thicket; before him the petals of torn flowers whirled high as if driven by a tempest. I heard her cry; I saw her spring with open arms in front of the white man. She was a woman of my country and of noble blood. They are so! I heard her shriek of anguish and fear—and all stood still! The fields, the house, the earth, the sky stood still—while Matara leaped at her with uplifted arm. I pulled the trigger, saw a spark, heard nothing; the smoke drove back into my face, and then I could see Matara roll over head first and lie with stretched arms at her feet. Ha! A sure shot! The sunshine fell on my back colder than the running water. A sure shot! I flung the gun after the shot. Those two stood over the dead man as though they had been bewitched by a charm. I shouted at her, 'Live and remember!' Then for a time I stumbled about in a cold darkness.

"Behind me there were great shouts, the running of many

feet; strange men surrounded me, cried meaningless words into my face, pushed me, dragged me, supported me . . . I stood before the big Dutchman: he stared as if bereft of his reason. He wanted to know, he talked fast, he spoke of gratitude, he offered me food, shelter, gold—he asked many questions. I laughed in his face. I said, 'I am a Korinchi traveller from Perak over there, and know nothing of that dead man. I was passing along the path when I heard a shot! and your senseless people rushed out and dragged me here.' He lifted his arms, he wondered, he could not believe, he could not understand, he clamoured in his own tongue! She had her arms clasped round his neck and over her shoulder stared back at me with wide eyes. I smiled and looked at her; I smiled and waited to hear the sound of her voice. The white man asked her suddenly, 'Do you know him?' I listened —my life was in my ears! She looked at me long, she looked at me with unflinching eyes, and said aloud, 'No! I never saw him before.' . . . What! Never before? Had she forgotten already? Was it possible? Forgotten already—after so many years—so many years of wandering, of companionship, of trouble, of tender words! Forgotten already! . . . I tore myself out from the hands that held me and went away without a word . . . They let me go.

"I was weary. Did I sleep? I do not know. I remember walking upon a broad path under a clear starlight; and that strange country seemed so big, the rice-fields so vast, that, as I looked around, my head swam with the fear of space. Then I saw a forest. The joyous starlight was heavy upon me. I turned off the path and entered the forest, which was very sombre and very sad."

V

Karain's tone had been getting lower and lower, as though he had been going away from us, till the last words sounded

Karain: A Memory

faint but clear, as if shouted on a calm day from a very great distance. He moved not. He stared fixedly past the motionless head of Hollis, who faced him, as still as himself. Jackson had turned sideways, and with elbow on the table shaded his eyes with the palm of his hand. And I looked on, surprised and moved; I looked at that man, loyal to a vision, betrayed by his dream, spurned by his illusion, and coming to us unbelievers for help—against a thought. The silence was profound; but it seemed full of noiseless phantoms, of things sorrowful, shadowy, and mute, in whose invisible presence the firm, pulsating beat of the two ship's chronometers ticking off steadily the seconds of Greenwich Time seemed to me a protection and a relief. Karain stared stonily; and looking at his rigid figure, I thought of his wanderings, of that obscure Odyssey of revenge, of all the men that wander amongst illusions; of the illusions as restless as men; of the illusions faithful, faithless; of the illusions that give joy, that give sorrow, that give pain, that give peace; of the invincible illusions that can make life and death appear serene, inspiring, tormented, or ignoble.

A murmur was heard; that voice from outside seemed to flow out of a dreaming world into the lamplight of the cabin. Karain was speaking.

"I lived in the forest.

"She came no more. Never! Never once! I lived alone. She had forgotten. It was well. I did not want her; I wanted no one. I found an abandoned house in an old clearing. Nobody came near. Sometimes I heard in the distance the voices of people going along a path. I slept; I rested; there was wild rice, water from a running stream—and peace! Every night I sat alone by my small fire before the hut. Many nights passed over my head.

"Then, one evening, as I sat by my fire after having eaten, I looked down on the ground and began to remember my wanderings. I lifted my head. I had heard no sound, no rustle, no footsteps—but I lifted my head. A man was coming towards me across the small clearing. I waited. He came up without a greeting and squatted down into the firelight. Then he turned his face to me. It was Matara. He stared at me fiercely with his big sunken eyes. The night was cold; the heat died suddenly out of the fire, and he stared at me. I rose and went away from there, leaving him by the fire that had no heat.

"I walked all that night, all next day, and in the evening made up a big blaze and sat down—to wait for him. He had not come into the light. I heard him in the bushes here and there, whispering, whispering. I understood at last—I had heard the words before, 'You are my friend—kill with a sure shot.'

"I bore it as long as I could—then leaped away, as on this very night I leaped from my stockade and swam to you. I ran—I ran crying like a child left alone and far from the houses. He ran by my side, without footsteps, whispering, whispering—invisible and heard. I sought people—I wanted men around me! Men who had not died! And again we two wandered. I sought danger, violence, and death. I fought in the Atjeh war, and a brave people wondered at the valiance of a stranger. But we were two; he warded off the blows . . . Why? I wanted peace not life. And no one could see him; no one knew—I dared tell no one. At times he would leave me, but not for long; then he would return and whisper or stare. My heart was torn with a strange fear, but could not die. Then I met an old man.

"You all knew him. People here called him my sorcerer, my servant and sword-bearer; but to me he was father, mother, protection, refuge and peace. When I met him he was returning from a pilgrimage, and I heard him intoning the prayer of sunset. He had gone to the holy place with his son, his son's wife, and a little child; and on their return, by the favour of the Most High, they all died: the strong man, the young mother, the little child—they died; and the old man

Karain: A Memory

reached his country alone. He was a pilgrim serene and pious, very wise and very lonely. I told him all. For a time we lived together. He said over me words of compassion, of wisdom, of prayer. He warded from me the shade of the dead. I begged him for a charm that would make me safe. For a long time he refused; but at last, with a sigh and a smile, he gave me one. Doubtless he could command a spirit stronger than the unrest of my dead friend, and again I had peace; but I had become restless, and a lover of turmoil and danger. The old man never left me. We travelled together. We were welcomed by the great; his wisdom and my courage are remembered where your strength, O white men, is forgotten! We served the Sultan of Sula. We fought the Spaniards. There were victories, hopes, defeats, sorrow, blood, women's tears . . . What for? . . . We fled. We collected wanderers of a warlike race and came here to fight again. The rest you know. I am the ruler of a conquered land, a lover of war and danger, a fighter and a plotter. But the old man has died, and I am again the slave of the dead. He is not here now to drive away the reproachful shade—to silence the lifeless voice! The power of his charm has died with him. And I know fear; and I hear the whisper, 'Kill! kill! kill!' . . . Have I not killed enough? . . ."

For the first time that night a sudden convulsion of madness and rage passed over his face. His wavering glances darted here and there like scared birds in a thunderstorm. He jumped up, shouting—

"By the spirits that drink blood: by the spirits that cry in the night: by all the spirits of fury, misfortune, and death, I swear—some day I will strike into every heart I meet—I . . ."

He looked so dangerous that we all three leaped to our feet, and Hollis, with the back of his hand, sent the kriss flying off the table. I believe we shouted together. It was a short scare, and the next moment he was again composed in his chair, with three white men standing over him in rather

Karain: A Memory

foolish attitudes. We felt a little ashamed of ourselves. Jackson picked up the kriss, and, after an inquiring glance at me, gave it to him. He received it with a stately inclination of the head and stuck it in the twist of his sarong, with punctilious care to give his weapon a pacific position. Then he looked up at us with an austere smile. We were abashed and reproved. Hollis sat sideways on the table and, holding his chin in his hand, scrutinized him in pensive silence. I said—

"You must abide with your people. They need you. And there is forgetfulness in life. Even the dead cease to speak in time."

"Am I a woman, to forget long years before an eyelid has had the time to beat twice?" he exclaimed, with bitter resentment. He startled me. It was amazing. To him his life—that cruel mirage of love and peace—seemed as real, as undeniable, as theirs would be to any saint, philosopher, or fool of us all. Hollis muttered—

"You won't soothe him with your platitudes."

Karain spoke to me.

"You know us. You have lived with us. Why?—we cannot know; but you understand our sorrows and our thoughts. You have lived with my people, and you understand our desires and our fears. With you I will go. To your land—to your people. To your people, who live in unbelief; to whom day is day, and night is night—nothing more, because you understand all things seen, and despise all else! To your land of unbelief, where the dead do not speak, where every man is wise, and alone—and at peace!"

"Capital description," murmured Hollis, with the flicker of a smile.

Karain hung his head.

"I can toil, and fight—and be faithful," he whispered, in a weary tone, "but I cannot go back to him who waits for me on the shore. No! Take me with you . . . Or else give me some of your strength—of your unbelief . . . A charm! . . ."

Karain: A Memory

He seemed utterly exhausted.

"Yes, take him home," said Hollis, very low, as if debating with himself. "That would be one way. The ghosts there are in society, and talk affably to ladies and gentlemen, but would scorn a naked human being like our princely friend. . . . Naked . . . Flayed! I should say. I am sorry for him. Impossible—of course. The end of all this shall be," he went on, looking up at us—"the end of this shall be, that some day he will run amuck amongst his faithful subjects and send *ad patres* ever so many of them before they make up their minds to the disloyalty of knocking him on the head."

I nodded. I thought it more than probable that such would be the end of Karain. It was evident that he had been hunted by his thought along the very limit of human endurance, and very little more pressing was needed to make him swerve over into the form of madness peculiar to his race. The respite he had during the old man's life made the return of the torment unbearable. That much was clear.

He lifted his head suddenly; we had imagined for a moment that he had been dozing.

"Give me your protection—or your strength!" he cried. "A charm . . . a weapon!"

Again his chin fell on his breast. We looked at him, then looked at one another with suspicious awe in our eyes, like men who come unexpectedly upon the scene of some mysterious disaster. He had given himself up to us; he had thrust into our hands his errors and his torment, his life and his peace; and we did not know what to do with that problem from the outer darkness. We three white men, looking at the Malay, could not find one word to the purpose amongst us— if indeed there existed a word that could solve that problem. We pondered, and our hearts sank. We felt as though we three had been called to the very gate of Infernal Regions to judge, to decide the fate of a wanderer coming suddenly from a world of sunshine and illusions.

Karain: A Memory

"By Jove, he seems to have a great idea of our power," whispered Hollis, hopelessly. And then again there was a silence, the feeble plash of water, the steady tick of chronometers. Jackson, with bare arms crossed, leaned his shoulders against the bulkhead of the cabin. He was bending his head under the deck beam; his fair beard spread out magnificently over his chest; he looked colossal, ineffectual, and mild. There was something lugubrious in the aspect of the cabin; the air in it seemed to become slowly charged with the cruel chill of helplessness, with the pitiless anger of egoism against the incomprehensible form of an intruding pain. We had no idea what to do; we began to resent bitterly the hard necessity to get rid of him.

Hollis mused, muttered suddenly with a short laugh, "Strength . . . Protection . . . Charm." He slipped off the table and left the cuddy without a look at us. It seemed a base desertion. Jackson and I exchanged indignant glances. We could hear him rummaging in his pigeon-hole of a cabin. Was the fellow actually going to bed? Karain sighed. It was intolerable!

Then Hollis reappeared, holding in both hands a small leather box. He put it down gently on the table and looked at us with a queer gasp, we thought, as though he had from some cause become speechless for a moment, or were ethically uncertain about producing that box. But in an instant the insolent and unerring wisdom of his youth gave him the needed courage. He said, as he unlocked the box with a very small key, "Look as solemn as you can, you fellows."

Probably we looked only surprised and stupid, for he glanced over his shoulder, and said angrily—

"This is no play; I am going to do something for him. Look serious. Confound it! . . . Can't you lie a little . . . for a friend!"

Karain seemed to take no notice of us, but when Hollis threw open the lid of the box his eyes flew to it—and so did

Karain: A Memory

ours. The quilted crimson satin of the inside put a violent patch of colour into the sombre atmosphere; it was something positive to look at—it was fascinating.

VI

Hollis looked smiling into the box. He had lately made a dash home through the Canal. He had been away six months and only joined us again just in time for this last trip. We had never seen the box before. His hands hovered above it; and he talked to us ironically, but his face became as grave as though he were pronouncing a powerful incantation over the things inside.

"Every one of us," he said, with pauses that somehow were more offensive than his words—"every one of us, you'll admit, has been haunted by some woman . . . And . . . as to friends . . . dropped by the way . . . Well! . . . ask yourselves . . ."

He paused. Karain stared. A deep rumble was heard high up under the deck. Jackson spoke seriously—

"Don't be so beastly cynical."

"Ah! You are without guile," said Hollis, sadly. "You will learn . . . Meantime this Malay has been our friend . . ."

He repeated several times thoughtfully, "Friend . . . Malay. Friend, Malay," as though weighing the words against one another, then went on more briskly—

"A good fellow—a gentleman in his way. We can't, so to speak, turn our backs on his confidence and belief in us. Those Malays are easily impressed—all nerves, you know—therefore . . ."

He turned to me sharply.

"You know him best," he said, in a practical tone. "Do you think he is fanatical—I mean very strict in his faith?"

I stammered in profound amazement that "I did not think so."

"It's on account of its being a likeness—an engraved

Karain: A Memory

image," muttered Hollis, enigmatically, turning to the box. He plunged his fingers into it. Karain's lips were parted and his eyes shone. We looked into the box.

There were there a couple of reels of cotton, a packet of needles, a bit of silk ribbon, dark blue; a cabinet photograph, at which Hollis stole a glance before laying it on the table face downwards. A girl's portrait, I could see. There were, amongst a lot of various small objects, a bunch of flowers, a narrow white glove with many buttons, a slim packet of letters carefully tied up. Amulets of white men! Charms and talismans! Charms that keep them straight, that drive them crooked, that have the power to make a young man sigh, an old man smile. Potent things that procure dreams of joy, thoughts of regret; that soften hard hearts and can temper a soft one to the hardness of steel. Gifts of heaven—things of earth . . .

Hollis rummaged in the box.

And it seemed to me, during that moment of waiting, that the cabin of the schooner was becoming filled with a stir invisible and living as of subtle breaths. All the ghosts driven out of the unbelieving West by men who pretend to be wise and alone and at peace—all the homeless ghosts of an unbelieving world—appeared suddenly round the figure of Hollis bending over the box; all the exiled and charming shades of loved women; all the beautiful and tender ghosts of ideals, remembered, forgotten, cherished, execrated; all the cast-out and reproachful ghosts of friends admired, trusted, traduced, betrayed, left dead by the way—they all seemed to come from the inhospitable regions of the earth to crowd into the gloomy cabin, as though it had been a refuge and, in all the unbelieving world, the only place of avenging belief. . . . It lasted a second—all disappeared. Hollis was facing us alone with something small that glittered between his fingers. It looked like a coin.

"Ah! here it is," he said.

84

Karain: A Memory

He held it up. It was a sixpence—a Jubilee sixpence. It was gilt; it had a hole punched near the rim. Hollis looked towards Karain.

"A charm for our friend," he said to us. "The thing itself is of great power—money, you know—and his imagination is struck. A loyal vagabond; if only his puritanism doesn't shy at a likeness . . ."

We said nothing. We did not know whether to be scandalized, amused, or relieved. Hollis advanced towards Karain, who stood up as if startled, and then, holding the coin up, spoke in Malay.

"This is the image of the Great Queen, and the most powerful thing the white men know," he said, solemnly.

Karain covered the handle of his kriss in sign of respect, and stared at the crowned head.

"The Invincible, the Pious," he muttered.

"She is more powerful than Suleiman the Wise, who commanded the genii, as you know," said Hollis, gravely. "I shall give this to you."

He held the sixpence in the palm of his hand, and looking at it thoughtfully, spoke to us in English.

"She commands a spirit, too—the spirit of her nation; a masterful, conscientious, unscrupulous, unconquerable devil . . . that does a lot of good—incidentally . . . a lot of good . . . at times—and wouldn't stand any fuss from the best ghost out for such a little thing as our friend's shot. Don't look thunderstruck, you fellows. Help me to make him believe—everything's in that."

"His people will be shocked," I murmured.

Hollis looked fixedly at Karain, who was the incarnation of the very essence of still excitement. He stood rigid, with head thrown back; his eyes rolled wildly, flashing; the dilated nostrils quivered.

"Hang it all!" said Hollis at last, "he is a good fellow. I'll give him something that I shall really miss."

Karain: A Memory

He took the ribbon out of the box, smiled at it scornfully, then with a pair of scissors cut out a piece from the palm of the glove.

"I shall make him a thing like those Italian peasants wear, you know."

He sewed the coin in the delicate leather, sewed the leather to the ribbon, tied the ends together. He worked with haste. Karain watched his fingers all the time.

"Now then," he said—then stepped up to Karain. They looked close into one another's eyes. Those of Karain stared in a lost glance, but Hollis's seemed to grow darker and looked out masterful and compelling. They were in violent contrast together—one motionless and the colour of bronze, the other dazzling white and lifting his arms, where the powerful muscles rolled slightly under a skin that gleamed like satin. Jackson moved near with the air of a man closing up to a chum in a tight place. I said impressively, pointing to Hollis——

"He is young, but he is wise. Believe him!"

Karain bent his head: Hollis threw lightly over it the dark-blue ribbon and stepped back.

"Forget, and be at peace!" I cried.

Karain seemed to wake up from a dream. He said, "Ha!" shook himself as if throwing off a burden. He looked round with assurance. Someone on deck dragged off the skylight cover, and a flood of light fell into the cabin. It was morning already.

"Time to go on deck," said Jackson.

Hollis put on a coat, and we went up, Karain leading.

The sun had risen beyond the hills, and their long shadows stretched far over the bay in the pearly light. The air was clear, stainless, and cool. I pointed at the curved line of yellow sands.

"He is not there," I said, emphatically, to Karain. "He waits no more. He has departed forever."

Karain: A Memory

A shaft of bright hot rays darted into the bay between the summits of two hills, and the water all round broke out as if by magic into a dazzling sparkle.

"No! He is not there waiting," said Karain, after a long look over the beach. "I do not hear him," he went on, slowly. "No!"

He turned to us.

"He has departed again—forever!" he cried.

We assented vigorously, repeatedly, and without compunction. The great thing was to impress him powerfully; to suggest absolute safety—the end of all trouble. We did our best; and I hope we affirmed our faith in the power of Hollis's charm efficiently enough to put the matter beyond the shadow of a doubt. Our voices rang around him joyously in the still air, and above his head the sky, pellucid, pure, stainless, arched its tender blue from shore to shore and over the bay, as if to envelop the water, the earth, and the man in the caress of its light.

The anchor was up, the sails hung still, and half-a-dozen big boats were seen sweeping over the bay to give us a tow out. The paddlers in the first one that came alongside lifted their heads and saw their ruler standing amongst us. A low murmur of surprise arose—then a shout of greeting.

He left us, and seemed straightway to step into the glorious splendour of his stage, to wrap himself in the illusion of unavoidable success. For a moment he stood erect, one foot over the gangway, one hand on the hilt of his kriss, in a martial pose; and relieved from the fear of outer darkness, he held his head high, he swept a serene look over his conquered foothold on the earth. The boats far off took up the cry of greeting; a great clamour rolled on the water; the hills echoed it, and seemed to toss back at him the words invoking long life and victories.

He descended into a canoe, and as soon as he was clear of the side we gave him three cheers. They sounded faint and

Karain: A Memory

orderly after the wild tumult of his loyal subjects, but it was the best we could do. He stood up in the boat, lifted up both his arms, then pointed to the infallible charm. We cheered again; and the Malays in the boats stared—very much puzzled and impressed. I wondered what they thought; what he thought; . . . what the reader thinks?

We towed out slowly. We saw him land and watch us from the beach. A figure approached him humbly but openly—not at all like a ghost with a grievance. We could see other men running towards him. Perhaps he had been missed? At any rate there was a great stir. A group formed itself rapidly near him, and he walked along the sands, followed by a growing *cortège* and kept nearly abreast of the schooner. With our glasses we could see the blue ribbon on his neck and a patch of white on his brown chest. The bay was waking up. The smokes of morning fires stood in faint spirals higher than the heads of palms; people moved between the houses; a herd of buffaloes galloped clumsily across a green slope; the slender figures of boys brandishing sticks appeared black and leaping in the long grass; a coloured line of women, with water bamboos on their heads, moved swaying through a thin grove of fruit-trees. Karain stopped in the midst of his men and waved his hand; then, detaching himself from the splendid group, walked alone to the water's edge and waved his hand again. The schooner passed out to sea between the steep headlands that shut in the bay, and at the same instant Karain passed out of our life forever.

But the memory remains. Some years afterwards I met Jackson, in the Strand. He was magnificent as ever. His head was high above the crowd. His beard was gold, his face red, his eyes blue; he had a wide-brimmed gray hat and no collar or waistcoat; he was inspiring; he had just come home—had landed that very day! Our meeting caused an eddy in the current of humanity. Hurried people would run against us, then walk round us, and turn back to look at that giant. We

Karain: A Memory

tried to compress seven years of life into seven exclamations; then, suddenly appeased, walked sedately along, giving one another the news of yesterday. Jackson gazed about him, like a man who looks for landmarks, then stopped before Bland's window. He always had a passion for firearms; so he stopped short and contemplated the row of weapons, perfect and severe, drawn up in a line behind the black-framed panes. I stood by his side. Suddenly he said—

"Do you remember Karain?"

I nodded.

"The sight of all this made me think of him," he went on, with his face near the glass . . . and I could see another man, powerful and bearded, peering at him intently from amongst the dark and polished tubes that can cure so many illusions. "Yes; it made me think of him," he continued, slowly. "I saw a paper this morning; they are fighting over there again. He's sure to be in it. He will make it hot for the caballeros. Well, good luck to him, poor devil! He was perfectly stunning."

We walked on.

"I wonder whether the charm worked—you remember Hollis's charm, of course. If it did . . . never was a sixpence wasted to better advantage! Poor devil! I wonder whether he got rid of that friend of his. Hope so. . . . Do you know, I sometimes think that——"

I stood still and looked at him.

"Yes . . . I mean, whether the thing was so, you know . . . whether it really happened to him. . . . What do you think?"

"My dear chap," I cried, "you have been too long away from home. What a question to ask! Only look at all this."

A watery gleam of sunshine flashed from the west and went out between two long lines of walls; and then the broken confusion of roofs, the chimney-stacks, the gold letters sprawling over the fronts of houses, the sombre polish of windows, stood resigned and sullen under the falling gloom. The whole length of the street, deep as a well and narrow

Karain: A Memory

like a corridor, was full of a sombre and ceaseless stir. Our ears were filled by a headlong shuffle and beat of rapid footsteps and an underlying rumour—a rumour vast, faint, pulsating, as of panting breaths, of beating hearts, of gasping voices. Innumerable eyes stared straight in front, feet moved hurriedly, blank faces flowed, arms swung. Over all, a narrow ragged strip of smoky sky wound about between the high roofs, extended and motionless, like a soiled streamer flying above the rout of a mob.

"Ye-e-e-s," said Jackson, meditatively.

The big wheels of hansoms turned slowly along the edge of side-walks; a pale-faced youth strolled, overcome by weariness, by the side of his stick and with the tails of his overcoat flapping gently near his heels; horses stepped gingerly on the greasy pavement, tossing their heads; two young girls passed by, talking vivaciously and with shining eyes; a fine old fellow strutted, red-faced, stroking a white moustache; and a line of yellow boards with blue letters on them approached us slowly, tossing on high behind one another like some queer wreckage adrift upon a river of hats.

"Ye-e-e-s," repeated Jackson. His clear blue eyes looked about, contemptuous, amused and hard, like the eyes of a boy. A clumsy string of red, yellow, and green omnibuses rolled swaying, monstrous and gaudy; two shabby children ran across the road; a knot of dirty men with red neckerchiefs round their bare throats lurched along, discussing filthily; a ragged old man with a face of despair yelled horribly in the mud the name of a paper; while far off, amongst the tossing heads of horses, the dull flash of harnesses, the jumble of lustrous panels and roofs of carriages, we could see a policeman, helmeted and dark, stretching out a rigid arm at the crossing of the streets.

"Yes; I see it," said Jackson, slowly. "It is there; it pants, it runs, it rolls; it is strong and alive; it would smash you if

Karain: A Memory

you didn't look out; but I'll be hanged if it is yet as real to me as . . . as the other thing . . . say, Karain's story."

I think that, decidedly, he had been too long away from home.

Commentary on 'Karain: A Memory'

Although *Karain* was completed less than a year after *An Outpost of Progress*, it marks a clear technical advance. For the first time Conrad uses a narrator who is also an actor in the drama. In *Youth*, published one year later, the inner narrator is named as Marlow, and Conrad found this invention so useful that he gave him an increasingly complex role in *Heart of Darkness* and *Lord Jim*. Such a character is often referred to as a choral character as he performs much the same role as the Chorus in Greek drama. The initial advantage of such a device is explained by Conrad's friend and collaborator, Ford Madox Ford, in *Joseph Conrad: A Personal Remembrance*: 'If your yearning to amend the human race is so great that you can't possibly keep your fingers out of the watch-springs there is a device that you can adopt.... You must then invent, justify, and set going in your novel a character who can convincingly express your views.' Joseph Conrad did not have Jonathan Swift's passionate desire to 'amend the human race', but he needed the opportunity to meditate aloud about the characters he developed and the situations that their interactions created. He frequently stressed his close relationship with his fictional narrator. In an Author's Note to an edition of *Youth* published in 1917 he wrote: 'He haunts my hours of solitude, when, in silence, we lay our heads together in great comfort and harmony.'

Commentary on 'Karain: A Memory'

Two additional advantages of this device are immediately apparent in *Karain*. The first is that the author is able to place a distance in time between the dramatic events of the story and the evaluating of them, and thus allow the narrator to probe, analyse and meditate upon these events and the states of mind of those engaged in them. Moreover, he can do this without breaking into the illusion of the story by obtruding the comments of an omniscient narrator. Secondly, he gives actuality and authenticity to the story—we are listening to someone who was there! We may notice how the narrator here withholds later knowledge and so recreates his own original puzzled state of mind.

In the final analysis it is not the events of the story that are of primary interest but the interpretation that the author, through his narrator, puts upon them. One should perhaps add a word of warning; as Conrad developed Marlow's role, he allowed him at times only a partial understanding of some of the events in which he was involved. As a result, Marlow's partial perception can serve as a foil to our own deeper understanding. But in doing this Conrad is not departing radically from his initial conception of Marlow as a choral character.

The importance of the narrator in this story is indicated by the full title, *Karain: A Memory*. The narrator spends the first half of the story, the first three chapters, creating a vivid visual impression of Karain and his land as he knew them many years before. The style has all the lush romanticism that one associates with early Conrad with its 'subtle and penetrating perfume as of land breezes breathing through the starlight of bygone nights.' But the tone is also one of nostalgia for a past when a young gun-runner in the Eastern seas lived dramatically and saw life as fresh, exciting and devoid of uncertainties. It is a world where 'green islets scattered through the calm of noon-day lie upon the level of a polished sea, like a handful of emeralds on a buckler of steel.' It is in-

Commentary on 'Karain: A Memory'

teresting to compare the imagery used here with that of the closing paragraphs describing London.

As the story unfolds, we see that the nostalgia is not merely for a lost youth of adventure and excitement but for the clearer moral standards of an earlier age: modern Englishmen are 'befogged' and 'timid', whereas their predecessors were 'imaginative' and 'courageous'. The contrast between the past and the present heralds the contrast between the illusion and reality that lies at the core of this story. The narrator introduces many images from drama and the illusory world of the stage as he leads us to see that illusions can in fact be salutary in that they have the power to conquer remorse and guilt. In describing Karain, he says: 'He was treated with a solemn respect accorded in the irreverent West only to the monarchs of the stage, and he accepted the profound homage with a sustained dignity seen nowhere else but behind the footlights and in the condensed falseness of some grossly tragic situations.' The narrator is clearly intent upon stressing both the theatrical nature of heroism and the power of illusions. Later, during a pause in Karain's confession, the narrator universalizes Karain's significance and reveals his own involvement to us:

> And I looked on, surprised and moved; I looked at that man, loyal to a vision, betrayed by his dream, spurned by his illusion, and coming to us unbelievers for help—against a thought.... I thought of his wanderings, of that obscure Odyssey of revenge, of all the men that wander amongst illusions; of the illusions as restless as men; of the illusions faithful, faithless; of the illusions that give pain, that give peace; of the invincible illusions that can make life and death appear serene, inspiring, tormented or ignoble.

After Karain leaves to return to his 'stage', to his 'illusion of unavoidable success', satisfied with the illusion of the talisman, the narrator addresses us directly for the first time:

Commentary on 'Karain: A Memory'

'I wonder what they [Karain's followers] thought; what he thought . . . what the reader thinks?' And it is seven years later when Jackson, met by chance in a London street, tells him that Karain's story was more real to him than the roar of London's traffic.

There is a close similarity between the heroes of *Karain* and *Lord Jim*; both are well intentioned men who commit impulsive crimes and then suffer from long periods of remorse as they attempt without avail to run away from the memory of their deeds. And both come at last to communicate their guilt to a narrator whose response is revealed to us. Conrad described *Karain* as 'magazine'ish' and was clearly not satisfied with the link he establishes between primitive and civilized, and East and West. *Lord Jim*, which was originally intended as a short story, shows the extent to which he benefited from a much larger canvas.

SUGGESTIONS FOR FURTHER READING
Almayer's Folly and *An Outcast of the Islands*—the first two 'Malayan' novels
The Lagoon—similar short story with betrayal and remorse theme
Youth—first appearance of Marlow
Lord Jim
Joseph Conrad's Fiction by John A. Palmer. Chapter 1, 'The Early Marlow Tales', is particularly relevant

The Secret Sharer

I

On my right hand there were lines of fishing-stakes resembling a mysterious system of half-submerged bamboo fences, incomprehensible in its division of the domain of tropical fishes, and crazy of aspect as if abandoned for ever by some nomad tribe of fishermen now gone to the other end of the ocean; for there was no sign of human habitation as far as the eye could reach. To the left a group of barren islets, suggesting ruins of stone walls, towers, and blockhouses, had its foundations set in a blue sea that itself looked solid, so still and stable did it lie below my feet; even the track of light from the westering sun shone smoothly, without that animated glitter which tells of an imperceptible ripple. And when I turned my head to take a parting glance at the tug which had just left us anchored outside the bar, I saw the straight line of the flat shore joined to the stable sea, edge to edge, with a perfect and unmarked closeness, in one levelled floor half brown, half blue under the enormous dome of the sky. Corresponding in their insignificance to the islets of the sea, two small clumps of trees, one on each side of the only fault in the impeccable joint, marked the mouth of the river Meinam we had just left on the first preparatory stage of our homeward journey; and, far back on the inland level, a larger and loftier mass, the grove surrounding the great Paknam pagoda, was the only thing on which the eye could rest from the vain task of exploring the momentous sweep of the horizon. Here and there gleams as of a few scattered

The Secret Sharer

pieces of silver marked the windings of the great river; and on the nearest of them, just within the bar, the tug steaming right into the land became lost to my sight, hull and funnel and masts, as though the impassive earth had swallowed her up without an effort, without a tremor. My eye followed the light cloud of her smoke, now here, now there, above the plain, according to the devious curves of the stream, but always fainter and farther away, till I lost it at last behind the mitre-shaped hill of the great pagoda. And then I was left alone with my ship, anchored at the head of the Gulf of Siam.

She floated at the starting-point of a long journey, very still in an immense stillness, the shadows of her spars flung far to the eastward by the setting sun. At that moment I was alone on her decks. There was not a sound in her—and around us nothing moved, nothing lived, not a canoe on the water, not a bird in the air, not a cloud in the sky. In this breathless pause at the threshold of a long passage we seemed to be measuring our fitness for a long and arduous enterprise, the appointed task of both our existences to be carried out, far from all human eyes, with only sky and sea for spectators and for judges.

There must have been some glare in the air to interfere with one's sight, because it was only just before the sun left us that my roaming eyes made out beyond the highest ridge of the principal islet of the group something which did away with the solemnity of perfect solitude. The tide of darkness flowed on swiftly; and with tropical suddenness a swarm of stars came out above the shadowy earth, while I lingered yet, my hand resting lightly on my ship's rail as if on the shoulder of a trusted friend. But, with all that multitude of celestial bodies staring down at one, the comfort of quiet communion with her was gone for good. And there were also disturbing sounds by this time—voices, footsteps forward, the steward flitted along the main-deck, a busily ministering spirit; a hand-bell tinkled urgently under the poop-deck. . . .

The Secret Sharer

I found my two officers waiting for me near the supper table, in the lighted cuddy. We sat down at once, and as I helped the chief mate, I said:

"Are you aware that there is a ship anchored inside the islands? I saw her mastheads above the ridge as the sun went down."

He raised sharply his simple face, overcharged by a terrible growth of whisker, and emitted his usual ejaculations: "Bless my soul, sir! You don't say so!"

My second mate was a round-cheeked, silent young man, grave beyond his years, I thought; but as our eyes happened to meet I detected a slight quiver on his lips. I looked down at once. It was not my part to encourage sneering on board my ship. It must be said, too, that I knew very little of my officers. In consequence of certain events of no particular significance, except to myself, I had been appointed to the command only a fortnight before. Neither did I know much of the hands forward. All these people had been together for eighteen months or so, and my position was that of the only stranger on board. I mention this because it has some bearing on what is to follow. But what I felt most was my being a stranger to the ship; and if all the truth must be told, I was somewhat of a stranger to myself. The youngest man on board (barring the second mate), and untried as yet by a position of the fullest responsibility, I was willing to take the adequacy of the others for granted. They had simply to be equal to their tasks; but I wondered how far I should turn out faithful to that ideal conception of one's own personality every man sets up for himself secretly.

Meantime the chief mate, with an almost visible effect of collaboration on the part of his round eyes and frightful whiskers, was trying to evolve a theory of the anchored ship. His dominant trait was to take all things into earnest consideration. He was of a painstaking turn of mind. As he

The Secret Sharer

used to say, he "liked to account to himself" for practically everything that came in his way, down to a miserable scorpion he had found in his cabin a week before. The why and the wherefore of that scorpion—how it got on board and came to select his room rather than the pantry (which was a dark place and more what a scorpion would be partial to), and how on earth it managed to drown itself in the ink-well of his writing-desk—had exercised him infinitely. The ship within the islands was much more easily accounted for; and just as we were about to rise from table he made his pronouncement. She was, he doubted not, a ship from home lately arrived. Probably she drew too much water to cross the bar except at the top of spring tides. Therefore she went into that natural harbour to wait for a few days in preference to remaining in an open roadstead.

"That's so, " confirmed the second mate, suddenly, in his slightly hoarse voice. "She draws over twenty feet. She's the Liverpool ship *Sephora* with a cargo of coal. Hundred and twenty-three days from Cardiff."

We looked at him in surprise.

"The tugboat skipper told me when he came on board for your letters, sir," explained the young man. "He expects to take her up the river the day after tomorrow."

After thus overwhelming us with the extent of his information he slipped out of the cabin. The mate observed regretfully that he "could not account for that young fellow's whims". What prevented him telling us all about it at once? he wanted to know.

I detained him as he was making a move. For the last two days the crew had had plenty of hard work, and the night before they had very little sleep. I felt painfully that I—a stranger—was doing something unusual when I directed him to let all hands turn in without setting an anchor-watch. I proposed to keep on deck myself till one o'clock or thereabouts. I would get the second mate to relieve me at that hour.

The Secret Sharer

"He will turn out the cook and the steward at four," I concluded, "and then give you a call. Of course at the slightest sign of any sort of wind we'll have the hands up and make a start at once."

He concealed his astonishment. "Very well, sir." Outside the cuddy he put his head in the second mate's door to inform him of my unheard-of caprice to take a five hours' anchor-watch on myself. I heard the other raise his voice incredulously—"What? The captain himself?" Then a few more murmurs, a door closed, then another. A few moments later I went on deck.

My strangeness, which had made me sleepless, had prompted that unconventional arrangement, as if I had expected in those solitary hours of the night to get on terms with the ship of which I knew nothing, manned by men of whom I knew very little more. Fast alongside a wharf, littered like any ship in port with a tangle of unrelated things, invaded by unrelated shore people, I had hardly seen her yet properly. Now, as she lay cleared for sea, the stretch of her main-deck seemed to me very fine under the stars. Very fine, very roomy for her size, and very inviting. I descended the poop and paced the waist, my mind picturing to myself the coming passage through the Malay Archipelago, down the Indian Ocean, and up the Atlantic. All its phases were familiar enough to me, every characteristic, all the alternatives which were likely to face me on the high seas—everything! . . . except the novel responsibility of command. But I took heart from the reasonable thought that the ship was like other ships, the men like other men, and that the sea was not likely to keep any special surprises expressly for my discomfiture.

Arrived at that comforting conclusion, I bethought myself of a cigar and went below to get it. All was still down there. Everybody at the after end of the ship was sleeping profoundly. I came out again on the quarter-deck, agreeably at ease in my sleeping-suit on that warm breathless night,

The Secret Sharer

barefooted, a glowing cigar in my teeth, and, going forward, I was met by the profound silence of the fore end of the ship. Only as I passed the door of the forecastle I heard a deep, quiet, trustful sigh of some sleeper inside. And suddenly I rejoiced in the great security of the sea as compared with the unrest of the land, in my choice of that untempted life presenting no disquieting problems, invested with an elementary moral beauty by the absolute straightforwardness of its appeal and by the singleness of its purpose.

The riding-light in the fore-rigging burned with a clear, untroubled, as if symbolic, flame, confident and bright in the mysterious shades of the night. Passing on my way aft along the other side of the ship, I observed that the rope sideladder, put over, no doubt, for the master of the tug when he came to fetch away our letters, had not been hauled in as it should have been. I became annoyed at this, for exactitude in small matters is the very soul of discipline. Then I reflected that I had myself peremptorily dismissed my officers from duty, and by my own act had prevented the anchor-watch being formally set and things properly attended to. I asked myself whether it was wise ever to interfere with the established routine of duties even from the kindest motives. My action might have made me appear eccentric. Goodness only knew how that absurdly whiskered mate would "account" for my conduct, and what the whole ship thought of that informality of their new captain. I was vexed with myself.

Not from compunction certainly, but, as it were mechanically, I proceeded to get the ladder in myself. Now a sideladder of that sort is a light affair and comes in easily, yet my vigorous tug, which should have brought it flying on board, merely recoiled upon my body in a totally unexpected jerk. What the devil! . . . I was so astounded by the immovableness of that ladder that I remained stock-still, trying to account for it to myself like that imbecile mate of mine. In the end, of course, I put my head over the rail.

The Secret Sharer

The side of the ship made an opaque belt of shadow on the darkling glassy shimmer of the sea. But I saw at once something elongated and pale floating very close to the ladder. Before I could form a guess a faint flash of phosphorescent light, which seemed to issue suddenly from the naked body of a man, flickered in the sleeping water with the elusive, silent play of summer lightning in a night sky. With a gasp I saw revealed to my stare a pair of feet, the long legs, a broad livid back immersed right up to the neck in a greenish cadaverous glow. One hand, awash, clutched the bottom rung of the ladder. He was complete but for the head. A headless corpse! The cigar dropped out of my gaping mouth with a tiny plop and a short hiss quite audible in the absolute stillness of all things under heaven. At that I suppose he raised up his face, a dimly pale oval in the shadow of the ship's side. But even then I could only barely make out down there the shape of his black-haired head. However, it was enough for the horrid, frost-bound sensation which had gripped me about the chest to pass off. The moment of vain exclamations was past, too. I only climbed on the spare spar and leaned over the rail as far as I could, to bring my eyes nearer to that mystery floating alongside.

As he hung by the ladder, like a resting swimmer, the sea-lightning played about his limbs at every stir; and he appeared in it ghastly, silvery, fish-like. He remained as mute as a fish, too. He made no motion to get out of the water, either. It was inconceivable that he should not attempt to come on board, and strangely troubling to suspect that perhaps he did not want to. And my first words were prompted by just that troubled incertitude.

"What's the matter?" I asked in my ordinary tone, speaking down to the face upturned exactly under mine.

"Cramp," it answered, no louder. Then slightly anxious, "I say, no need to call anyone."

"I was not going to," I said.

The Secret Sharer

"Are you alone on deck?"

"Yes."

I had somehow the impression that he was on the point of letting go the ladder to swim away beyond my ken—mysterious as he came. But, for the moment, this being appearing as if he had risen from the bottom of the sea (it was certainly the nearest land to the ship) wanted only to know the time. I told him. And he, down there, tentatively:

"I suppose your captain's turned in?"

"I am sure he isn't," I said.

He seemed to struggle with himself, for I heard something like the low, bitter murmur of doubt. "What's the good?" His next words came out with a hesitating effort.

"Look here, my man. Could you call him out quietly?"

I thought the time had come to declare myself.

"*I* am the captain."

I heard a "By Jove!" whispered at the level of the water. The phosphorescence flashed in the swirl of the water all about his limbs, his other hand seized the ladder.

"My name's Leggatt."

The voice was calm and resolute. A good voice. The self-possession of that man had somehow induced a corresponding state in myself. It was very quietly that I remarked:

"You must be a good swimmer."

"Yes. I've been in the water practically since nine o'clock. The question for me now is whether I am to let go this ladder and go on swimming till I sink from exhaustion, or—to come on board here."

I felt this was no mere formula of desperate speech, but a real alternative in the view of a strong soul. I should have gathered from this that he was young; indeed, it is only the young who are ever confronted by such clear issues. But at the time it was pure intuition on my part. A mysterious communication was established already between us two—in the face of that silent, darkened tropical sea. I was young, too; young enough to make no comment. The man in the water began suddenly to climb up the ladder, and I hastened away from the rail to fetch some clothes.

Before entering the cabin I stood still, listening in the lobby at the foot of the stairs. A faint snore came through the closed door of the chief mate's room. The second mate's door was on the hook, but the darkness in there was absolutely soundless. He, too, was young and could sleep like a stone. Remained the steward, but he was not likely to wake up before he was called. I got a sleeping-suit out of my room and, coming back on deck saw the naked man from the sea sitting on the main-hatch, glimmering white in the darkness, his elbows on his knees and his head in his hands. In a moment he had concealed his damp body in a sleeping-suit of the same grey-stripe pattern as the one I was wearing and followed me like my double on the poop. Together we moved right aft, barefooted, silent.

"What is it?" I asked in a deadened voice, taking the lighted lamp out of the binnacle and raising it to his face.

"An ugly business."

He had rather regular features; a good mouth; light eyes under somewhat heavy, dark eyebrows; a smooth, square forehead; no growth on his cheeks; a small brown moustache, and a well-shaped, round chin. His expression was concentrated, meditative, under the inspecting light of the lamp I held up to his face, such as a man thinking hard in solitude might wear. My sleeping-suit was just right for his size. A well-knit young fellow of twenty-five at most. He caught his lower lip with the edge of white, even teeth.

"Yes," I said, replacing the lamp in the binnacle. The warm, heavy tropical night closed upon his head again.

"There's a ship over there," he murmured.

"Yes, I know. The *Sephora*. Did you know of us?"

"Hadn't the slightest idea. I am the mate of her——" He paused and corrected himself. "I should say I *was*."

"Aha! Something wrong?"

"Yes. Very wrong indeed. I've killed a man."

"What do you mean? Just now?"

"No, on the passage. Weeks ago. Thirty-nine south. When I say a man——"

"Fit of temper," I suggested, confidently.

The shadowy, dark head, like mine, seemed to nod imperceptibly above the ghostly grey of my sleeping-suit. It was, in the night, as though I had been faced by my own reflection in the depths of a sombre and immense mirror.

"A pretty thing to have to own up to for a Conway boy," murmured my double, distinctly.

"You're a Conway boy?"

"I am," he said, as if startled. Then, slowly—"Perhaps you too——"

It was so; but being a couple of years older I had left before he joined. After a quick interchange of dates a silence fell; and I thought suddenly of my absurd mate with his terrific whiskers and the "Bless my soul—you don't say so" type of intellect. My double gave me an inkling of his thoughts by saying:

"My father's a parson in Norfolk. Do you see me before a judge and jury on that charge? For myself I can't see the necessity. There are fellows that an angel from heaven—— And I am not that. He was one of those creatures that are just simmering all the time with a silly sort of wickedness. Miserable devils that have no business to live at all. He wouldn't do his duty and wouldn't let anybody else do theirs. But what's the good of talking! You know well enough the sort of ill-conditioned snarling cur——"

He appealed to me as if our experiences had been as identical as our clothes. And I knew well enough the pestiferous danger of such a character where there are no means of legal repression. And I knew well enough also that my double there was no homicidal ruffian. I did not think of asking him for details, and he told me the story roughly in brusque, disconnected sentences. I needed no more. I saw it all going on as though I were myself inside that other sleeping-suit.

"It happened while we were setting a reefed foresail at dusk. Reefed foresail! You understand the sort of weather. The only sail we had left to keep the ship running; so you may guess what it had been like for days. Anxious sort of job, that. He gave me some of his cursed insolence at the sheet. I tell you I was over-done with this terrific weather that seemed to have no end to it. Terrific, I tell you—and a deep ship. I believe the fellow himself was half crazed with funk. It was no time for gentlemanly reproof, so I turned round and felled him like an ox. He up and at me. We closed just as an awful sea made for the ship. All hands saw it coming and took to the rigging, but I had him by the throat, and went on shaking him like a rat, the men above us yelling, 'Look out! look out!' Then a crash as if the sky had fallen on my head. They say that for over ten minutes hardly anything was to be seen of the ship—just the three masts and a bit of the forecastle head and of the poop all awash driving along in a smother of foam. It was a miracle that they found us, jammed together behind the forebits. It's clear that I meant business, because I was holding him by the throat still when they picked us up. He was black in the face. It was too much for them. It seems they rushed us aft together, gripped as we were, screaming 'Murder!' like a lot of lunatics, and broke into the cuddy. And the ship running for her life, touch and go all the time, any minute her last in a sea fit to turn your hair grey only a-looking at it. I understand that the skipper, too, started raving like the rest of them. The man had been deprived of sleep for more than a week, and to have this sprung on him at the height of a furious gale nearly drove him out of his mind. I wonder they didn't fling me overboard after getting the carcase of their precious shipmate out of my fingers. They had rather a job to separate us, I've been told. A

The Secret Sharer

sufficiently fierce story to make an old judge and a respectable jury sit up a bit. The first thing I heard when I came to myself was the maddening howling of that endless gale, and on that the voice of the old man. He was hanging on to my bunk, staring into my face out of his sou'wester.

"'Mr Leggatt, you have killed a man. You can act no longer as chief mate of this ship.'"

His care to subdue his voice made it sound monotonous. He rested a hand on the end of the skylight to steady himself with, and all that time did not stir a limb, so far as I could see. "Nice little tale for a quiet tea-party," he concluded in the same tone.

One of my hands, too, rested on the end of the skylight; neither did I stir a limb, so far as I knew. We stood less than a foot from each other. It occurred to me that if old "Bless my soul—you don't say so" were to put his head up the companion and catch sight of us, he would think he was seeing double, or imagine himself come upon a scene of weird witchcraft; the strange captain having a quiet confabulation by the wheel with his own grey ghost. I became very much concerned to prevent anything of the sort. I heard the other's soothing undertone.

"My father's a parson in Norfolk," it said. Evidently he had forgotten he had told me this important fact before. Truly a nice little tale.

"You had better slip down into my stateroom now," I said, moving off stealthily. My double followed my movements; our bare feet made no sound; I let him in, closed the door with care, and, after giving a call to the second mate, returned on deck for my relief.

"Not much sign of any wind yet," I remarked when he approached.

"No, sir. Not much," he assented sleepily, in his hoarse voice, with just enough deference, no more, and barely suppressing a yawn.

107

The Secret Sharer

"Well, that's all you have to look out for. You have got your orders."

"Yes, sir."

I paced a turn or two on the poop and saw him take up his position face forward with his elbow in the rat-lines of the mizzen-rigging before I went below. The mate's faint snoring was still going on peacefully. The cuddy lamp was burning over the table on which stood a vase with flowers, a polite attention from the ship's provision merchant—the last flowers we should see for the next three months at the very least. Two bunches of bananas hung from the beam symmetrically, one on each side of the rudder-casing. Everything was as before in the ship—except that two of her captain's sleeping-suits were simultaneously in use, one motionless in the cuddy, the other keeping very still in the captain's stateroom.

It must be explained here that my cabin had the form of the capital letter L, the door being within the angle and opening into the short part of the letter. A couch was to the left, the bed-place to the right; my writing-desk and the chronometers' table faced the door. But anyone opening it, unless he stepped right inside, had no view of what I call the long (or vertical) part of the letter. It contained some lockers surmounted by a bookcase; and a few clothes, a thick jacket or two, caps, oilskin coat, and such like, hung on hooks. There was at the bottom of that part a door opening into my bathroom, which could be entered also directly from the saloon. But that way was never used.

The mysterious arrival had discovered the advantage of this particular shape. Entering my room, lighted strongly by a big bulkhead lamp swung on gimbals above my writing-desk, I did not see him anywhere till he stepped out quietly from behind the coats hung in the recessed part.

"I heard somebody moving about, and went in there at once," he whispered.

I, too, spoke under my breath.

The Secret Sharer

"Nobody is likely to come in here without knocking and getting permission."

He nodded. His face was thin and the sunburn faded, as though he had been ill. And no wonder. He had been, I heard presently, kept under arrest in his cabin for nearly seven weeks. But there was nothing sickly in his eyes or in his expression. He was not a bit like me, really; yet, as we stood leaning over my bed-place, whispering side by side, with our dark heads together and our backs to the door, anybody bold enough to open it stealthily would have been treated to the uncanny sight of a double captain busy talking in whispers with his other self.

"But all this doesn't tell me how you came to hang on to our side-ladder," I inquired, in the hardly audible murmurs we used, after he had told me something more of the proceedings on board the *Sephora* once the bad weather was over.

"When we sighted Java Head I had had time to think all those matters out several times over. I had six weeks of doing nothing else, and with only an hour or so every evening for a tramp on the quarter-deck".

He whispered, his arms folded on the side of my bed-place, staring through the open port. And I could imagine perfectly the manner of this thinking out—a stubborn if not a steadfast operation; something of which I should have been perfectly incapable.

"I reckoned it would be dark before we closed with the land," he continued, so low that I had to strain my hearing, near as we were to each other, shoulder touching shoulder almost. "So I asked to speak to the old man. He always seemed very sick when he came to see me—as if he could not look me in the face. You know, that foresail saved the ship. She was too deep to have run long under bare poles. And it was I that managed to set it for him. Anyway, he came. When I had him in my cabin—he stood by the door

The Secret Sharer

looking at me as if I had the halter round my neck already—I asked him right away to leave my cabin door unlocked at night while the ship was going through Sunda Straits. There would be the Java coast within two or three miles, off Angier Point. I wanted nothing more. I've had a prize for swimming my second year in the Conway."

"I can believe it," I breathed out.

"God only knows why they locked me in every night. To see some of their faces you'd have thought they were afraid I'd go about at night strangling people. Am I a murdering brute? Do I look it? By Jove! if I had been he wouldn't have trusted himself like that into my room. You'll say I might have chucked him aside and bolted out, there and then—it was dark already. Well, no. And for the same reason I wouldn't think of trying to smash the door. There would have been a rush to stop me at the noise, and I did not mean to get into a confounded scrimmage. Somebody else might have got killed—for I would not have broken out only to get chucked back, and I did not want any more of that work. He refused, looking more sick than ever. He was afraid of the men, and also of that old second mate of his who had been sailing with him for years—a grey-headed old humbug; and his steward, too, had been with him devil knows how long—seventeen years or more—a dogmatic sort of loafer who hated me like poison, just because I was the chief mate. No chief mate ever made more than one voyage in the *Sephora*, you know. Those two old chaps ran the ship. Devil only knows what the skipper wasn't afraid of (all his nerve went to pieces altogether in that hellish spell of bad weather we had)—of what the law would do to him—of his wife, perhaps. Oh, yes! she's on board. Though I don't think she would have meddled. She would have been only too glad to have me out of the ship in any way. The 'brand of Cain' business, don't you see. That's all right. I was ready enough to go off wandering on the face of the earth—and that was

110

The Secret Sharer

price enough to pay for an Abel of that sort. Anyhow, he wouldn't listen to me. 'This thing must take its course. I represent the law here.' He was shaking like a leaf. 'So you won't?' 'No!' 'Then I hope you will be able to sleep on that,' I said, and turned my back on him. 'I wonder that *you* can,' cries he, and locks the door.

"Well, after that, I couldn't. Not very well. That was three weeks ago. We have had a slow passage through the Java Sea; drifted about Carimata for ten days. When we anchored here they thought, I suppose, it was all right. The nearest land (and that's five miles) is the ship's destination; the consul would soon set about catching me; and there would have been no object in bolting to these islets there. I don't suppose there's a drop of water on them. I don't know how it was, but tonight that steward, after bringing me my supper, went out to let me eat it, and left the door unlocked. And I ate it—all there was, too. After I had finished I strolled out on the quarter-deck. I don't know that I meant doing anything. A breath of fresh air was all I wanted, I believe. Then a sudden temptation came over me. I kicked off my slippers and was in the water before I had made up my mind fairly. Somebody heard the splash and they raised an awful hullabaloo. 'He's gone! Lower the boats! He's committed suicide! No, he's swimming.' Certainly I was swimming. It's not so easy for a swimmer like me to commit suicide by drowning. I landed on the nearest islet before the boat left the ship's side. I heard them pulling about in the dark, hailing and so on, but after a bit they gave up. Everything quieted down and the anchorage became as still as death. I sat down on a stone and began to think. I felt certain they would start searching for me at daylight. There was no place to hide on those stony things—and if there had been, what would have been the good? But now I was clear of that ship, I was not going back. So after a while I took off all my clothes, tied them up in a bundle with a stone inside, and dropped them

The Secret Sharer

in the deep water on the outer side of that islet. That was suicide enough for me. Let them think what they liked, but I didn't mean to drown myself. I meant to swim till I sank—but that's not the same thing. I struck out for another of these little islands, and it was from that one that I first saw your riding-light. Something to swim for. I went on easily, and on the way I came upon a flat rock a foot or two above the water. In the daytime, I dare say, you might make it out with a glass from your poop. I scrambled up on it and rested myself for a bit. Then I made another start. That last spell must have been over a mile."

His whisper was getting fainter and fainter, and all the time he stared straight out through the port-hole, in which there was not even a star to be seen. I had not interrupted him. There was something that made comment impossible in his narrative, or perhaps in himself; a sort of feeling, a quality, which I can't find a name for. And when he ceased, all I found was a futile whisper: "So you swam for our light?"

"Yes—straight for it. It was something to swim for. I couldn't see any stars low down because the coast was in the way, and I couldn't see the land, either. The water was like glass. One might have been swimming in a confounded thousand-feet deep cistern with no place for scrambling out anywhere; but what I didn't like was the notion of swimming round and round like a crazed bullock before I gave out; and as I didn't mean to go back . . . No. Do you see me being hauled back, stark naked, off one of these little islands by the scruff of the neck and fighting like a wild beast? Somebody would have got killed for certain, and I did not want any of that. So I went on. Then your ladder——"

"Why didn't you hail the ship?" I asked, a little louder.

He touched my shoulder lightly. Lazy footsteps came right over our heads and stopped. The second mate had crossed from the other side of the poop and might have been hanging over the rail, for all we knew.

The Secret Sharer

"He couldn't hear us talking—could he?" my double breathed into my very ear, anxiously.

His anxiety was an answer, a sufficient answer, to the question I had put to him. An answer containing all the difficulty of that situation. I closed the port-hole quietly, to make sure. A louder word might have been overheard.

"Who's that?" he whispered then.

"My second mate. But I don't know much more of the fellow than you do."

And I told him a little about myself. I had been appointed to take charge while I least expected anything of the sort, not quite a fortnight ago. I didn't know either the ship or the people. Hadn't had the time in port to look about me or size anybody up. And as to the crew, all they knew was that I was appointed to take the ship home. For the rest, I was almost as much of a stranger on board as himself, I said. And at the moment I felt it most acutely. I felt that it would take very little to make me a suspect person in the eyes of the ship's company.

He had turned about meantime; and we, the two strangers in the ship, faced each other in identical attitudes.

"Your ladder——" he murmured, after a silence. "Who'd have thought of finding a ladder hanging over at night in a ship anchored out here! I felt just then a very unpleasant faintness. After the life I've been leading for nine weeks, anybody would have got out of condition. I wasn't capable of swimming round as far as your rudder-chains. And, lo and behold! there was a ladder to get hold of. After I gripped it I said to myself, 'What's the good?' When I saw a man's head looking over I thought I would swim away presently and leave him shouting—in whatever language it was. I didn't mind being looked at. I—I liked it. And then you speaking to me so quietly—as if you had expected me—made me hold on a little longer. It had been a confounded lonely time—I don't mean while swimming. I was glad to talk a little to somebody that didn't belong to the *Sephora*. As to asking

The Secret Sharer

for the captain, that was a mere impulse. It could have been no use, with all the ship knowing about me and the other people pretty certain to be round here in the morning. I don't know—I wanted to be seen, to talk with somebody, before I went on. I don't know what I would have said. . . . 'Fine night, isn't it?' or something of the sort."

"Do you think they will be round here presently?" I asked with some incredulity.

"Quite likely," he said, faintly.

He looked extremely haggard all of a sudden. His head rolled on his shoulders.

"H'm. We shall see then. Meantime get into that bed," I whispered. "Want help? There."

It was a rather high bed-place with a set of drawers underneath. This amazing swimmer really needed the lift I gave him by seizing his leg. He tumbled in, rolled over on his back, and flung one arm across his eyes. And then, with his face nearly hidden, he must have looked exactly as I used to look in that bed. I gazed upon my other self for a while before drawing across carefully the two green serge curtains which ran on a brass rod. I thought for a moment of pinning them together for greater safety, but I sat down on the couch, and once there I felt unwilling to rise and hunt for a pin. I would do it in a moment. I was extremely tired, in a peculiarly intimate way, by the strain of stealthiness, by the effort of whispering and the general secrecy of this excitement. It was three o'clock by now and I had been on my feet since nine, but I was not sleepy; I could not have gone to sleep. I sat there, fagged out, looking at the curtains, trying to clear my mind of the confused sensation of being in two places at once, and greatly bothered by an exasperating knocking in my head. It was a relief to discover suddenly that it was not my head at all, but on the outside of the door. Before I could collect myself the words "Come in" were out of my mouth, and the steward entered with a tray, bringing in my morning

The Secret Sharer

coffee. I had slept, after all, and I was so frightened that I shouted, "This way! I am here, steward," as though he had been miles away. He put down the tray on the table next the couch and only then said, very quietly, "I can see you are here, sir." I felt him give me a keen look, but I dared not meet his eyes just then. He must have wondered why I had drawn the curtains of my bed before going to sleep on the couch. He went out, hooking the door open as usual.

I heard the crew washing decks above me. I knew I would have been told at once if there had been any wind. Calm, I thought, and I was doubly vexed. Indeed, I felt dual more than ever. The steward reappeared suddenly in the doorway. I jumped up from the couch so quickly that he gave a start.

"What do you want here?"

"Close your port, sir—they are washing decks."

"It is closed," I said, reddening.

"Very well, sir." But he did not move from the doorway and returned my stare in an extraordinary, equivocal manner for a time. Then his eyes wavered, all his expression changed, and in a voice unusually gentle, almost coaxingly:

"May I come in to take the empty cup away, sir?"

"Of course!" I turned my back on him while he popped in and out. Then I unhooked and closed the door and even pushed the bolt. This sort of thing could not go on very long. The cabin was as hot as an oven, too. I took a peep at my double, and discovered that he had not moved, his arm was still over his eyes; but his chest heaved; his hair was wet; his chin glistened with perspiration. I reached over him and opened the port.

"I must show myself on deck," I reflected.

Of course, theoretically, I could do what I liked, with no one to say nay to me within the whole circle of the horizon; but to lock my cabin door and take the key away I did not dare. Directly I put my head out of the companion I saw the group of my two officers, the second mate barefooted, the

The Secret Sharer

chief mate in long india-rubber boots, near the break of the poop, and the steward half-way down the poop-ladder talking to them eagerly. He happened to catch sight of me and dived, the second ran down on the main-deck shouting some order or other, and the chief mate came to meet me, touching his cap.

There was a sort of curiosity in his eye that I did not like. I don't know whether the steward had told them that I was "queer" only, or downright drunk, but I know the man meant to have a good look at me. I watched him coming with a smile which, as he got into point-blank range, took effect and froze his very whiskers. I did not give him time to open his lips.

"Square the yards by lifts and braces before the hands go to breakfast."

It was the first particular order I had given on board that ship; and I stayed on deck to see it executed, too. I had felt the need of asserting myself without loss of time. That sneering young cub got taken down a peg or two on that occasion, and I also seized the opportunity of having a good look at the face of every foremast man as they filed past me to go to the after braces. At breakfast-time, eating nothing myself, I presided with such frigid diginity that the two mates were only too glad to escape from the cabin as soon as decency permitted, and all the time the dual working of my mind distracted me almost to the point of insanity. I was constantly watching myself, my secret self, as dependent on my actions as my own personality, sleeping in that bed, behind that door which faced me as I sat at the head of the table. It was very much like being mad, only it was worse because one was aware of it.

I had to shake him for a solid minute, but when at last he opened his eyes it was in the full possession of his senses, with an inquiring look.

"All's well so far," I whispered. "Now you must vanish into the bathroom."

The Secret Sharer

He did so, as noiseless as a ghost, and I then rang for the steward, and facing him boldly, directed him to tidy up my stateroom while I was having my bath—"and be quick about it." As my tone admitted of no excuses, he said, "Yes, sir," and ran off to fetch his dust-pan and brushes. I took a bath and did most of my dressing, splashing, and whistling softly for the steward's edification, while the secret sharer of my life stood drawn up bolt upright in that little space, his face looking very sunken in daylight, his eyelids lowered under the stern, dark line of his eyebrows drawn together by a slight frown.

When I left him there to go back to my room the steward was finishing dusting. I sent for the mate and engaged him in some insignificant conversation. It was, as it were, trifling with the terrific character of his whiskers; but my object was to give him an opportunity for a good look at my cabin. And then I could at last shut, with a clear conscience, the door of my stateroom and get my double back into the recessed part. There was nothing else for it. He had to sit still on a small folding-stool, half smothered by the heavy coats hanging there. We listened to the steward going into the bathroom out of the saloon, filling the water-bottles there, scrubbing the bath, setting things to rights, whisk, bang, clatter—out again into the saloon—turn the key—click. Such was my scheme for keeping my second self invisible. Nothing better could be contrived under the circumstances. And there we sat; I at my writing-desk ready to appear busy with some papers, he behind me, out of sight of the door. It would not have been prudent to talk in daytime; and I could not have stood the excitement of that queer sense of whispering to myself. Now and then, glancing over my shoulder, I saw him far back there, sitting rigidly on the low stool, his bare feet close together, his arms folded, his head hanging on his breast—and perfectly still. Anybody would have taken him for me.

I was fascinated by it myself. Every moment I had to

glance over my shoulder. I was looking at him when a voice outside the door said:

"Beg pardon, sir."

"Well!" . . . I kept my eyes on him, and so, when the voice outside the door announced, "There's a ship's boat coming our way, sir," I saw him give a start—the first movement he had made for hours. But he did not raise his bowed head.

"All right. Get the ladder over."

I hesitated. Should I whisper something to him? But what? His immobility seemed to have been never disturbed. What could I tell him he did not know already? . . . Finally I went on deck.

II

The skipper of the *Sephora* had a thin red whisker all round his face, and the sort of complexion that goes with hair of that colour; also the particular, rather smeary shade of blue in the eyes. He was not exactly a showy figure; his shoulders were high, his stature but middling—one leg slightly more bandy than the other. He shook hands, looking vaguely around. A spiritless tenacity was his main characteristic, I judged. I behaved with a politeness which seemed to disconcert him. Perhaps he was shy. He mumbled to me as if he were ashamed of what he was saying; gave his name (it was something like Archbold—but at this distance of years I hardly am sure), his ship's name, and a few other particulars of that sort, in the manner of a criminal making a reluctant and doleful confession. He had had terrible weather on the passage out—terrible—terrible—wife aboard, too.

By this time we were seated in the cabin and the steward brought in a tray with a bottle and glasses.

"Thanks! No." Never took liquor. Would have some water, though. He drank two tumblerfuls. Terrible thirsty work. Ever since daylight had been exploring the islands round his ship.

The Secret Sharer

"What was that for—fun?" I asked, with an appearance of polite interest.

"No!" He sighed. "Painful duty."

As he persisted in his mumbling and I wanted my double to hear every word, I hit upon the notion of informing him that I regretted to say I was hard of hearing.

"Such a young man, too!" he nodded, keeping his smeary blue, unintelligent eyes fastened upon me. What was the cause of it—some disease? he inquired, without the least sympathy and as if he thought that, if so, I'd got no more than I deserved.

"Yes; disease," I admitted in a cheerful tone which seemed to shock him. But my point was gained, because he had to raise his voice to give me his tale. It is not worth while to record that version. It was just over two months since all this had happened, and he had thought so much about it that he seemed completely muddled as to its bearings, but still immensely impressed.

"What would you think of such a thing happening on board your own ship? I've had the *Sephora* for these fifteen years. I am a well-known shipmaster."

He was densely distressed—and perhaps I should have sympathized with him if I had been able to detach my mental vision from the unsuspected sharer of my cabin as though he were my second self. There he was on the other side of the bulkhead, four or five feet from us, no more, as we sat in the saloon. I looked politely at Captain Archbold (if that was his name), but it was the other I saw, in a grey sleeping-suit, seated on a low stool, his bare feet close together, his arms folded, and every word said between us falling into the ears of his dark head bowed on his chest.

"I have been at sea now, man and boy, for seven-and-thirty years, and I've never heard of such a thing happening in an English ship. And that it should be my ship. Wife on board, too."

The Secret Sharer

I was hardly listening to him.

"Don't you think," I said, "that the heavy sea which, you told me, came aboard just then might have killed the man? I have seen the sheer weight of a sea kill a man very neatly, by simply breaking his neck."

"Good God!" he uttered, impressively, fixing his smeary blue eyes on me. "The sea! No man killed by the sea ever looked like that." He seemed positively scandalized at my suggestion. And as I gazed at him, certainly not prepared for anything original on his part, he advanced his head close to mine and thrust his tongue out at me so suddenly that I couldn't help starting back.

After scoring over my calmness in this graphic way he nodded wisely. If I had seen the sight, he assured me, I would never forget it as long as I lived. The weather was too bad to give the corpse a proper sea burial. So next day at dawn they took it up on the poop, covering its face with a bit of bunting; he read a short prayer, and then, just as it was, in its oilskins and long boots, they launched it amongst those mountainous seas that seemed ready every moment to swallow up the ship herself and the terrified lives on board of her.

"That reefed foresail saved you," I threw in.

"Under God—it did," he exclaimed fervently. "It was by a special mercy, I firmly believe, that it stood some of those hurricane squalls."

"It was the setting of that sail which——" I began.

"God's own hand in it," he interrupted me. "Nothing less could have done it. I don't mind telling you that I hardly dared give the order. It seemed impossible that we could touch anything without losing it, and then our last hope would have been gone."

The terror of that gale was on him yet. I let him go on for a bit, then said, casually—as if returning to a minor subject:

"You were very anxious to give up your mate to the shore people, I believe?"

The Secret Sharer

He was. To the law. His obscure tenacity on that point had in it something incomprehensible and a little awful; something, as it were, mystical, quite apart from his anxiety that he should not be suspected of "countenancing any doings of that sort." Seven-and-thirty virtuous years at sea, of which over twenty of immaculate command, and the last fifteen in the *Sephora*, seemed to have laid him under some pitiless obligation.

"And you know," he went on, groping shamefacedly amongst his feelings, "I did not engage that young fellow. His people had some interest with my owners. I was in a way forced to take him on. He looked very smart, very gentlemanly, and all that. But do you know—I never liked him, somehow. I am a plain man. You see, he wasn't exactly the sort for the chief mate of a ship like the *Sephora*."

I had become so connected in thoughts and impressions with the secret sharer of my cabin that I felt as if I, personally, were being given to understand that I, too, was not the sort that would have done for the chief mate of a ship like the *Sephora*. I had no doubt of it in my mind.

"Not at all the style of man. You understand," he insisted, superfluously, looking hard at me.

I smiled urbanely. He seemed at a loss for a while.

"I suppose I must report a suicide."

"Beg pardon?"

"Sui—cide! That's what I'll have to write to my owners directly I get in."

"Unless you manage to recover him before tomorrow," I assented, dispassionately.... "I mean, alive."

He mumbled something which I really did not catch, and I turned my ear to him in a puzzled manner. He fairly bawled:

"The land—I say, the mainland is at least seven miles off my anchorage."

"About that."

My lack of excitement, of curiosity, of surprise, of any sort

The Secret Sharer

of pronounced interest, began to arouse his distrust. But except for the felicitous pretence of deafness I had not tried to pretend anything, I had felt utterly incapable of playing the part of ignorance properly, and therefore was afraid to try. It is also certain that he had brought some ready-made suspicions with him, and that he viewed my politeness as a strange and unnatural phenomenon. And yet how else could I have received him? Not heartily! That was impossible for psychological reasons, which I need not state here. My only object was to keep off his inquiries. Surlily? Yes, but surliness might have provoked a point-blank question. From its novelty to him and from its nature, punctilious courtesy was the manner best calculated to restrain the man. But there was the danger of his breaking through my defence bluntly. I could not, I think, have met him by a direct lie, also for psychological (not moral) reasons. If he had only known how afraid I was of his putting my feeling of identity with the other to the test! But, strangely enough—I thought of it only afterward—I believe that he was not a little disconcerted by the reverse side of that weird situation, by something in me that reminded him of the man he was seeking—suggested a mysterious similitude to the young fellow he had distrusted and disliked from the first.

However that might have been, the silence was not very prolonged. He took another oblique step.

"I reckon I had no more than a two-mile pull to your ship. Not a bit more."

"And quite enough, too, in this awful heat," I said.

Another pause full of mistrust followed. Necessity, they say, is mother of invention, but fear, too, is not barren of ingenious suggestions. And I was afraid he would ask me point-blank for news of my other self.

"Nice little saloon, isn't it?" I remarked, as if noticing for the first time the way his eyes roamed from one closed door to the other. "And very well fitted out, too. Here, for instance," I continued reaching over the back of my seat negligently and flinging the door open, "is my bathroom."

He made an eager movement, but hardly gave it a glance. I got up, shut the door of the bathroom, and invited him to have a look round, as if I were very proud of my accommodation. He had to rise and be shown round, but he went through the business without any raptures whatever.

"And now we'll have a look at my stateroom," I declared, in a voice as loud as I dared to make it, crossing the cabin to the starboard side with purposely heavy steps.

He followed me in and gazed around. My intelligent double had vanished. I played my part.

"Very convenient—isn't it?"

"Very nice. Very comf . . ." He didn't finish, and went out brusquely as if to escape from some unrighteous wiles of mine. But it was not to be. I had been too frightened not to feel vengeful; I felt I had him on the run, and I meant to keep him on the run. My polite insistence must have had something menacing in it, because he gave in suddenly. And I did not let him off a single item; mate's room, pantry, storerooms, the very sail-locker which was also under the poop—he had to look into them all. When at last I showed him out on the quarter-deck he drew a long, spiritless sigh, and mumbled dismally that he must really be going back to his ship now. I desired my mate, who had joined us, to see to the captain's boat.

The man of whiskers gave a blast on the whistle which he used to wear hanging round his neck, and yelled, "*Sephoras* away!" My double down there in my cabin must have heard, and certainly could not feel more relieved than I. Four fellows came running out from somewhere forward and went over the side, while my own men, appearing on deck too, lined the rail. I escorted my visitor to the gangway ceremoniously, and nearly overdid it. He was a tenacious beast. On the very ladder he lingered, and in that unique, guiltily conscientious manner of sticking to the point:

The Secret Sharer

"I say . . . you . . . you don't think that——"

I covered his voice loudly:

"Certainly not. . . . I am delighted. Good-bye."

I had an idea of what he meant to say, and just saved myself by the privilege of defective hearing. He was too shaken generally to insist, but my mate, close witness of that parting, looked mystified and his face took on a thoughtful cast. As I did not want to appear as if I wished to avoid all communication with my officers, he had the opportunity to address me.

"Seems a very nice man. His boat's crew told our chaps a very extraordinary story, if what I am told by the steward is true. I suppose you had it from the captain, sir?"

"Yes. I had a story from the captain."

"A very horrible affair—isn't it, sir?"

"It is."

"Beats all these tales we hear about murders in Yankee ships."

"I don't think it beats them. I don't think it resembles them in the least."

"Bless my soul—you don't say so! But of course I've no acquaintance whatever with American ships, not I, so I couldn't go against your knowledge. It's horrible enough for me. . . . But the queerest part is that those fellows seemed to have some idea the man was hidden aboard here. They had really. Did you ever hear of such a thing?"

"Preposterous—isn't it?"

We were walking to and fro athwart the quarter-deck. No one of the crew forward could be seen (the day was Sunday), and the mate pursued:

"There was some little dispute about it. Our chaps took offence. 'As if we would harbour a thing like that,' they said. 'Wouldn't you like to look for him in our coal-hole?' Quite a tiff. But they made it up in the end. I suppose he did drown himself. Don't you, sir?"

The Secret Sharer

"I don't suppose anything."

"You have no doubt in the matter, sir?"

"None whatever."

I left him suddenly. I felt I was producing a bad impression but with my double down there it was most trying to be on deck. And it was almost as trying to be below. Altogether a nerve-trying situation. But on the whole I felt less torn in two when I was with him. There was no one in the whole ship whom I dared take into my confidence. Since the hands had got to know his story, it would have been impossible to pass him off for anyone else, and an accidental discovery was to be dreaded now more than ever. . . .

The steward being engaged in laying the table for dinner, we could talk only with our eyes when I first went down. Later in the afternoon we had a cautious try at whispering. The Sunday quietness of the ship was against us; the stillness of air and water around her was against us; the elements, the men were against us—everything was against us in our secret partnership; time itself—for this could not go on for ever. The very trust in Providence was, I suppose, denied to his guilt. Shall I confess that this thought cast me down very much? And as to the chapter of accidents which counts for so much in the book of success, I could only hope that it was closed. For what favourable accident could be expected?

"Did you hear everything?" were my first words as soon as we took up our position side by side, leaning over my bed-place.

He had. And the proof of it was his earnest whisper, "The man told you he hardly dared to give the order."

I understood the reference to be to that saving fore-sail.

"Yes. He was afraid of it being lost in the setting."

"I assure you he never gave the order. He may think he did but he never gave it. He stood there with me on the break of the poop after the maintopsail blew away, and whimpered about our last hope—positively whimpered about it and

The Secret Sharer

nothing else—and the night coming on! To hear one's skipper go on like that in such weather was enough to drive any fellow out of his mind. It worked me up into a sort of desperation. I just took it into my own hands and went away from him, boiling, and—— But what's the use telling you? *You* know! . . . Do you think that if I had not been pretty fierce with them I should have got the men to do anything? Not it! The bo's'n perhaps? Perhaps! It wasn't a heavy sea—it was a sea gone mad! I suppose the end of the world will be something like that; and a man may have the heart to see it coming once and be done with it—but to have to face it day after day——I don't blame anybody. I was precious little better than the rest. Only—I was an officer of that old coal-wagon, anyhow——"

"I quite understand," I conveyed that sincere assurance into his ear. He was out of breath with whispering; I could hear him pant slightly. It was all very simple. The same strung-up force which had given twenty-four men a chance, at least, for their lives, had, in a sort of recoil, crushed an unworthy mutinous existence.

But I had no leisure to weigh the merits of the matter—footsteps in the saloon, a heavy knock. "There's enough wind to get under way with, sir." Here was the call of a new claim upon my thoughts and even upon my feelings.

"Turn the hands up," I cried through the door. "I'll be on deck directly."

I was going out to make the acquaintance of my ship. Before I left the cabin our eyes met—the eyes of the only two strangers on board. I pointed to the recessed part where the little camp-stool awaited him and laid my finger on my lips. He made a gesture—somewhat vague—a little mysterious, accompanied by a faint smile, as if of regret.

This is not the place to enlarge upon the sensations of a man who feels for the first time a ship move under his feet to his own independent word. In my case they were not unal-

The Secret Sharer

loyed. I was not wholly alone with my command; for there was that stranger in my cabin. Or rather, I was not completely and wholly with her. Part of me was absent. That mental feeling of being in two places at once affected me physically as if the mood of secrecy had penetrated my very soul. Before an hour had elapsed since the ship begun to move, having occasion to ask the mate (he stood by my side) to take a compass bearing of the Pagoda, I caught myself reaching up to his ear in whispers. I say I caught myself, but enough had escaped to startle the man. I can't describe it otherwise than by saying that he shied. A grave, preoccupied manner, as though he were in possession of some perplexing intelligence, did not leave him henceforth. A little later I moved away from the rail to look at the compass with such a stealthy gait that the helmsman noticed it—and I could not help noticing the unusual roundness of his eyes. These are trifling instances, though it's to no commander's advantage to be suspected of ludicrous eccentricities. But I was also more seriously affected. There are to a seaman certain words, gestures, that should in given conditions come as naturally, as instinctively as the winking of a menaced eye. A certain order should spring on to his lips without thinking; a cetrain sign should get itself made, so to speak, without reflection. But all unconscious alertness had abandoned me. I had to make an effort of will to recall myself back (from the cabin) to the conditions of the moment. I felt that I was appearing an irresolute commander to those people who were watching me more or less critically.

And, besides, there were the scares. On the second day out, for instance, coming off the deck in the afternoon (I had straw slippers on my bare feet) I stopped at the open pantry door and spoke to the steward. He was doing something there with his back to me. At the sound of my voice he nearly jumped out of his skin, as the saying is, and incidentally broke a cup.

"What on earth's the matter with you?" I asked, astonished.

He was extremely confused. "Beg your pardon, sir. I made sure you were in your cabin."

"You see I wasn't."

"No, sir. I could have sworn I had heard you moving in there not a moment ago. It's most extraordinary . . . very sorry, sir."

I passed on with an inward shudder. I was so identified with my secret double that I did not even mention the fact in those scanty, fearful whispers we exchanged. I suppose he had made some slight noise of some kind or other. It would have been miraculous if he hadn't at one time or another. And yet, haggard as he appeared, he looked always perfectly self-controlled, more than calm—almost invulnerable. On my suggestion he remained almost entirely in the bathroom, which, upon the whole, was the safest place. There could be really no shadow of an excuse for anyone ever wanting to go in there, once the steward had done with it. It was a very tiny place. Sometimes he reclined on the floor, his legs bent, his head sustained on one elbow. At others I would find him on the camp-stool, sitting in his grey sleeping-suit and with his cropped dark hair like a patient, unmoved convict. At night I would smuggle him into my bed-place, and we would whisper together, with the regular footfalls of the officer of the watch passing and repassing over our heads. It was an infinitely miserable time. It was lucky that some tins of fine preserves were stowed in a locker in my stateroom; hard bread I could always get hold of; and so he lived on stewed chicken, pâté de foie gras, asparagus, cooked oysters, sardines—on all sorts of abominable sham delicacies out of tins. My early morning coffee he always drank; and it was all I dared do for him in that respect.

Every day there was the horrible manoeuvring to go through so that my room and then the bathroom should be

The Secret Sharer

done in the usual way. I came to hate the sight of the steward, to abhor the voice of that harmless man. I felt that it was he who would bring on the disaster of discovery. It hung like a sword over our heads.

The fourth day out, I think (we were then working down the east side of the Gulf of Siam, tack for tack, in light winds and smooth water)—the fourth day, I say, of this miserable juggling with the unavoidable, as we sat at our evening meal, that man, whose slightest movement I dreaded, after putting down the dishes ran up on deck busily. This could not be dangerous. Presently he came down again; and then it appeared that he had remembered a coat of mine which I had thrown over a rail to dry after having been wetted in a shower which had passed over the ship in the afternoon. Sitting stolidly at the head of the table I became terrified at the sight of the garment on his arm. Of course he made for my door. There was no time to lose.

"Steward," I thundered. My nerves were so shaken that I could not govern my voice and conceal my agitation. This was the sort of thing that made my terrifically whiskered mate tap his forehead with his forefinger. I had detected him using that gesture while talking on deck with a confidential air to the carpenter. It was too far to hear a word, but I had no doubt that this pantomime could only refer to the strange new captain.

"Yes, sir," the pale-faced steward turned resignedly to me. It was this maddening course of being shouted at, checked without rhyme or reason, arbitrarily chased out of my cabin, suddenly called into it, sent flying out of his pantry on incomprehensible errands, that accounted for the growing wretchedness of his expression.

"Where are you going with that coat?"

"To your room, sir."

"Is there another shower coming?"

"I'm sure I don't know, sir. Shall I go up again and see, sir?"

"No! Never mind."

E   129

The Secret Sharer

My object was attained, as of course my other self in there would have heard everything that passed. During this interlude my two officers never raised their eyes off their respective plates; but the lip of that confounded cub, the second mate, quivered visibly.

I expected the steward to hook my coat on and come out at once. He was very slow about it; but I dominated my nervousness sufficiently not to shout after him. Suddenly I became aware (it could be heard plainly enough) that the fellow for some reason or other was opening the door of the bathroom. It was the end. The place was literally not big enough to swing a cat in. My voice died in my throat and I went stony all over. I expected to hear a yell of surprise and terror, and made a movement, but had not the strength to get on my legs. Everything remained still. Had my second self taken the poor wretch by the throat? I don't know what I would have done next moment if I had not seen the steward come out of my room, close the door, and then stand quietly by the sideboard.

"Saved," I thought. "But, no! Lost! Gone! He was gone!"

I laid my knife and fork down and leaned back in my chair. My head swam. After a while, when sufficiently recovered to speak in a steady voice, I instructed my mate to put the ship round at eight o'clock himself.

"I won't come on deck," I went on. "I think I'll turn in, and unless the wind shifts I don't want to be disturbed before midnight. I feel a bit seedy."

"You did look middling bad a little while ago," the chief mate remarked without showing any great concern.

They both went out, and I stared at the steward clearing the table. There was nothing to be read on that wretched man's face. But why did he avoid my eyes? I asked myself. Then I thought I should like to hear the sound of his voice.

"Steward!"

"Sir!" Startled as usual.

The Secret Sharer

"Where did you hang up that coat?"

"In the bathroom, sir." The usual anxious tone. "It's not quite dry yet, sir."

For some time longer I sat in the cuddy. Had my double vanished as he had come? But of his coming there was an explanation, whereas his disappearance would be inexplicable. . . . I went slowly into my dark room, shut the door, lighted the lamp, and for a time dared not turn round. When at last I did I saw him standing bolt upright in the narrow recessed part. It would not be true to say I had a shock, but an irresistible doubt of his bodily existence flitted through my mind. Can it be, I asked myself, that he is not visible to other eyes than mine? It was like being haunted. Motionless, with a grave face, he raised his hands slightly at me in a gesture which meant clearly, "Heavens! what a narrow escape!" Narrow, indeed. I think I had come creeping quietly as near insanity as any man who has not actually gone over the border. That gesture restrained me, so to speak.

The mate with the terrific whiskers was now putting the ship on the other tack. In the moment of profound silence which follows upon the hands going to their stations I heard on the poop his raised voice: "Hard alee!" and the distant shout of the order repeated on the main-deck. The sails, in that light breeze, made but a faint fluttering noise. It ceased. The ship was coming round slowly; I held my breath in the renewed stillness of expectation; one wouldn't have thought that there was a single living soul on her decks. A sudden brisk shout, "Mainsail haul!" broke the spell, and in the noisy cries and rush overhead of the men running away with the main-brace we two, down in my cabin, came together in our usual position by the bed-place.

He did not wait for my question. "I heard him fumbling here and just managed to squat myself down in the bath," he whispered to me. "The fellow only opened the door and put his arm in to hang the coat up. All the same——"

The Secret Sharer

"I never thought of that," I whispered back, even more appalled than before at the closeness of the shave, and marvelling at that something unyielding in his character which was carrying him through so finely. There was no agitation in his whisper. Whoever was being driven distracted, it was not he. He was sane. And the proof of his sanity was continued when he took up the whispering again.

"It would never do for me to come to life again."

It was something that a ghost might have said. But what he was alluding to was his old captain's reluctant admission of the theory of suicide. It would obviously serve his turn—if I had understood at all the view which seemed to govern the unalterable purpose of his action.

"You must maroon me as soon as ever you can get amongst these islands off the Cambodje shore," he went on.

"Maroon you! We are not living in a boy's adventure tale," I protested. His scornful whispering took me up.

"We aren't indeed! There's nothing of a boy's tale in this. But there's nothing else for it. I want no more. You don't suppose I am afraid of what can be done to me? Prison or gallows or whatever they may please. But you don't see me coming back to explain such things to an old fellow in a wig and twelve respectable tradesmen, do you? What can they know whether I am guilty or not—or of *what* I am guilty, either? That's my affair. What does the Bible say? 'Driven off the face of the earth.' Very well. I am off the face of the earth now. As I came at night so I shall go."

"Impossible!" I murmured. "You can't."

"Can't... Not naked like a soul on the Day of Judgment. I shall freeze on to this sleeping-suit. The Last Day is not yet—and .. you have understood thoroughly. Didn't you?"

I felt suddenly ashamed of myself. I may say truly that I understood—and my hesitation in letting that man swim away from my ship's side had been a mere sham sentiment, a sort of cowardice.

The Secret Sharer

"It can't be done now till next night," I breathed out. "The ship is on the off-shore tack and the wind may fail us."

"As long as I know that you understand," he whispered. "But of course you do. It's a great satisfaction to have got somebody to understand. You seem to have been there on purpose." And in the same whisper, as if we two whenever we talked had to say things to each other which were not fit for the world to hear, he added, "It's very wonderful."

We remained side by side talking in our secret way—but sometimes silent or just exchanging a whispered word or two at long intervals. And as usual he stared through the port. A breath of wind came now and again into our faces. The ship might have been moored in dock, so gently and on an even keel she slipped through the water, and did not murmur even at our passage, shadowy and silent like a phantom sea.

At midnight I went on deck, and to my mate's great surprise put the ship round on the other tack. His terrible whiskers flitted round me in silent criticism. I certainly should not have done it if it had been only a question of getting out of that sleepy gulf as quickly as possible. I believe he told the second mate, who relieved him, that it was a great want of judgement. The other only yawned. That intolerable cub shuffled about so sleepily and lolled against the rails in such a slack, improper fashion that I came down on him sharply.

"Aren't you properly awake yet?"

"Yes, sir! I am awake."

"Well, then, be good enough to hold yourself as if you were. And keep a look-out. If there's any current we'll be closing with some islands before daylight."

The east side of the gulf is fringed with islands, some solitary, others in groups. On the blue background of the high coast they seem to float on silvery patches of calm water, arid and grey, or dark green and rounded like clumps of evergreen bushes, with the larger ones, a mile or two long,

The Secret Sharer

showing the outlines of ridges, ribs of grey rock under the dank mantle of matted leafage. Unknown to trade, to travel, almost to geography, the manner of life they harbour is an unsolved secret. There must be villages—settlements of fishermen at least—on the largest of them, and some communication with the world is probably kept up by native craft. But all that forenoon, as we headed for them, fanned along by the faintest of breezes, I saw no sign of man or canoe in the field of the telescope I kept on pointing at the scattered group.

At noon I gave no orders for a change of course, and the mate's whiskers became much concerned and seemed to be offering themselves unduly to my notice. At last I said:

"I am going to stand right in. Quite in—as far as I can take her."

The stare of extreme surprise imparted an air of ferocity also to his eyes, and he looked truly terrific for a moment.

"We're not doing well in the middle of the gulf," I continued, casually. "I am going to look for the land breezes tonight."

"Bless my soul! Do you mean, sir, in the dark amongst the lot of all them islands and reefs and shoals?"

"Well—if there are any regular land breezes at all on this coast one must get close inshore to find them, mustn't one?"

"Bless my soul!" he exclaimed again under his breath. All that afternoon he wore a dreamy, contemplative appearance which in him was a mark of perplexity. After dinner I went into my stateroom as if I meant to take some rest. There we two bent our dark heads over a half-unrolled chart lying on my bed.

"There," I said. "It's got to be Koh-ring. I've been looking at it ever since sunrise. It has got two hills and a low point. It must be inhabited. And on the coast opposite there is what looks like the mouth of a biggish river—with some town, no doubt, not far up. It's the best chance for you that I can see."

The Secret Sharer

"Anything. Koh-ring let it be."

He looked thoughtfully at the chart as if surveying chances and distances from a lofty height—and following with his eyes his own figure wandering on the blank land of Cochin-China, and then passing off that piece of paper clean out of sight into uncharted regions. And it was as if the ship had two captains to plan her course for her. I had been so worried and restless running up and down that I had not had the patience to dress that day. I had remained in my sleeping-suit with straw slippers and a soft floppy hat. The closeness of the heat in the gulf had been most oppressive, and the crew were used to see me wandering in that airy attire.

"She will clear the south point as she heads now," I whispered into his ear. "Goodness only knows when, though, but certainly after dark. I'll edge her in to half a mile, as far as I may be able to judge in the dark——"

"Be careful," he murmured, warningly—and I realized suddenly that all my future, the only future for which I was fit, would perhaps go irretrievably to pieces in any mishap to my first command.

I could not stop a moment longer in the room. I motioned him to get out of sight and made my way on the poop. That unplayful cub had the watch. I walked up and down for a while thinking things out, then beckoned him over.

"Send a couple of hands to open the two quarter-deck ports," I said, mildly.

He actually had the impudence, or else so forgot himself in his wonder at such an incomprehensible order, as to repeat:

"Open the quarter-deck ports! What for, sir?"

"The only reason you need concern yourself about is because I tell you to do so. Have them open wide and fastened properly."

He reddened and went off, but I believe made some jeering remark to the carpenter as to the sensible practice of ventilating a ship's quarter-deck. I know he popped into the mate's

The Secret Sharer

cabin to impart the fact to him because the whiskers came on deck, as it were by chance, and stole glances at me from below—for signs of lunacy or drunkenness, I suppose.

A little before supper, feeling more restless than ever, I rejoined, for a moment, my second self. And to find him sitting so quietly was surprising, like something against nature, inhuman.

I developed my plan in a hurried whisper.

"I shall stand in as close as I dare and then put her round. I shall presently find means to smuggle you out of here into the sail-locker, which communicates with the lobby. But there is an opening, a sort of square for hauling the sails out, which gives straight on the quarter-deck and which is never closed in fine weather, so as to give air to the sails. When the ship's way is deadened in stays and all the hands are aft at the main-braces you shall have a clear road to slip out and get overboard through the open quarter-deck port. I've had them both fastened up. Use a rope's end to lower yourself into the water so as to avoid a splash—you know. It could be heard and cause some beastly complication."

He kept silent for a while, then whispered, "I understand."

"I won't be there to see you go," I began with an effort. "The rest . . . I only hope I have understood, too."

"You have. From first to last"—and for the first time there seemed to be a faltering, something strained in his whisper. He caught hold of my arm, but the ringing of the supper bell made me start. He didn't though; he only released his grip.

After supper I didn't come below again till well past eight o'clock. The faint, steady breeze was loaded with dew; and the wet, darkened sails held all there was of propelling power in it. The night, clear and starry, sparkled darkly, and the opaque, lightless patches shifting slowly against the low stars were the drifting islets. On the port bow there was a big one more distant and shadowily imposing by the great space of sky it eclipsed.

The Secret Sharer

On opening the door I had a back view of my very own self looking at a chart. He had come out of the recess and was standing near the table.

"Quite dark enough," I whispered.

He stepped back and leaned against my bed with a level, quiet glance. I sat on the couch. We had nothing to say to each other. Over our heads the officer of the watch moved here and there. Then I heard him move quickly. I knew what that meant. He was making for the companion; and presently his voice was outside my door.

"We are drawing in pretty fast, sir. Land looks rather close."

"Very well," I answered. "I am coming on deck directly."

I waited till he was gone out of the cuddy, then rose. My double moved too. The time had come to exchange our last whispers, for neither of us was ever to hear each other's natural voice.

"Look here!" I opened a drawer and took out three sovereigns. "Take this, anyhow. I've got six and I'd give you the lot only I must keep a little money to buy some fruit and vegetables for the crew from native boats as we go through Sunda Straights."

He shook his head.

"Take it," I urged him, whispering desperately. "No one can tell what——"

He smiled and slapped meaningly the only pocket of the sleeping-jacket. It was not safe, certainly. But I produced a large old silk handkerchief of mine, and tying the three pieces of gold in a corner, pressed it on him. He was touched, I suppose, because he took it at last and tied it quickly round his waist under the jacket, on his bare skin.

Our eyes met; several seconds elapsed, till, our glances still mingled, I extended my hand and turned the lamp out. Then I passed through the cuddy, leaving the door of my room wide open.... "Steward!"

137

The Secret Sharer

He was still lingering in the pantry in the greatness of his zeal, giving a rub-up to a plated cruet-stand the last thing before going to bed. Being careful not to wake up the mate, whose room was opposite, I spoke in an undertone.

He looked round anxiously. "Sir!"

"Can you get me a little hot water from the galley?"

"I am afraid, sir, the galley fire's been out for some time now."

"Go and see."

He fled up the stairs.

"Now," I whispered, loudly, into the saloon—too loudly, perhaps, but I was afraid I couldn't make a sound. He was by my side in an instant—the double captain slipped past the stairs—through a tiny dark passage . . . a sliding door. We were in the sail-locker, scrambling on our knees over the sails. A sudden thought struck me. I saw myself wandering barefooted, bareheaded, the sun beating on my dark poll. I snatched off my floppy hat and tried hurriedly in the dark to ram it on my other self. He dodged and fended off silently. I wonder what he thought had come to me before he understood and suddenly desisted. Our hands met gropingly, lingered united in a steady, motionless clasp for a second. . . . No word was breathed by either of us when they separated.

I was standing quietly by the pantry door when the steward returned.

"Sorry, sir. Kettle barely warm. Shall I light the spirit-lamp?"

"Never mind."

I came out on deck slowly. It was now a matter of conscience to shave the land as close as possible—for now he must go overboard whenever the ship was put in stays. Must! There could be no going back for him. After a moment I walked over to leeward and my heart flew into my mouth at the nearness of the land on the bow. Under any other circum-

138

The Secret Sharer

stances I would not have held on a minute longer. The second mate had followed me anxiously.

I looked on till I felt I could command my voice.

"She will weather," I said then in a quiet tone.

"Are you going to try that, sir?" he stammered out incredulously.

I took no notice of him and raised my tone just enough to be heard by the helmsman.

"Keep her good full."

"Good full, sir."

The wind fanned my cheek, the sails slept, the world was silent. The strain of watching the dark loom of the land grow bigger and denser was too much for me. I had shut my eyes—because the ship must go closer. She must! The stillness was intolerable. Were we standing still?

When I opened my eyes the second view started my heart with a thump. The black southern hill of Koh-ring seemed to hang right over the ship like a towering fragment of the everlasting night. On that enormous mass of blackness there was not a gleam to be seen, not a sound to be heard. It was gliding irresistibly toward us and yet seemed already within reach of the hand. I saw the vague figures of the watch grouped in the waist, gazing in awed silence.

"Are you going on, sir?" inquired an unsteady voice at my elbow.

I ignored it. I had to go on.

"Keep her full. Don't check her way. That won't do now," I said, warningly.

"I can't see the sails very well," the helmsman answered me, in strange, quavering tones.

Was she close enough? Already she was, I won't say in the shadow of the land, but in the very blackness of it, already swallowed up as it were, gone too close to be recalled, gone from me altogether.

"Give the mate a call," I said to the young man who stood

The Secret Sharer

at my elbow as still as death. "And turn all hands up."

My tone had a borrowed loudness reverberated from the height of the land. Several voices cried out together: "We are all on deck, sir."

Then stillness again, with the great shadow gliding closer, towering higher, without a light, without a sound. Such a hush had fallen on the ship that she might have been a bark of the dead floating in slowly under the very gate of Erebus.

"My God! Where are we?"

It was the mate moaning at my elbow. He was thunderstruck, and as it were deprived of the moral support of his whiskers. He clapped his hands and absolutely cried out, "Lost!"

"Be quiet," I said, sternly.

He lowered his tone, but I saw the shadowy gesture of his despair. "What are we doing here?"

"Looking for the land wind."

He made as if to tear his hair, and addressed me recklessly.

"She will never get out. You have done it, sir. I knew it'd end in something like this. She will never weather, and you are too close now to stay. She'll drift ashore before she's round. Oh my God!"

I caught his arm as he was raising it to batter his poor devoted head, and shook it violently.

"She's ashore already," he wailed, trying to tear himself away.

"Is she? . . . Keep good full there!"

"Good full, sir," cried the helmsman in a frightened, thin, child-like voice.

I hadn't let go the mate's arm and went on shaking it. "Ready about, do you hear? You go forward"—shake—"and stop there"—shake—"and hold your noise"—shake—"and see these head-sheets properly overhauled"—shake, shake—shake.

And all the time I dared not look toward the land lest my heart should fail me. I released my grip at

The Secret Sharer

last and he ran forward as if fleeing for dear life.

I wondered what my double there in the sail-locker thought of this commotion. He was able to hear everything—and perhaps he was able to understand why, on my conscience, it had to be thus close—no less. My first order "Hard alee!" re-echoed ominously under the towering shadow of Koh-ring as If I had shouted in a mountain gorge. And then I watched the land intently. In that smooth water and light wind it was impossible to feel the ship coming-to. No! I could not feel her. And my second self was making now ready to slip out and lower himself overboard. Perhaps he was gone already . . . ?

The great black mass brooding over our very mast-heads began to pivot away from the ship's side silently. And now I forgot the secret stranger ready to depart, and remembered only that I was a total stranger to the ship. I did not know her. Would she do it? How was she to be handled?

I swung the mainyard and waited helplessly. She was perhaps stopped, and her very fate hung in the balance, with the black mass of Koh-ring like the gate of the everlasting night towering over her taffrail. What would she do now? Had she way on her yet? I stepped to the side swiftly, and on the shadowy water I could see nothing except a faint phosphorescent flash revealing the glassy smoothness of the sleeping surface. It was impossible to tell—and I had not learned yet the feel of my ship. Was she moving? What I needed was something easily seen, a piece of paper, which I could throw overboard and watch. I had nothing on me. To run down for it I didn't dare. There was no time. All at once my strained, yearning stare distinguished a white object floating within a yard of the ship's side. White on the black water. A phosphorescent flash passed under it. What was that thing? I recognized my own floppy hat. It must have fallen off his head . . . and he didn't bother. Now I had what I wanted—the saving mark for my eyes. But I hardly thought of my other self, now gone from the ship, to be hidden for

The Secret Sharer

ever from all friendly faces, to be a fugitive and a vagabond on the earth, with no brand of the curse on his sane forehead to stay a slaying hand . . . too proud to explain.

And I watched the hat—the expression of my sudden pity for his mere flesh. It had been meant to save his homeless head from the dangers of the sun. And now—behold—it was saving the ship, by serving me for a mark to help out the ignorance of my strangeness. Ha! It was drifting forward, warning me just in time that the ship had gathered sternway.

"Shift the helm," I said in a low voice to the seaman standing still like a statue.

The man's eyes glistened wildly in the binnacle light as he jumped round to the other side and spun round the wheel.

I walked to the break of the poop. On the overshadowed deck all hands stood by the forebraces waiting for my order. The stars ahead seemed to be gliding from right to left. And all was so still in the world that I heard the quiet remark "She's round" passed in a tone of intense relief between two seamen.

"Let go and haul."

The foreyards ran round with a great noise, amidst cheery cries. And now the frightful whiskers made themselves heard giving various orders. Already the ship was drawing ahead. And I was alone with her. Nothing! no one in the world should stand now between us, throwing a shadow on the way of silent knowledge and mute affection, the perfect communion of a seaman with his first command.

Walking to the taffrail, I was in time to make out, on the very edge of a darkness thrown by a towering black mass like the very gateway of Erebus—yes, I was in time to catch an evanescent glimpse of my white hat left behind to mark the spot where the secret sharer of my cabin and of my thoughts as though he were my second self, had lowered himself into the water to take his punishment: a free man, a proud swimmer striking out for a new destiny.

Commentary on
'The Secret Sharer'

This is Conrad's most commented-on tale, but it can be more simply interpreted than some commentators lead us to believe. Clearly it is basically a story of a young man's initiation. In the second paragraph the young captain describes his feeling that he and his ship seemed to be measuring their fitness for a long and arduous enterprise, and shortly afterwards admits that he is not only a stranger to the ship but 'somewhat a stranger to myself.' And he wonders how far he should turn out 'faithful to that ideal conception of one's own personality every man sets up for himself secretly.' By the end of the ordeal recounted in the story he has achieved at least part of the self-knowledge essential for true maturity. In resolving the complex moral problem at the heart of the tale and then acting decisively to give effect to his decision, the young captain proves to himself that he is fitted to command.

If the theme of a young man facing a test or ordeal is reminiscent of *Lord Jim*, it is perhaps not altogether surprising, for both stories had their origins in actual sea crimes that were reported upon in the same edition of the *Straits Times* in September 1880 while Conrad was serving on the *Loch Etive* bound for Sydney. It seems likely that both incidents would have been discussed during that voyage and have been linked in Conrad's memory and imagination as a result. In the case that concerns us here, the chief mate of the

Commentary on 'The Secret Sharer'

Cutty Sark seized a capstan bar with which he was being threatened by a seaman and struck the man a blow from the effects of which he ultimately died. The mate then persuaded his captain to allow him to escape when they reached the Eastern port of Anjer. The changes Conrad made in the story are interesting for they are clearly designed to intensify the moral dilemma that is one part of the young captain's ordeal. The mate of the *Cutty Sark* was apparently a brutal character with a sinister reputation, but Leggatt was obviously an exemplary young officer whose crime was merely a part of his instinctive action to save his ship in a crisis. And it was virtually *his* ship for his captain had clearly lost his nerve.

Conrad's reiterations of the fact that Leggatt was a man with whom the young captain could easily identify become tedious. In a letter to his agent, J. B. Pinker, he suggested 'The Second Self', 'The Secret Self' and 'The Other Self' as possible titles—and he makes use of all these phrases in the story. Not surprisingly, many critics have revelled in the possible psychological interpretations of this process of identification and I have listed two in the suggestions for further reading at the end of this commentary. The gradual deepening of this process of identification is revealed in the narrator's use of imagery. When Leggatt first boards the ship the narrator uses straightforward similes: 'He followed me like my double on the poop.' But he soon moves to the more intimate metaphor: Leggatt becomes 'my own grey ghost' and 'my other self' and then 'the secret sharer of my life.' The metaphors are then used to indicate that the notion of separate identities has been dropped altogether: 'I felt torn in two', 'part of me was absent'. In the end the two characters share the position of grammatical subject: 'The double captain slipped past the stairs.' Alongside this gradual linguistic integration one notices a steadily developing dramatic and emotional identification until that final, silent, symbolic union: 'Our hands met gropingly, lingered united

Commentary on 'The Secret Sharer'

in a steady, motionless clasp for a second. . . . No word was breathed by either of us when they separated.'

The reason for the stress on identification is not hard to see; here is a man who has acted precisely as the narrator might have acted and he subsequently demonstrates a self-possession that the young captain has yet to acquire. A careful reading reveals a clear contrast in the behaviour of the two men. At first when the captain hears Leggatt's 'calm and resolute' voice he records, 'the self-possession of that man had somehow induced a corresponding state in myself.' But at each new threat of exposure the captain becomes increasingly nervous while Leggatt remains 'perfectly self-controlled, more than calm—almost invulnerable.' After the closest shave when the steward opens the bathroom door, the captain almost faints and then when Leggatt explains how the steward had only put his arm in to hang up his coat he marvels at 'something unyielding' in Leggatt's character 'which was carrying him through so finely.'

The contrast between the young captain and Captain Archbold is much more obvious as Conrad wants to indicate the other way in which the moral dilemma could have been handled. Where the narrator chooses personal loyalty Captain Archbold chooses public duty. But it is hardly an equal contest; the *Sephora*'s captain's failure of nerve in the storm is hardly redeemed in our eyes by his determination to give up to the Law the man who saved his ship. The narrator comments, 'His obscure tenacity on that point had in it something incomprehensible and a little awful.' In fact it never really seems to occur to the narrator that he has a choice to make; Captain Archbold may have had 'over twenty years of immaculate command' but they count for little when set against his inflexible response to his chief mate's predicament and contrasted with that young man's assurance in a crisis.

In accepting that Leggatt must be put ashore the captain is also asserting his own ability to go it alone and we notice

Commentary on 'The Secret Sharer'

a new decisiveness in his captaincy. Leggatt's example of how to stand up under pressure inspires the captain to act boldly and decisively himself. In a final, self-imposed test in his ordeal of initiation in command, the young captain puts his faith in the fortune that favours the brave in order to give a fellow human the best possible chance of survival. As if to confirm that an act of courage and generosity will bring its own reward, the floppy hat given to save Leggatt's homeless head from the dangers of the sun turns out instead to save the ship. The young captain's dramatic example of commitment to another demonstrates the great virtue of human solidarity—for Conrad a higher ideal than any other embodied in conventional morality, and the only possible counter to the spectre of human betrayal that so frequently haunts his stories.

SUGGESTIONS FOR FURTHER READING

The Shadow Line—a closer working of Conrad's first experience of command

Under Western Eyes—the novel Conrad was writing when he took a month off to write *The Secret Sharer*, and an interesting contrast

Conrad the Novelist by Albert J. Guerard—perhaps the best of the psychological interpretations

Conrad: A Reassessment by Douglas Hewitt. Chapter 6 takes basically the same line as Guerard but is briefer and simpler

Conrad's Eastern World by Norman Sherry. Chapter 14 is a mine of factual information

The Planter of Malata

I

In the private editorial office of the principal newspaper in a great colonial city two men were talking. They were both young. The stouter of the two, fair, and with more of an urban look about him, was the editor and part-owner of the important newspaper.

The other's name was Renouard. That he was exercised in his mind about something was evident on his fine bronzed face. He was a lean, lounging, active man. The journalist continued the conversation.

"And so you were dining yesterday at old Dunster's."

He used the word old not in the endearing sense in which it is sometimes applied to intimates, but as a matter of sober fact. The Dunster in question was old. He had been an eminent colonial statesman, but had now retired from active politics after a tour in Europe and a lengthy stay in England, during which he had had a very good press indeed. The colony was proud of him.

"Yes. I dined there," said Renouard. "Young Dunster asked me just as I was going out of his office. It seemed to be like a sudden thought. And yet I can't help suspecting some purpose behind it. He was very pressing. He swore that his uncle would be very pleased to see me. Said his uncle had mentioned lately that the granting to me of the Malata concession was the last act of his official life."

"Very touching. The old boy sentimentalizes over the past now and then."

The Planter of Malata

"I really don't know why I accepted," continued the other. "Sentiment does not move me very easily. Old Dunster was civil to me of course, but he did not even inquire how I was getting on with my silk plants. Forgot there was such a thing probably. I must say there were more people there than I expected to meet. Quite a big party."

"I was asked," remarked the newspaper man. "Only I couldn't go. But when did you arrive from Malata?"

"I arrived yesterday at daylight. I am anchored out there in the bay—off Garden Point. I was in Dunster's office before he had finished reading his letters. Have you ever seen young Dunster reading his letters? I had a glimpse of him through the open door. He holds the paper in both hands, hunches his shoulders up to his ugly ears, and brings his long nose and his thick lips on to it like a sucking apparatus. A commercial monster."

"Here we don't consider him a monster," said the newspaper man looking at his visitor thoughtfully.

"Probably not. You are used to see his face and to see other faces. I don't know how it is that, when I come to town, the appearance of the people in the street strike me with such force. They seem so awfully expressive."

"And not charming."

"Well—no. Not as a rule. The effect is forcible without being clear. . . . I know that you think it's because of my solitary manner of life away there."

"Yes. I do think so. It is demoralizing. You don't see anyone for months at a stretch. You're leading an unhealthy life."

The other hardly smiled and murmured the admission that true enough it was a good eleven months since he had been in town last.

"You see," insisted the other. "Solitude works like a sort of poison. And then you perceive suggestions in faces—mysterious and forcible, that no sound man would be bothered with. Of course you do."

148

The Planter of Malata

Geoffrey Renouard did not tell his journalist friend that the suggestions of his own face, the face of a friend, bothered him as much as the others. He detected a degrading quality in the touches of age which every day adds to a human countenance. They moved and disturbed him, like the signs of a horrible inward travail which was frightfully apparent to the fresh eye he had brought from his isolation in Malata, where he had settled after five strenuous years of adventure and exploration.

"It's a fact," he said, "that when I am at home in Malata I see no one consciously. I take the plantation boys for granted."

"Well, and we here take the people in the streets for granted. And that's sanity."

The visitor said nothing to this for fear of engaging a discussion. What he had come to seek in the editorial office was not controversy, but information. Yet somehow he hesitated to approach the subject. Solitary life makes a man reticent in respect of anything in the nature of gossip, which those to whom chatting about their kind is an everyday exercise regard as the commonest use of speech.

"You very busy?" he asked.

The Editor making red marks on a long slip of printed paper threw the pencil down.

"No. I am done. Social paragraphs. This office is the place where everything is known about everybody—including even a great deal of nobodies. Queer fellows drift in and out of this room. Waifs and strays from home, from up-country, from the Pacific. And, by the way, last time you were here you picked up one of that sort for your assistant—didn't you?"

"I engaged an assistant only to stop your preaching about the evils of solitude," said Renouard hastily; and the pressman laughed at the half-resentful tone. His laugh was not very loud, but his plump person shook all over. He was aware that his younger friend's deference to his advice was based only on an imperfect belief in his wisdom—or his sagacity. But it was

The Planter of Malata

he who had first helped Renouard in his plans of exploration: the five-years' programme of scientific adventure, of work, of danger and endurance, carried out with such distinction and rewarded modestly with the lease of Malata island by the frugal colonial government. And this reward, too, had been due to the journalist's advocacy with word and pen—for he was an influential man in the community. Doubting very much if Renouard really liked him, he was himself without great sympathy for a certain side of that man which he could not quite make out. He only felt it obscurely to be his real personality—the true—and, perhaps, the absurd. As, for instance in that case of the assistant. Renouard had given way to the arguments of his friend and backer—the argument against the unwholesome effect of solitude, the argument for the safety of companionship even if quarrelsome. Very well. In this docility he was sensible and even likeable. But what did he do next? Instead of taking counsel as to the choice with his old backer and friend, and a man, besides, knowing everybody employed and unemployed on the pavements of the town, this extraordinary Renouard suddenly and almost surreptitiously picked up a fellow—God knows who—and sailed away with him back to Malata in a hurry; a proceeding obviously rash and at the same time not quite straight. That was the sort of thing. The secretly unforgiving journalist laughed a little longer and then ceased to shake all over.

"Oh, yes. About that assistant of yours...."

"What about him," said Renouard, after waiting a while, with a shadow of uneasiness on his face.

"Have you nothing to tell me of him?"

"Nothing except...." Incipient grimness vanished out of Renouard's aspect and his voice, while he hesitated as if reflecting seriously before he changed his mind. "No. Nothing whatever."

"You haven't brought him along with you by chance—for a change."

The Planter of Malata

The Planter of Malata stared, then shook his head, and finally murmured carelessly: "I think he's very well where he is. But I wish you could tell me why young Dunster insisted so much on my dining with his uncle last night. Everybody knows I am not a society man."

The Editor exclaimed at so much modesty. Didn't his friend know that he was their one and only explorer—that he was the man experimenting with the silk plant. . . .

"Still, that doesn't tell me why I was invited yesterday. For young Dunster never thought of this civility before. . . ."

"Our Willie," said the popular journalist, "never does anything without a purpose, that's a fact."

"And to his uncle's house too!"

"He lives there."

"Yes. But he might have given me a feed somewhere else. The extraordinary part is that the old man did not seem to have anything special to say. He smiled kindly on me once or twice, and that was all. It was quite a party, sixteen people."

The Editor then, after expressing his regret that he had not been able to come, wanted to know if the party had been entertaining.

Renouard regretted that his friend had not been there. Being a man whose business or at least whose profession was to know everything that went on in this part of the globe, he could probably have told him something of some people lately arrived from home, who were amongst the guests. Young Dunster (Willie) with his large shirt front and streaks of white skin shining unpleasantly through the thin black hair plastered over the top of his head, bore down on him and introduced him to that party, as if he had been a trained dog or a child phenomenon. Decidedly, he said, he disliked Willie— one of these large oppressive men. . . .

A silence fell, and it was as if Renouard were not going to say anything more when, suddenly, he came out with the real object of his visit to the editorial room.

The Planter of Malata

"They looked to me like people under a spell."

The Editor gazed at him appreciatively, thinking that, whether the effect of solitude or not, this was a proof of a sensitive perception of the expression of faces.

"You omitted to tell me their name, but I can make a guess. You mean Professor Moorsom, his daughter and sister—don't you?"

Renouard assented. Yes, a white-haired lady. But from his silence, with his eyes fixed, yet avoiding his friend, it was easy to guess that it was not in the white-haired lady that he was interested.

"Upon my word," he said, recovering his usual bearing. "It looks to me as if I had been asked there only for the daughter to talk to me."

He did not conceal that he had been greatly struck by her appearance. Nobody could have helped being impressed. She was different from everybody else in that house, and it was not only the effect of her London clothes. He did not take her down to dinner. Willie did that. It was afterwards, on the terrace.... The evening was delightfully calm. He was sitting apart and alone, and wishing himself somewhere else—on board the schooner for choice, with the dinner-harness off. He hadn't exchanged forty words altogether during the evening with the other guests. He saw her suddenly all by herself coming towards him along the dimly lighted terrace, quite from a distance.

She was tall and supple, carrying nobly on her straight body a head of a character which to him appeared peculiar, something—well—pagan, crowned with a great wealth of hair. He had been about to rise, but her decided approach caused him to remain on the seat. He had not looked much at her that evening. He had not that freedom of gaze acquired by the habit of society and the frequent meetings with strangers. It was not shyness, but the reserve of a man not used to the world and to the practice of covert staring, with careless

The Planter of Malata

curiosity. All he had captured by his first, keen, instantly lowered glance was the impression that her hair was magnificently red and her eyes very black. It was a troubling effect, but it had been evanescent; he had forgotten it almost till very unexpectedly he saw her coming down the terrace slow and eager, as if she were restraining herself, and with a rhythmic upward undulation of her whole figure. The light from an open window fell across her path, and suddenly all that mass of arranged hair appeared incandescent, chiselled and fluid, with the daring suggestion of a helmet of burnished copper and the flowing lines of molten metal. It kindled in him an astonished admiration. But he said nothing of it to his friend the Editor. Neither did he tell him that her approach woke up in his brain the image of love's infinite grace and the sense of the inexhaustible joy that lives in beauty. No! What he imparted to the Editor were no emotions, but mere facts conveyed in a deliberate voice and in uninspired words.

"That young lady came and sat down by me. She said: 'Are you French, Mr. Renouard?'"

He had breathed a whiff of perfume of which he said nothing either—of some perfume he did not know. Her voice was low and distinct. Her shoulders and her bare arms gleamed with an extraordinary splendour, and when she advanced her head into the light he saw the admirable contour of the face, the straight fine nose with delicate nostrils, the exquisite crimson brush-stroke of the lips on this oval without colour. The expression of the eyes was lost in a shadowy mysterious play of jet and silver, stirring under the red coppery gold of the hair as though she had been a being made of ivory and precious metals changed into living tissue.

"... I told her my people were living in Canada, but that I was brought up in England before coming out here. I can't imagine what interest she could have in my history."

The Planter of Malata

"And you complain of her interest?"

The accent of the all-knowing journalist seemed to jar on the Planter of Malata.

"No!" he said, in a deadened voice that was almost sullen. But after a short silence he went on. "Very extraordinary. I told her I came out to wander at large in the world when I was nineteen, almost directly after I left school. It seems that her late brother was in the same school a couple of years before me. She wanted me to tell her what I did at first when I came out here; what other men found to do when they came out—where they went, what was likely to happen to them—as if I could guess and foretell from my experience the fates of men who come out here with a hundred different projects, for hundreds of different reasons—for no reason but restlessness—who come, and go, and disappear! Preposterous. She seemed to want to hear their histories. I told her that most of them were not worth telling."

The distinguished journalist leaning on his elbow, his head resting against the knuckles of his left hand, listened with great attention, but gave no sign of that surprise which Renouard, pausing, seemed to expect.

"You know something," the latter said brusquely. The all-knowing man moved his head slightly and said, "Yes. But go on."

"It's just this. There is no more to it. I found myself talking to her of my adventures, of my early days. It couldn't possibly have interested her. Really," he cried, "this is most extraordinary. Those people have something on their minds. We sat in the light of the window, and her father prowled about the terrace, with his hands behind his back and his head drooping. The white-haired lady came to the dining-room window twice—to look at us I am certain. The other guests began to go away—and still we sat there. Apparently these people are staying with the Dunsters. It was old Mrs. Dunster who put an end to the thing. The father and the aunt circled about as if

154

The Planter of Malata

they were afraid of interfering with the girl. Then she got up all at once, gave me her hand, and said she hoped she would see me again."

While he was speaking Renouard saw again the sway of her figure in a movement of grace and strength—felt the pressure of her hand—heard the last accents of the deep murmur that came from her throat so white in the light of the window, and remembered the black rays of her steady eyes passing off his face when she turned away. He remembered all this visually, and it was not exactly pleasurable. It was rather startling like the discovery of a new faculty in himself. There are faculties one would rather do without—such, for instance, as seeing through a stone wall or remembering a person with this uncanny vividness. And what about those two people belonging to her with their air of expectant solicitude! Really, those figures from home got in front of one. In fact, their persistence in getting between him and the solid forms of the everyday material world had driven Renouard to call on his friend at the office. He hoped that a little common, gossipy information would lay the ghost of that unexpected dinner-party. Of course the proper person to go to would have been young Dunster, but he couldn't stand Willie Dunster—not at any price.

In the pause the Editor had changed his attitude, faced his desk, and smiled a faint knowing smile.

"Striking girl—eh?" he said.

The incongruity of the word was enough to make one jump out of the chair. Striking! That girl striking! Stri . . . ! But Renouard restrained his feelings. His friend was not a person to give oneself away to. And, after all, this sort of speech was what he had come there to hear. As, however, he had made a movement he re-settled himself comfortably and said, with very creditable indifference, that yes—she was, rather. Especially amongst a lot of over-dressed frumps. There wasn't one woman under forty there.

The Planter of Malata

"Is that the way to speak of the cream of our society; the 'top of the basket,' as the French say," the Editor remonstrated with mock indignation. "You aren't moderate in your expressions—you know."

"I express myself very little," interjected Renouard seriously.

"I will tell you what you are. You are a fellow that doesn't count the cost. Of course you are safe with me, but will you never learn...."

"What struck me most," interrupted the other, "is that she should pick me out for such a long conversation."

"That's perhaps because you were the most remarkable of the men there."

Renouard shook his head.

"This shot doesn't seem to me to hit the mark, " he said calmly. "Try again."

"Don't you believe me? Oh, you modest creature. Well, let me assure you that under ordinary circumstances it would have been a good shot. You are sufficiently remarkable. But you seem a pretty acute customer too. The circumstances are extraordinary. By Jove they are!"

He mused. After a time the Planter of Malata dropped a negligent—

"And you know them."

"And I know them," assented the all-knowing Editor, soberly, as though the occasion were too special for a display of professional vanity; a vanity so well known to Renouard that its absence augmented his wonder and almost made him uneasy as if portending bad news of some sort.

"You have met those people?" he asked.

"No. I was to have met them last night, but I had to send an apology to Willie in the morning. It was then that he had the bright idea to invite you to fill the place, from a muddled notion that you could be of use. Willie is stupid sometimes. For it is clear that you are the last man able to help."

156

The Planter of Malata

"How on earth do I come to be mixed up in this—whatever it is?" Renouard's voice was slightly altered by nervous irritation. "I only arrived here yesterday morning."

II

His friend the Editor turned to him squarely.

"Willie took me into consultation, and since he seems to have let you in I may just as well tell you what is up. I shall try to be as short as I can. But in confidence—mind!"

He waited. Renouard, his uneasiness growing on him unreasonably, assented by a nod, and the other lost no time in beginning. Professor Moorsom—physicist and philosopher—fine head of white hair, to judge from the photographs—plenty of brains in the head too—all these famous books—surely even Renouard would know....

Renouard muttered moodily that it wasn't his sort of reading, and his friend hastened to assure him earnestly that neither was it his sort—except as a matter of business and duty, for the literary page of that newspaper which was his property (and the pride of his life). The only literary newspaper in the Antipodes could not ignore the fashionable philosopher of the age. Not that anybody read Moorsom at the Antipodes, but everybody had heard of him—women, children, dock labourers, cabmen. The only person (besides himself) who had read Moorsom, as far as he knew, was old Dunster, who used to call himself a Moorsomian (or was it Moorsomite) years and years ago, long before Moorsom had worked himself up into the great swell he was now, in every way.... Socially too. Quite the fashion in the highest world.

Renouard listened with profoundly concealed attention. "A charlatan," he muttered languidly.

"Well—no. I should say not. I shouldn't wonder though if most of his writing had been done with his tongue in his cheek.

The Planter of Malata

Of course. That's to be expected. I tell you what: the only really honest writing is to be found in newspapers and nowhere else—and don't you forget it."

The Editor paused with a basilisk stare till Renouard had conceded a casual: "I dare say," and only then went on to explain that old Dunster, during his European tour, had been made rather a lion of in London, where he stayed with the Moorsoms—he meant the father and the girl. The professor had been a widower for a long time.

"She doesn't look just a girl," muttered Renouard. The other agreed. Very likely not. Had been playing the London hostess to tip-top people ever since she put her hair up, probably.

"I don't expect to see any girlish bloom on her when I do have the privilege," he continued. "Those people are staying with the Dunsters *incog.*, in a manner, you understand—something like royalties. They don't deceive anybody, but they want to be left to themselves. We have even kept them out of the paper—to oblige old Dunster. But we shall put your arrival in—our local celebrity."

"Heavens!"

"Yes. Mr. G. Renouard, the explorer, whose indomitable energy, etc., and who is now working for the prosperity of our country in another way on his Malata plantation . . . And, by the by, how's the silk plant—flourishing?"

"Yes."

"Did you bring any fibre?"

"Schooner-full."

"I see To be transshipped to Liverpool for experimental manufacture, eh? Eminent capitalists at home very much interested, aren't they?"

"They are."

A silence fell. Then the Editor uttered slowly—

"You will be a rich man some day."

Renouard's face did not betray his opinion of that confident prophecy. He didn't say anything till his friend suggested in the same meditative voice—

"You ought to interest Moorsom in the affair too—since Willie has let you in."

"A philosopher!"

"I suppose he isn't above making a bit of money. And he may be clever at it for all you know. I have a notion that he's a fairly practical old cove.... Anyhow," and here the tone of the speaker took on a tinge of respect, "he has made philosophy pay."

Renouard raised his eyes, repressed an impulse to jump up, and got out of the arm-chair slowly. "It isn't perhaps a bad idea," he said. "I'll have to call there in any case."

He wondered whether he had managed to keep his voice steady, its tone unconcerned enough; for his emotion was strong though it had nothing to do with the business aspect of this suggestion. He moved in the room in vague preparation for departure, when he heard a soft laugh. He spun about quickly with a frown, but the Editor was not laughing at him. He was chuckling across the big desk at the wall: a preliminary of some speech for which Renouard, recalled to himself, waited silent and mistrustful.

"No! You would never guess! No one would ever guess what these people are after. Willie's eyes bulged out when he came to me with the tale."

"They always do," remarked Renouard with disgust. "He's stupid."

"He was startled. And so was I after he told me. It's a search party. They are out looking for a man. Willie's soft heart's enlisted in the cause."

Renouard repeated: "Looking for a man." He sat down suddenly as if on purpose to stare. "Did Willie come to you to borrow the lantern?" he asked sarcastically, and got up again for no apparent reason.

"What lantern?" snapped the puzzled Editor, and his face

darkened with suspicion. "You, Renouard, are always alluding to things that aren't clear to me. If you were in politics, I as a party journalist, wouldn't trust you further than I could see you. Not an inch further. You are such a sophisticated beggar. Listen: the man is the man Miss Moorsom was engaged to for a year. He couldn't have been a nobody, anyhow. But he doesn't seem to have been very wise. Hard luck for the young lady."

He spoke with feeling. It was clear that what he had to tell appealed to his sentiment. Yet, as an experienced man of the world, he marked his amused wonder. Young man of good family and connections, going everywhere, yet not merely a man about town, but with a foot in the two big F's.

Renouard lounging aimlessly in the room turned round: "And what the devil's that?" he asked faintly.

"Why Fashion and Finance," explained the Editor. "That's how I call it. There are the three R's at the bottom of the social edifice and the two F's on the top. See?"

"Ha! Ha! Excellent! Ha! Ha!" Renouard laughed with stony eyes.

"And you proceed from one set to the other in this democratic age," the Editor went on with unperturbed complacency. "That is if you are clever enough. The only danger is in being too clever. And I think something of the sort happened here. That swell I am speaking of got himself into a mess. Apparently a very ugly mess of a financial character. You will understand that Willie did not go into details with me. They were not imparted to him with very great abundance either. But a bad mess—something of the criminal order. Of course he was innocent. But he had to quit all the same."

"Ha! Ha!" Renouard laughed again abruptly, staring as before. "So there's one more big F in the tale."

"What do you mean?" inquired the Editor quickly, with an air as if his patent were being infringed.

The Planter of Malata

"I mean—Fool."

"No. I wouldn't say that. I wouldn't say that."

"Well—let him be a scoundrel then. What the devil do I care."

"But hold on! You haven't heard the end of the story."

Renouard, his hat on his head already, sat down with the disdainful smile of a man who had discounted the moral of the story. Still he sat down and the Editor swung his revolving chair right round. He was full of unction.

"Imprudent, I should say. In many ways money is as dangerous to handle as gunpowder. You can't be too careful either as to who you are working with. Anyhow, there was a mighty flashy burst up, a sensation, and—his familiar haunts knew him no more. But before he vanished he went to see Miss Moorsom. That very fact argues for his innocence—don't it? What was said between them no man knows—unless the professor had the confidence from his daughter. There couldn't have been much to say. There was nothing for it but to let him go—was there?—for the affair had got into the papers. And perhaps the kindest thing would have been to forget him. Anyway the easiest. Forgiveness would have been more difficult, I fancy, for a young lady of spirit and position drawn into an ugly affair like that. Any ordinary young lady, I mean. Well, the fellow asked nothing better than to be forgotten, only he didn't find it easy to do so himself, because he would write home now and then. Not to any of his friends though. He had no near relations. The professor had been his guardian. No, the poor devil wrote now and then to an old retired butler of his late father, somewhere in the country, forbidding him at the same time to let anyone know of his whereabouts. So that worthy old ass would go up and dodge about the Moorsoms' town house, perhaps waylay Miss Moorsom's maid, and then would write to 'Master Arthur' that the young lady looked well and happy, or some such cheerful intelligence. I dare say he wanted to be forgotten,

The Planter of Malata

but I shouldn't think he was much cheered by the news. What would you say?"

Renouard, his legs stretched out and his chin on his breast, said nothing. A sensation which was not curiosity, but rather a vague nervous anxiety, distinctly unpleasant, like a mysterious symptom of some malady, prevented him from getting up and going away.

"Mixed feelings," the Editor opined. "Many fellows out here receive news from home with mixed feelings. But what will his feelings be when he hears what I am going to tell you now? For we know he has not heard yet. Six months ago a city clerk, just a common drudge of finance, gets himself convicted of a common embezzlement or something of that kind. Then seeing he's in for a long sentence he thinks of making his conscience comfortable, and makes a clean breast of an old story of tampered with, or else suppressed, documents, a story which clears altogether the honesty of our ruined gentleman. That embezzling fellow was in a position to know, having been employed by the firm before the smash. There was no doubt about the character being cleared—but where the cleared man was nobody could tell. Another sensation in society. And then Miss Moorsom says: 'He will come back to claim me, and I'll marry him.' But he didn't come back. Between you and me I don't think he was much wanted—except by Miss Moorsom. I imagine she's used to have her own way. She grew impatient, and declared that if she knew where the man was she would go to him. But all that could be got out of the old butler was that the last envelope bore the postmark of our beautiful city; and that this was the only address of 'Master Arthur' that he ever had. That and no more. In fact the fellow was at his last gasp—with a bad heart. Miss Moorsom wasn't allowed to see him. She had gone herself into the country to learn what she could, but she had to stay downstairs while the old chap's wife went up to the invalid. She brought down the scrap of intelligence I've told you of. He

The Planter of Malata

was already too far gone to be cross-examined on it, and that very night he died. He didn't leave behind him much to go by, did he? Our Willie hinted to me that there had been pretty stormy days in the professor's house, but—here they are. I have a notion she isn't the kind of everyday young lady who may be permitted to gallop about the world all by herself —eh? Well, I think it rather fine of her, but I quite understand that the professor needed all his philosophy under the circumstances. She is his only child now—and brilliant—what? Willie positively spluttered trying to describe her to me; and I could see directly you came in that you had an uncommon experience."

Renouard, with an irritated gesture, tilted his hat more forward on his eyes, as though he were bored. The Editor went on with the remark that to be sure neither he (Renouard) nor yet Willie were much used to meet girls of that remarkable superiority. Willie when learning business with a firm in London, years before, had seen none but boarding-house society, he guessed. As to himself in the good old days, when he trod the glorious flags of Fleet Street, he neither had access to, nor yet would have cared for the swells. Nothing interested him then but parliamentary politics and the oratory of the House of Commons.

He paid to this not very distant past the tribute of a tender, reminiscent smile, and returned to his first idea that for a society girl her action was rather fine. All the same the professor could not be very pleased. The fellow if he was as pure as a lily now was just about as devoid of the goods of the earth. And there were misfortunes, however undeserved, which damaged a man's standing permanently. On the other hand, it was difficult to oppose cynically a noble impulse—not to speak of the great love at the root of it. Ah! Love! And then the lady was quite capable of going off by herself. She was of age, she had money of her own, plenty of pluck too. Moorsom must have concluded that it was more truly paternal, more

The Planter of Malata

prudent too, and generally safer all round to let himself be dragged into this chase. The aunt came along for the same reasons. It was given out at home as a trip round the world of the usual kind.

Renouard had risen and remained standing with his heart beating, and strangely affected by this tale, robbed as it was of all glamour by the prosaic personality of the narrator. The Editor added: "I've been asked to help in the search—you know."

Renouard muttered something about an appointment and went out into the street. His inborn sanity could not defend him from a misty, creeping jealousy. He thought that obviously no man of that sort could be worthy of such a woman's devoted fidelity. Renouard, however, had lived long enough to reflect that a man's activities, his views, and even his ideals may be very inferior to his character; and moved by a delicate consideration for that splendid girl he tried to think out for the man a character of inward excellence and outward gifts—some extraordinary seduction. But in vain. Fresh from months of solitude and from days at sea, her splendour presented itself to him absolutely unconquerable in its perfection, unless by her own folly. It was easier to suspect her of this than to imagine in the man qualities which would be worthy of her. Easier and less degrading. Because folly may be generous—could be nothing else but generosity in her; whereas to imagine her subjugated by something common was intolerable.

Because of the force of the physical impression he had received from her personality (and such impressions are the real origins of the deepest movements of our soul) this conception of her was even inconceivable. But no Prince Charming has ever lived out of a fairy tale. He doesn't walk the worlds of Fashion and Finance—and with a stumbling gait at that. Generosity. Yes. It was her generosity. But this generosity was altogether regal in its splendour, almost absurd in its lavishness—or, perhaps, divine.

The Planter of Malata

In the evening, on board his schooner, sitting on the rail, his arms folded on his breast and his eyes fixed on the deck, he let the darkness catch him unawares in the midst of a meditation on the mechanism of sentiment and the springs of passion. And all the time he had an abiding consciousness of her bodily presence. The effect on his senses had been so penetrating that in the middle of the night, rousing up suddenly, wide-eyed in the darkness of his cabin, he did not create a faint mental vision of her person for himself, but, more intimately affected, he scented distinctly the faint perfume she used, and could almost have sworn that he had been awakened by the soft rustle of her dress. He even sat up listening in the dark for a time, then sighed and lay down again, not agitated but, on the contrary, oppressed by the sensation of something that had happened to him and could not be undone.

III

In the afternoon he lounged into the editorial office carrying with affected nonchalance that weight of the irremediable he had felt laid on him suddenly in the small hours of the night—that consciousness of something that could no longer be helped. His patronising friend informed him at once that he had made the acquaintance of the Moorsom party last night. At the Dunsters, of course. Dinner.

"Very quiet. Nobody there. It was much better for the business. I say..."

Renouard, his hand grasping the back of a chair, stared down at him dumbly.

"Phew! That's a stunning girl.... Why do you want to sit on that chair? It's uncomfortable!"

"I wasn't going to sit on it." Renouard walked slowly to the window, glad to find in himself enough self-control to let go the chair instead of raising it on high and bringing it down on the Editor's head.

The Planter of Malata

"Willie kept on gazing at her with tears in his boiled eyes. You should have seen him bending sentimentally over her at dinner."

"Don't," said Renouard in such an anguished tone that the Editor turned right round to look at his back.

"You push your dislike of young Dunster too far. It's positively morbid," he disapproved mildly. "We can't all be beautiful after thirty.... I talked a little, about you mostly, to the professor. He appeared to be interested in the silk plant—if only as a change from the great subject. Miss Moorsom didn't seem to mind when I confessed to her that I had taken you into the confidence of the thing. Our Willie approved too. Old Dunster with his white beard seemed to give me his blessing. All those people have a great opinion of you, simply because I told them that you've led every sort of life one can think of before you got struck on exploration. They want you to make suggestions. What do you think 'Master Arthur' is likely to have taken to?"

"Something easy," muttered Renouard without unclenching his teeth.

"Hunting man. Athlete. Don't be hard on the chap. He may be riding boundaries, or droving cattle, or humping his swag about the back-blocks away to the devil—somewhere. He may be even prospecting at the back of beyond—this very moment."

"Or lying dead drunk in a roadside pub. It's late enough in the day for that."

The Editor looked up instinctively. The clock was pointing at a quarter to five. "Yes, it is," he admitted. "But it needn't be. And he may have lit out into the Western Pacific all of a sudden—say in a trading schooner. Though I really don't see in what capacity. Still..."

"Or he may be passing at this very moment under this very window."

"Not he... and I wish you would get away from it to where

The Planter of Malata

one can see your face. I hate talking to a man's back. You stand there like a hermit on a seashore growling to yourself. I tell you what it is, Geoffrey, you don't like mankind."

"I don't make my living by talking about mankind's affairs," Renouard defended himself. But he came away obediently and sat down in the armchair. "How can you be so certain that your man isn't down there in the street?" he asked. "It's neither more nor less probable than every single one of your other suppositions."

Placated by Renouard's docility the Editor gazed at him for a while. "Aha! I'll tell you how. Learn then that we have begun the campaign. We have telegraphed his description to the police of every township up and down the land. And what's more we've ascertained definitely that he hasn't been in this town for the last three months at least. How much longer he's been away we can't tell."

"That's very curious."

"It's very simple. Miss Moorsom wrote to him, to the post office here, directly she returned to London after her excursion into the country to see the old butler. Well—her letter is still lying there. It has not been called for. Ergo, this town is not his usual abode. Personally, I never thought it was. But he cannot fail to turn up some time or other. Our main hope lies just in the certitude that he must come to town sooner or later. Remember, he doesn't know that the butler is dead, and he will want to inquire for a letter. Well, he'll find a note from Miss Moorsom."

Renouard, silent, thought that it was likely enough. His profound distaste for this conversation was betrayed by an air of weariness darkening his energetic sun-tanned features, and by the augmented dreaminess of his eyes. The Editor noted it as a further proof of that immoral detachment from mankind, of that callousness of sentiment fostered by the unhealthy conditions of solitude—according to his own favourite theory. Aloud he observed that as long as a man had not

The Planter of Malata

given up correspondence he could not be looked upon as lost. Fugitive criminals had been tracked in that way by justice, he reminded his friend; then suddenly changed the bearing of the subject somewhat by asking if Renouard had heard from his people lately, and if every member of his large tribe was well and happy.

"Yes, thanks."

The tone was curt, as if repelling a liberty. Renouard did not like being asked about his people, for whom he had a profound and remorseful affection. He had not seen a single human being to whom he was related for many years, and he was extremely different from them all.

On the very morning of his arrival from his island he had gone to a set of pigeon-holes in Willie Dunster's outer office and had taken out from a compartment labelled "Malata" a very small accumulation of envelopes, a few addressed to himself, and one addressed to his assistant, all to the care of the firm, W. Dunster and Co. As opportunity offered, the firm used to send them on to Malata either by a man-of-war schooner going on a cruise, or by some trading craft proceeding that way. But for the last four months there had been no opportunity.

"You going to stay here some time?" asked the Editor, after a longish silence.

Renouard, perfunctorily, did see no reason why he should make a long stay.

"For health, for your mental health, my boy," rejoined the newspaper man. "To get used to human faces so that they don't hit you in the eye so hard when you walk about the streets. To get friendly with your kind. I suppose that assistant of yours can be trusted to look after things?"

"There's the half-caste, too. The Portuguese. He knows what's to be done."

"Aha!" The Editor looked sharply at his friend. "What's his name?"

The Planter of Malata

"Whose name?"

"The assistant's you picked up on the sly behind my back."

Renouard made a slight movement of impatience.

"I met him unexpectedly one evening. I thought he would do as well as another. He had come from up country and didn't seem happy in a town. He told me his name was Walter. I did not ask him for proofs, you know."

"I don't think you get on very well with him."

"Why? What makes you think so."

"I don't know. Something reluctant in your manner when he's in question."

"Really. My manner! I don't think he's a great subject for conversation, perhaps. Why not drop him?"

"Of course! You wouldn't confess to a mistake. Not you. Nevertheless, I have my suspicions about it."

Renouard got up to go, but hesitated, looking down at the seated Editor.

"How funny," he said at last with the utmost seriousness, and was making for the door, when the voice of his friend stopped him.

"You know what has been said of you? That you couldn't get on with anybody you couldn't kick. Now, confess—is there any truth in the soft impeachment?"

"No," said Renouard. "Did you print that in your paper?"

"No. I didn't quite believe it. But I will tell you what I believe. I believe that when your heart is set on some object you are a man that doesn't count the cost to yourself or others. And this shall get printed some day."

"Obituary notice?" Renouard dropped negligently.

"Certain—some day."

"Do you then regard yourself as immortal?"

"No, my boy. I am not immortal. But the voice of the press goes on for ever. . . . And it will say that this was the secret of your great success in a task where better men than you— meaning no offence—did fail repeatedly."

The Planter of Malata

"Success," muttered Renouard, pulling-to the office door after him with considerable energy. And the letters of the word PRIVATE like a row of white eyes seemed to stare after his back sinking down the staircase of that temple of publicity.

Renouard had no doubt that all the means of publicity would be put at the service of love and used for the discovery of the loved man. He did not wish him dead. He did not wish him any harm. We are all equipped with a fund of humanity which is not exhausted without many and repeated provocations—and this man had done him no evil. But before Renouard had left old Dunster's house, at the conclusion of the call he made there that very afternoon, he had discovered in himself the desire that the search might last long. He never really flattered himself that it might fail. It seemed to him that there was no other course in this world for himself, for all mankind, but resignation. And he could not help thinking that Professor Moorsom had arrived at the same conclusion, too.

Professor Moorsom, slight frame of middle height, a thoughtful keen head under the thick wavy hair, veiled dark eyes under straight eyebrows, and with an inward gaze which, when disengaged and arriving at one, seemed to issue from an obscure dream of books, from the limbo of meditation, showed himself extremely gracious to him. Renouard guessed in him a man whom an incurable habit of investigation and analysis had made gentle and indulgent; inapt for action, and more sensitive to the thoughts than to the events of existence. Withal not crushed, sub-ironic without a trace of acidity, and with a simple manner which put people at ease quickly. They had a long conversation on the terrace commanding an extended view of the town and the harbour.

The splendid immobility of the bay resting under his gaze, with its grey spurs and shining indentations, helped Renouard to regain his self-possession, which he had felt shaken, in coming out on the terrace, into the setting of the most powerful emotion of his life, when he had sat within a foot of Miss

The Planter of Malata

Moorsom with fire in his breast, a humming in his ears, and in a complete disorder of his mind. There was the very garden seat on which he had been enveloped in the radiant spell. And presently he was sitting on it again with the professor talking of her. Nearby, the patriarchal Dunster leaned forward in a wicker armchair, benign and a little deaf, his big hand to his ear with the innocent eagerness of his advanced age remembering the fires of life.

It was with a sort of apprehension that Renouard looked forward to seeing Miss Moorsom. And strangely enough it resembled the state of mind of a man who fears disenchantment more than sortilege. But he need not have been afraid. Directly he saw her in the distance at the other end of the terrace he shuddered to the roots of his hair. With her approach the power of speech left him for a time. Mrs. Dunster and her aunt were accompanying her. All these people sat down; it was an intimate circle into which Renouard felt himself cordially admitted; and the talk was of the great search which occupied all their minds. Discretion was expected by these people, but of reticence as to the object of the journey there could be no question. Nothing but ways and means and arrangements could be talked about.

By fixing his eyes obstinately on the ground, which gave him an air of reflective sadness, Renouard managed to recover his self-possession. He used it to keep his voice in a low key and to measure his words on the great subject. And he took care with a great inward effort to make them reasonable without giving them a discouraging complexion. For he did not want the quest to be given up, since it would mean her going away with her two attendant grey-heads to the other side of the world.

He was asked to come again, to come often and take part in the counsels of all these people captivated by the sentimental enterprise of a declared love. On taking Miss Moorsom's hand he looked up, would have liked to say something, but found himself voiceless, with his lips suddenly sealed. She returned the pressure of his fingers, and he left her with her eyes vaguely staring beyond him, an air of listening for an expected sound, and the faintest possible smile on her lips. A smile not for him, evidently, but the reflection of some deep and inscrutable thought.

IV

He went on board his schooner. She lay white, and as if suspended, in the crepuscular atmosphere of sunset mingling with the ashy gleam of the vast anchorage. He tried to keep his thoughts as sober, as reasonable, as measured as his words had been, lest they should get away from him and cause some sort of moral disaster. What he was afraid of in the coming night was sleeplessness and the endless strain of that wearisome task. It had to be faced, however. He lay on his back, sighing profoundly in the dark, and suddenly beheld his very own self, carrying a small bizarre lamp, reflected in a long mirror inside a room in an empty and unfurnished palace. In this startling image of himself he recognized somebody he had to follow—the frightened guide of his dream. He traversed endless galleries, no end of lofty halls, innumerable doors. He lost himself utterly—he found his way again. Room succeeded room. At last the lamp went out, and he stumbled against some object which, when he stooped for it, he found to be very cold and heavy to lift. The sickly white light of dawn showed him the head of a statue. Its marble hair was done in the bold lines of a helmet, on its lips the chisel had left a faint smile, and it resembled Miss Moorsom. While he was staring at it fixedly, the head began to grow light in his fingers, to diminish and crumble to pieces, and at last turned into a handful of dust, which was blown away by a puff of wind so chilly that he woke up with a desperate shiver and leaped headlong out of his bed-place. The day had really come. He sat down by the cabin table,

The Planter of Malata

and taking his head between his hands, did not stir for a very long time.

Very quiet, he set himself to review this dream. The lamp, of course, he connected with the search for a man. But on closer examination he perceived that the reflection of himself in the mirror was not really the true Renouard, but somebody else whose face he could not remember. In the deserted palace he recognized a sinister adaptation by his brain of the long corridors with many doors, in the great building in which his friend's newspaper was lodged on the first floor. The marble head with Miss Moorsom's face! Well! What other face could he have dreamed of? And her complexion was fairer than Parian marble, than the heads of angels. The wind at the end was the morning breeze entering through the open porthole and touching his face before the schooner could swing to the chilly gust.

Yes! And all this rational explanation of the fantastic made it only more mysterious and weird. There was something daemonic in that dream. It was one of those experiences which throw a man out of conformity with the established order of his kind and make him a creature of obscure suggestions.

Henceforth, without ever trying to resist, he went every afternoon to the house where she lived. He went there as passively as if in a dream. He could never make out how he had attained the footing of intimacy in the Dunster mansion above the bay—whether on the ground of personal merit or as the pioneer of the vegetable silk industry. It must have been the last, because he remembered distinctly, as distinctly as in a dream, hearing old Dunster once telling him that his next public task would be a careful survey of the Northern Districts to discover tracts suitable for the cultivation of the silk plant. The old man wagged his beard at him sagely. It was indeed as absurd as a dream.

Willie of course would be there in the evening. But he was more of a figure out of a nightmare, hovering about the circle

The Planter of Malata

of chairs in his dress-clothes like a gigantic, repulsive, and sentimental bat. "Do away with the beastly cocoons all over the world," he buzzed in his blurred, water-logged voice. He affected a great horror of insects of all kinds. One evening he appeared with a red flower in his button-hole. Nothing could have been more disgustingly fantastic. And he would also say to Renouard: "You may yet change the history of our country. For economic conditions do shape the history of nations. Eh? What?" And he would turn to Miss Moorsom for approval, lowering protectingly his spatulous nose and looking up with feeling from under his absurd eyebrows, which grew thin, in the manner of canebrakes, out of his spongy skin. For this large, bilious creature was an economist and a sentimentalist, facile to tears, and a member of the Cobden Club.

In order to see as little of him as possible Renouard began coming earlier so as to get away before his arrival without curtailing too much the hours of secret contemplation for which he lived. He had given up trying to deceive himself. His resignation was without bounds. He accepted the immense misfortune of being in love with a woman who was in search of another man only to throw herself into his arms. With such desperate precision he defined in his thoughts the situation, the consciousness of which traversed like a sharp arrow the sudden silences of general conversation. The only thought before which he quailed was the thought that this could not last; that it must come to an end. He feared it instinctively as a sick man may fear death. For it seemed to him that it must be the death of him followed by a lightless, bottomless pit. But his resignation was not spared the torments of jealousy: the cruel, insensate, poignant, and imbecile jealousy, when it seems that a woman betrays us simply by this that she exists, that she breathes—and when the deep movements of her nerves or her soul become a matter of distracting suspicion, of killing doubt, of mortal anxiety.

The Planter of Malata

In the peculiar condition of their sojourn Miss Moorsom went out very little. She accepted this seclusion at the Dunsters' mansion as in a hermitage, and lived there, watched over by a group of old people, with the lofty endurance of a condescending and strong-headed goddess. It was impossible to say if she suffered from anything in the world, and whether this was the insensibility of a great passion concentrated on itself, or a perfect restraint of manner, or the indifference of superiority so complete as to be sufficient to itself. But it was visible to Renouard that she took some pleasure in talking to him at times. Was it because he was the only person near her age? Was this, then, the secret of his admission to the circle?

He admired her voice as well poised as her movements, as her attitudes. He himself had always been a man of tranquil tones. But the power of fascination had torn him out of his very nature so completely that to preserve his habitual calmness from going to pieces had become a terrible effort. He used to go from her on board the schooner exhausted, broken, shaken up, as though he had been put to the most exquisite torture. When he saw her approaching he always had a moment of hallucination. She was a misty and fair creature, fitted for invisible music, for the shadows of love, for the murmurs of waters. After a time (he could not be always staring at the ground) he would summon up all his resolution and look at her. There was a sparkle in the clear obscurity of her eyes; and when she turned them on him they seemed to give a new meaning to life. He would say to himself that another man would have found long before the happy release of madness, his wits burnt to cinders in that radiance. But no such luck for him. His wits had come unscathed through the furnaces of hot suns of blazing deserts, of flaming angers against the weaknesses of men and the obstinate cruelties of hostile nature.

Being sane he had to be constantly on his guard against falling into adoring silences or breaking out into wild speeches. He had to keep watch on his eyes, his limbs, on the muscles of his face. Their conversations were such as they could be between these two people: she a young lady fresh from the thick twilight of four million people and the artificiality of several London seasons; he the man of definite conquering tasks, the familiar of wide horizons, and in his very repose holding aloof from these agglomerations of units in which one loses one's importance even to oneself. They had no common conversational small change. They had to use the great pieces of general ideas, but they exchanged them trivially. It was no serious commerce. Perhaps she had not much of that coin. Nothing significant came from her. It could not be said that she had received from the contacts of the external world impressions of a personal kind, different from other women. What was ravishing in her was her quietness and, in her grave attitudes, the unfailing brilliance of her femininity. He did not know what there was under that ivory forehead so splendidly shaped, so gloriously crowned. He could not tell what were her thoughts, her feelings. Her replies were reflective, always preceded by a short silence, while he hung on her lips anxiously. He felt himself in the presence of a mysterious being in whom spoke an unknown voice, like the voice of oracles, bringing everlasting unrest to the heart.

He was thankful enough to sit in silence with secretly clenched teeth, devoured by jealousy—and nobody could have guessed that his quiet deferential bearing to all these grey-heads was the supreme effort of stoicism, that the man was engaged in keeping a sinister watch on his tortures lest his strength should fail him. As before, when grappling with other forces of nature, he could find in himself all sorts of courage except the courage to run away.

It was perhaps from the lack of subjects they could have in common that Miss Moorsom made him so often speak of his own life. He did not shrink from talking about himself, for he was free from that exacerbated, timid vanity which seals so many vain-glorious lips. He talked to her in his restrained

The Planter of Malata

voice, gazing at the tip of her shoe, and thinking that the time was bound to come soon when her very inattention would get weary of him. And indeed on stealing a glance he would see her dazzling and perfect, her eyes vague, staring in mournful immobility, with a drooping head that made him think of a tragic Venus arising before him, not from the foam of the sea, but from a distant, still more formless, mysterious, and potent immensity of mankind.

V

One afternoon Renouard stepping out on the terrace found nobody there. It was for him, at the same time, a melancholy disappointment and a poignant relief.

The heat was great, the air was still, all the long windows of the house stood wide open. At the further end, grouped round a lady's work-table, several chairs disposed sociably suggested invisible occupants, a company of conversing shades. Renouard looked towards them with a sort of dread. A most elusive, faint sound of ghostly talk issuing from one of the rooms added to the illusion and stopped his already hesitating footsteps. He leaned over the balustrade of stone near a squat vase holding a tropical plant of a bizarre shape. Professor Moorsom coming up from the garden with a book under his arm and a white parasol held over his bare head, found him there and, closing the parasol, leaned over by his side with a remark on the increasing heat of the season. Renouard assented and changed his position a little; the other, after a short silence, administered unexpectedly a question which, like the blow of a club on the head, deprived Renouard of the power of speech and even thought, but, more cruel, left him quivering with apprehension, not of death but of everlasting torment. Yet the words were extremely simple.

"Something will have to be done soon. We can't remain in

a state of suspended expectation for ever. Tell me what do you think of our chances?"

Renouard, speechless, produced a faint smile. The professor confessed in a jocular tone his impatience to complete the circuit of the globe and be done with it. It was impossible to remain quartered on the dear excellent Dunsters for an indefinite time. And then there were the lectures he had arranged to deliver in Paris. A serious matter.

That lectures by Professor Moorsom were a European event and that brilliant audiences would gather to hear them Renouard did not know. All he was aware of was the shock of this hint of departure. The menace of separation fell on his head like a thunderbolt. And he saw the absurdity of his emotion, for hadn't he lived all these days under the very cloud? The professor, his elbows spread out, looked down into the garden and went on unburdening his mind. Yes. The department of sentiment was directed by his daughter, and she had plenty of volunteered moral support, but he had to look after the practical side of life without assistance.

"I have the less hesitation in speaking to you about my anxiety, because I feel you are friendly to us and at the same time you are detached from all these sublimities—confound them."

"What do you mean?" murmured Renouard.

"I mean that you are capable of calm judgement. Here the atmosphere is simply detestable. Everybody has knuckled under to sentiment. Perhaps your deliberate opinion could influence . . ."

"You want Miss Moorsom to give it up?"

The professor turned to the young man dismally.

"Heaven only knows what I want."

Renouard, leaning his back against the balustrade, folded his arms on his breast, appeared to meditate profoundly. His face, shaded softly by the broad brim of a planter's panama hat, with the straight line of the nose level with the forehead, the eyes lost in the depth of the setting, and the chin well forward, had such a profile as may be seen amongst the bronzes of classical museums, pure under a crested helmet—recalled vaguely a Minerva's head.

"This is the most troublesome time I ever had in my life," exclaimed the professor testily.

"Surely the man must be worth it," muttered Renouard with a pang of jealousy traversing his breast like a self-inflicted stab.

Whether enervated by the heat or giving way to pent-up irritation the professor surrendered himself to the mood of sincerity.

"He began by being a pleasantly dull boy. He developed into a pointlessly clever young man, without, I suspected, ever trying to understand anything. My daughter knew him from childhood. I am a busy man, and I confess that their engagement was a complete surprise to me. I wish their reasons for that step had been more naïve. But simplicity was out of fashion in their set. From a worldly point of view he seems to have been a mere baby. Of course, now, I am assured that he is the victim of his noble confidence in the rectitude of his kind. But that's mere idealizing of a sad reality. For my part I will tell you that from the very beginning I had the gravest doubts of his dishonesty. Unfortunately my clever daughter hadn't. And now we behold the reaction. No. To be earnestly dishonest one must be really poor. This was only a manifestation of his extremely refined cleverness. The complicated simpleton. He had an awful awakening though."

In such words did Professor Moorsom give his "young friend" to understand the state of his feelings towards the lost man. It was evident that the father of Miss Moorsom wished him to remain lost. Perhaps the unprecedented heat of the season made him long for the cool spaces of the Pacific, the sweep of the ocean's free wind along the promenade decks, cumbered with long chairs, of a ship steaming towards the

The Planter of Malata

Californian coast. To Renouard the philosopher appeared simply the most treacherous of fathers. He was amazed. But he was not at the end of his discoveries.

"He may be dead," the professor murmured.

"Why? People don't die here sooner than in Europe. If he had gone to hide in Italy, for instance, you wouldn't think of saying that."

"Well! And suppose he has become morally disintegrated. You know he was not a strong personality," the professor suggested moodily. "My daughter's future is in question here."

Renouard thought that the love of such a woman was enough to pull any broken man together—to drag a man out of his grave. And he thought this with inward despair, which kept him silent as much almost as his astonishment. At last he managed to stammer out a generous—

"Oh! Don't let us even suppose . . ."

The professor struck in with a sadder accent than before—

"It's good to be young. And then you have been a man of action, and necessarily a believer in success. But I have been looking too long at life not to distrust its surprises. Age! Age! Here I stand before you, a man full of doubts and hesitation—*spe lentus, timidus futuri*."

He made a sign to Renouard not to interrupt, and in a lowered voice, as if afraid of being overheard, even there, in the solitude of the terrace—

"And the worst is that I am not even sure how far this sentimental pilgrimage is genuine. Yes. I doubt my own child. It's true that she's a woman. . . ."

Renouard detected with horror a tone of resentment, as if the professor had never forgiven his daughter for not dying instead of his son. The latter noticed the young man's stony stare.

"Ah! You don't understand. Yes, she's clever, open-minded, popular, and—well, charming. But you don't know what it is to have moved, breathed, existed, and even

The Planter of Malata

triumphed in the mere smother and froth of life—the brilliant froth. There thoughts, sentiments, opinions, feelings, actions too, are nothing but agitation in empty space—to amuse life—a sort of superior debauchery, exciting and fatiguing, meaning nothing, leading nowhere. She is the creature of that circle. And I ask myself if she is obeying the uneasiness of an instinct seeking its satisfaction, or is it a revulsion of feeling, or is she merely deceiving her own heart by this dangerous trifling with romantic images. And everything is possible—except sincerity, such as only stark, struggling humanity can know. No woman can stand that mode of life in which women rule, and remain a perfectly genuine, simple human being. . . . Ah! There's some people coming out."

He moved off a pace, then, turning his head: "Upon my word! I would be infinitely obliged to you if you could throw a little cold water . . ." and at a vaguely dismayed gesture of Renouard, he added: "Don't be afraid. You wouldn't be putting out a sacred fire."

Renouard could hardly find words for a protest: "I assure you that I never talk with Miss Moorsom—on—on—that. And if you, her father . . ."

"I envy you your innocence," sighed the professor. "A father is only an everyday person. Flat. Stale. Moreover, my child would naturally mistrust me. We belong to the same set. Whereas you carry with you the prestige of the unknown. You have proved yourself to be a force."

Thereupon the professor, followed by Renouard, joined the circle of all the inmates of the house assembled at the other end of the terrace about a tea-table; three white heads and that resplendent vision of woman's glory, the sight of which had the power to flutter his heart like a reminder of the mortality of his frame.

He avoided the seat by the side of Miss Moorsom. The others were talking together languidly. Unnoticed he looked at that woman so marvellous that centuries seemed to lie between them. He was oppressed and overcome at the thought of what she could give to some man who really would be a force! What a glorious struggle with this amazon. What noble burden for the victorious strength.

Dear old Mrs. Dunster was dispensing tea, looking from time to time with interest towards Miss Moorsom. The aged statesman having eaten a raw tomato and drunk a glass of milk (a habit of his early farming days, long before politics, when, pioneer of wheat-growing, he demonstrated the possibility of raising crops on ground looking barren enough to discourage a magician), smoothed his white beard, and struck lightly Renouard's knee with his big wrinkled hand.

"You had better come back tonight and dine with us quietly."

He liked this young man, a pioneer, too, in more than one direction. Mrs. Dunster added: "Do. It will be very quiet. I don't even know if Willie will be home for dinner." Renouard murmured his thanks, and left the terrace to go on board the schooner. While lingering in the drawing-room doorway he heard the resonant voice of old Dunster uttering oracularly—

"... the leading man here some day.... Like me."

Renouard let the thin summer portière of the doorway fall behind him. The voice of Professor Moorsom said—

"I am told that he has made an enemy of almost every man who had to work with him."

"That's nothing. He did his work.... Like me."

"He never counted the cost they say. Not even of lives."

Renouard understood that they were talking of him. Before he could move away, Mrs. Dunster struck in placidly—

"Don't let yourself be shocked by the tales you may hear of him, my dear. Most of it is envy."

Then he heard Miss Moorsom's voice replying to the old lady—

"Oh! I am not easily deceived. I think I may say I have an instinct for truth."

The Planter of Malata

He hastened away from that house with his heart full of dread.

VI

On board the schooner, lying on the settee on his back with the knuckles of his hands pressed over his eyes, he made up his mind that he would not return to that house for dinner —that he would never go back there any more. He made up his mind some twenty times. The knowledge that he had only to go up on the quarter deck, utter quietly the words: "Man the windlass", and that the schooner springing into life would run a hundred miles out to sea before sunrise, deceived his struggling will. Nothing easier! Yet, in the end, this young man, almost ill-famed for his ruthless daring, the inflexible leader of two tragically successful expeditions, shrank from that act of savage energy, and began, instead, to hunt for excuses.

No! It was not for him to run away like an incurable who cuts his throat. He finished dressing and looked at his own impassive face in the saloon mirror scornfully. While being pulled on shore in the gig, he remembered suddenly the wild beauty of a waterfall seen when hardly more than a boy, years ago, in Menado. There was a legend of a governor-general of the Dutch East Indies, on official tour, committing suicide on that spot by leaping into the chasm. It was supposed that a painful disease had made him weary of life. But was there ever a visitation like his own, at the same time binding one to life and so cruelly mortal!

The dinner was indeed quiet. Willie, given half an hour's grace, failed to turn up, and his chair remained vacant by the side of Miss Moorsom. Renouard had the professor's sister on his left, dressed in an expensive gown becoming her age. That maiden lady in her wonderful preservation reminded Renouard somehow of a wax flower under glass. There were no traces of the dust of life's battles on her anywhere. She did

The Planter of Malata

not like him very much in the afternoons, in his white drill suit and planter's hat, which seemed to her an unduly Bohemian costume for calling in a house where there were ladies. But in the evening, lithe and elegant in his dress clothes and with his pleasant, slightly veiled voice, he always made her conquest afresh. He might have been anybody distinguished —the son of a duke. Falling under that charm probably (and also because her brother had given her a hint), she attempted to open her heart to Renouard, who was watching with all the power of his soul her niece across the table. She spoke to him as frankly as though that miserable mortal envelope, emptied of everything but hopeless passion, were indeed the son of a duke.

Inattentive, he heard her only in snatches, till the final confidential burst: ". . . glad if you would express an opinion. Look at her, so charming, such a great favourite, so generally admired It would be too sad. We all hoped she would make a brilliant marriage with somebody very rich and of high position, have a house in London and in the country, and entertain us all splendidly. She's so eminently fitted for it. She has such hosts of distinguished friends! And then—this instead! . . . My heart really aches."

Her well-bred if anxious whisper was covered by the voice of Professor Moorsom discoursing subtly down the short length of the dinner table on the Impermanency of the Measurable to his venerable disciple. It might have been a chapter in a new and popular book of Moorsomian philosophy. Patriarchal and delighted, old Dunster leaned forward a little, his eyes shining youthfully, two spots of colour at the roots of his white beard; and Renouard, glancing at the senile excitement, recalled the words heard on those subtle lips, adopted their scorn for his own, saw their truth before this man ready to be amused by the side of the grave. Yes! Intellectual debauchery in the froth of existence! Froth and fraud!

On the same side of the table Miss Moorsom never once

looked towards her father, all her grace as if frozen, her red lips compressed, the faintest rosiness under her dazzling complexion, her black eyes burning motionless, and the very coppery gleams of light lying still on the waves and undulation of her hair. Renouard fancied himself overturning the table, smashing crystal and china, treading fruit and flowers under foot, seizing her in his arms, carrying her off in a tumult of shrieks from all these people, a silent frightened mortal, into some profound retreat as in the age of Cavern men. Suddenly everybody got up, and he hastened to rise too, finding himself out of breath and quite unsteady on his feet.

On the terrace the philosopher, after lighting a cigar, slipped his hand condescendingly under his "dear young friend's" arm. Renouard regarded him now with the profoundest mistrust. But the great man seemed really to have a liking for his young friend—one of those mysterious sympathies, disregarding the differences of age and position, which in this case might have been explained by the failure of philosophy to meet a very real worry of a practical kind.

After a turn or two and some casual talk the professor said suddenly: "My late son was in your school—do you know? I can imagine that had he lived and you had ever met you would have understood each other. He too was inclined to action."

He sighed, then, shaking off the mournful thought and with a nod at the dusky part of the terrace where the dress of his daughter made a luminous stain: "I really wish you would drop in that quarter a few sensible, discouraging words."

Renouard disengaged himself from that most perfidious of men under the pretence of astonishment, and stepping back a pace—

"Surely you are making fun of me, Professor Moorsom," he said with a low laugh, which was really a sound of rage.

"My dear young friend! It's no subject for jokes, to me.... You don't seem to have any notion of your prestige," he added, walking away towards the chairs.

The Planter of Malata

"Humbug!" thought Renouard, standing still and looking after him. "And yet! And yet! What if it were true?"

He advanced then towards Miss Moorsom. Posed on the seat on which they had first spoken to each other, it was her turn to watch him coming on. But many of the windows were not lighted that evening. It was dark over there. She appeared to him luminous in her clear dress, a figure without shape, a face without features, awaiting his approach, till he got quite near to her, sat down, and they had exchanged a few insignificant words. Gradually she came out like a magic painting of charm, fascination, and desire, glowing mysteriously on the dark background. Something imperceptible in the lines of her attitude, in the modulations of her voice, seemed to soften that suggestion of calm unconscious pride which enveloped her always like a mantle. He, sensitive like a bond slave to the moods of the master, was moved by the subtle relenting of her grace to an infinite tenderness. He fought down the impulse to seize her by the hand, lead her down into the garden away under the big trees, and throw himself at her feet uttering words of love. His emotion was so strong that he had to cough slightly, and not knowing what to talk to her about he began to tell her of his mother and sisters. All the family were coming to London to live there, for some little time at least.

"I hope you will go and tell them something of me. Something seen," he said pressingly.

By this miserable subterfuge, like a man about to part with his life, he hoped to make her remember him a little longer.

"Certainly," she said. "I'll be glad to call when I get back. But that 'when' may be a long time."

He heard a light sigh. A cruel jealous curiosity made him ask—

"Are you growing weary, Miss Moorsom?"

A silence fell on his low-spoken question.

"Do you mean heart-weary?" sounded Miss Moorsom's voice. "You don't know me, I see."

The Planter of Malata

"Ah! Never despair," he muttered.

"This, Mr. Renouard, is a work of reparation. I stand for truth here. I can't think of myself."

He could have taken her by the throat for every word seemed an insult to his passion; but he only said—

"I never doubted the—the—nobility of your purpose."

"And to hear the word weariness pronounced in this connection surprises me. And from a man too who, I understand, has never counted the cost."

"You are pleased to tease me," he said, directly he had recovered his voice and had mastered his anger. It was as if Professor Moorsom had dropped poison in his ear which was spreading now and tainting his passion, his very jealousy. He mistrusted every word that came from those lips on which his life hung. "How can you know anything of men who do not count the cost?" he asked in his gentlest tones.

"From hearsay—a little."

"Well, I assure you they are like the others, subject to suffering, victims of spells. . . ."

"One of them, at least, speaks very strangely."

She dismissed the subject after a short silence. "Mr. Renouard, I had a disappointment this morning. This mail brought me a letter from the widow of the old butler—you know. I expected to learn that she had heard from—from here. But no. No letter arrived home since we left."

Her voice was calm. His jealousy couldn't stand much more of this sort of talk; but he was glad that nothing had turned up to help the search; glad blindly, unreasonably—only because it would keep her longer in his sight—since she wouldn't give up.

"I am too near her," he thought, moving a little further on the seat. He was afraid in the revulsion of feeling of flinging himself on her hands, which were lying on her lap, and covering them with kisses. He was afraid. Nothing, nothing could shake that spell—not if she were ever so false, stupid, or de-

187

The Planter of Malata

graded. She was fate itself. The extent of his misfortune plunged him in such a stupor that he failed at first to hear the sound of voices and footsteps inside the drawing-room. Willie had come home—and the Editor was with him.

They burst out on the terrace babbling noisily, and then pulling themselves together stood still, surprising—and as if themselves surprised.

VII

They had been feasting a poet from the bush, the latest discovery of the Editor. Such discoveries were the business, the vocation, the pride and delight of the only apostle of letters in the hemisphere, the solitary patron of culture, the Slave of the Lamp—as he subscribed himself at the bottom of the weekly literary page of his paper. He had had no difficulty in persuading the virtuous Willie (who had festive instincts) to help in the good work, and now they had left the poet lying asleep on the hearthrug of the editorial room and had rushed to the Dunster mansion wildly. The Editor had another discovery to announce. Swaying a little where he stood he opened his mouth very wide to shout the one word "Found!" Behind him Willie flung both his hands above his head and let them fall dramatically. Renouard saw the four white-headed people at the end of the terrace rise all together from their chairs with an effect of sudden panic.

"I tell you—he—is—found," the patron of letters shouted emphatically.

"What is this!" exclaimed Renouard in a choked voice. Miss Moorsom seized his wrist suddenly, and at that contact fire ran though all his veins, a hot stillness descended upon him in which he heard the blood—or the fire—beating in his ears. He made a movement as if to rise, but was restrained by the convulsive pressure on his wrist.

"No, no." Miss Moorsom's eyes stared black as night, searching the space before her. Far away the Editor strutted

The Planter of Malata

forward, Willie following with his ostentatious manner of carrying his bulky and oppressive carcass which, however, did not remain exactly perpendicular for two seconds together.

"The innocent Arthur . . . Yes. We've got him," the Editor became very business-like. "Yes, this letter has done it."

He plunged into an inside pocket for it, slapped the scrap of paper with his open palm. "From that old woman. William had it in his pocket since this morning when Miss Moorsom gave it to him to show me. Forgot all about it till an hour ago. Thought it was of no importance. Well, no! Not till it was properly read."

Renouard and Miss Moorsom emerged from the shadows side by side, a well-matched couple, animated yet statuesque in their calmness and in their pallor. She had let go his wrist. On catching sight of Renouard the Editor exclaimed: "What —you here!" in a quite shrill voice.

There came a dead pause. All the faces had in them something dismayed and cruel.

"He's the very man we want," continued the Editor. "Excuse my excitement. You are the very man, Renouard. Didn't you tell me that your assistant called himself Walter? Yes? Thought so. But here's that old woman—the butler's wife—listen to this. She writes: All I can tell you, Miss, is that my poor husband directed his letters to the name of H. Walter."

Renouard's violent but repressed exclamation was lost in a general murmur and shuffle of feet. The Editor made a step forward, bowed with creditable steadiness.

"Miss Moorsom, allow me to congratulate you from the bottom of my heart on the happy—er—issue . . ."

"Wait," muttered Renouard irresolutely.

The Editor jumped on him in the manner of their old friendship. "Ah, you! You are a fine fellow too. With your solitary ways of life you will end by having no more discrimination than a savage. Fancy living with a gentleman for

The Planter of Malata

months and never guessing. A man, I am certain, accomplished, remarkable, out of the common, since he had been distinguished" (he bowed again) "by Miss Moorsom, whom we all admire."

She turned her back on him.

"I hope to goodness you haven't been leading him a dog's life, Geoffrey," the Editor addressed his friend in a whispered aside.

Renouard seized a chair violently, sat down, and propping his elbow on his knee leaned his head on his hand. Behind him the sister of the professor looked up to heaven and wrung her hands stealthily. Mrs. Dunster's hands were clasped forcibly under her chin, but she, dear soul, was looking sorrowfully at Willie. The model nephew! In this strange state! So very much flushed! The careful disposition of the thin hairs across Willie's bald spot was deplorably disarranged, and the spot itself was red and, as it were, steaming.

"What's the matter, Geoffrey?" The Editor seemed disconcerted by the silent attitudes round him, as though he had expected all these people to shout and dance. "You have him on the island—haven't you?"

"Oh, yes: I have him there," said Renouard, without looking up.

"Well, then!" The Editor looked helplessly around as if begging for response of some sort. But the only response that came was very unexpected. Annoyed at being left in the background, and also because very little drink made him nasty, the emotional Willie turned malignant all at once, and in a bibulous tone surprising in a man able to keep his balance so well—

"Aha! But you haven't got him here—not yet!" he sneered. "No! You haven't got him yet."

This outrageous exhibition was to the Editor like the lash to a jaded horse. He positively jumped.

"What of that? What do you mean? We—haven't—got—

The Planter of Malata

him—here. Of course he isn't here! But Geoffrey's schooner is here. She can be sent at once to fetch him here. No! Stay! There's a better plan. Why shouldn't you all sail over to Malata, professor? Save time! I am sure Miss Moorsom would prefer..."

With a gallant flourish of his arm he looked for Miss Moorsom. She had disappeared. He was taken aback somewhat.

"Ah! H'm. Yes.... Why not? A pleasure cruise, delightful ship, delightful season, delightful errand, del... No! There are no objections. Geoffrey, I understand, has indulged in a bungalow three sizes too large for him. He can put you all up. It will be a pleasure for him. It will be the greatest privilege. Any man would be proud of being an agent of this happy reunion. I am proud of the little part I've played. He will consider it the greatest honour. Geoff, my boy, you had better be stirring tomorrow bright and early about the preparations for the trip. It would be criminal to lose a single day."

He was as flushed as Willie, the excitement keeping up the effect of the festive dinner. For a time Renouard, silent, as if he had not heard a word of all that babble, did not stir. But when he got up it was to advance towards the Editor and give him such a hearty slap on the back that the plump little man reeled in his tracks and looked quite frightened for a moment.

"You are a heaven-born discoverer and a first-rate manager.... He's right. It's the only way. You can't resist the claim of sentiment, and you must even risk the voyage to Malata...." Renouard's voice sank. "A lonely spot," he added, and fell into thought under all these eyes converging on him in the sudden silence. His slow glance passed over all the faces in succession, remaining arrested on Professor Moorsom, stony eyed, a smouldering cigar in his fingers, and with his sister standing by his side.

"I shall be infinitely gratified if you consent to come. But, of course, you will. We shall sail tomorrow evening, then. And now let me leave you to your happiness."

The Planter of Malata

He bowed, very grave, pointed suddenly his finger at Willie who was swaying about with a sleepy frown. . . . "Look at him. He's overcome with happiness. You had better put him to bed . . ." and disappeared while every head on the terrace was turned to Willie with varied expressions.

Renouard ran through the house. Avoiding the carriage road he fled down the steep short cut to the shore, where his gig was waiting. At his loud shout the sleeping Kanakas jumped up. He leaped in. "Shove off. Give way!" and the gig darted through the water. "Give way! Give way!" She flew past the wool-clippers sleeping at their anchors, each with the open unwinking eye of the lamp in the rigging; she flew past the flagship of the Pacific squadron, a great mass all dark and silent, heavy with the slumbers of five hundred men, and where the invisible sentries heard his urgent "Give way! Give way!" in the night. The Kanakas, panting, rose off the thwarts at every stroke. Nothing could be fast enough for him! And he ran up the side of his schooner shaking the ladder noisily with his rush.

On deck he stumbled and stood still.

Wherefore this haste? To what end, since he knew well before he started that he had a pursuer from whom there was no escape.

As his foot touched the deck his will, his purpose he had been hurrying to save, died out within him. It had been nothing less than getting the schooner under-way, letting her vanish silently in the night from amongst these sleeping ships. And now he was certain he could not do it. It was impossible! And he reflected that whether he lived or died such an act would lay him under a dark suspicion from which he shrank. No, there was nothing to be done.

He went down into the cabin and, before even unbuttoning his overcoat, took out of the drawer the letter addressed to his assistant; that letter which he had found in the pigeon-hole labelled "Malata" in young Dunster's outer office, where it had been waiting for three months some occasion for being forwarded. From the moment of dropping it in the drawer he had utterly forgotten its existence—till now, when the man's name had come out so clamorously. He glanced at the common envelope, noted the shaky and laborious handwriting: H. Walter, Esqre. Undoubtedly the very last letter the old butler had posted before his illness, and in answer clearly to one from "Master Arthur" instructing him to address in the future: "Care of Messrs. W. Dunster and Co." Renouard made as if to open the envelope, but paused, and, instead, tore the letter deliberately in two, in four, in eight. With his hand full of pieces of paper he returned on deck and scattered them overboard on the dark water, in which they vanished instantly.

He did it slowly, without hesitation or remorse. H. Walter, Esqre, in Malata. The innocent Arthur—— What was his name? The man sought for by that woman who as she went by seemed to draw all the passion of the earth to her, without effort, not deigning to notice, naturally, as other women breathed the air. But Renouard was no longer jealous of her very existence. Whatever its meaning it was not for that man he had picked up casually on obscure impulse, to get rid of the tiresome expostulations of a so-called friend; a man of whom he really knew nothing—and now a dead man. In Malata. Oh, yes! He was there secure enough, untroubled in his grave. In Malata. To bury him was the last service Renouard had rendered to his assistant before leaving the island on this trip to town.

Like many men ready enough for arduous enterprises Renouard was inclined to evade the small complications of existence. This trait of his character was composed of a little indolence, some disdain, and a shrinking from contests with certain forms of vulgarity—like a man who would face a lion and go out of his way to avoid a toad. His intercourse with the meddlesome journalist was that merely outward intimacy

The Planter of Malata

without sympathy some young men get drawn into easily. It had amused him rather to keep that "friend" in the dark about the fate of his assistant. Renouard had never needed other company than his own, for there was in him something of the sensitiveness of a dreamer who is easily jarred. He had said to himself that the all-knowing one would only preach again about the evils of solitude and worry his head off in favour of some forlornly useless protégé of his. Also the inquisitiveness of the Editor had irritated him and had closed his lips in sheer disgust.

And now he contemplated the noose of consequences drawing tight around him.

It was the memory of that diplomatic reticence which on the terrace had stifled his first cry which would have told them all that the man sought for was not to be met on earth any more. He shrank from the absurdity of hearing the all-knowing one, and not very sober at that, turning on him with righteous reproaches—

"You never told me. You gave me to understand that your assistant was alive, and now you say he's dead. Which is it? Were you lying then or are you lying now?" No! the thought of such a scene was not to be borne. He had sat down appalled, thinking: "What shall I do now?"

His courage had oozed out of him. Speaking the truth meant the Moorsoms going away at once—while it seemed to him that he would give the last shred of his rectitude to secure a day more of her company. He sat on—silent. Slowly, from confused sensations, from his talk with the professor, the manner of the girl herself, the intoxicating familiarity of her sudden hand-clasp, there had come to him a half glimmer of hope. The other man was dead. Then! . . . Madness, of course—but he could not give it up. He had listened to that confounded busybody arranging everything—while all these people stood around assenting, under the spell of that dead romance. He had listened scornful and silent. The glimmers of

The Planter of Malata

hope, of opportunity, passed before his eyes. He had only to sit still and say nothing. That and no more. And what was truth to him in the face of that great passion which had flung him prostrate in spirit at her adored feet!

And now it was done! Fatality had willed it! With the eyes of a mortal struck by the maddening thunderbolt of the gods, Renouard looked up to the sky, an immense black pall dusted over with gold, on which great shudders seemed to pass from the breath of life affirming its sway.

VIII

At last, one morning, in a clear spot of a glassy horizon charged with heraldic masses of black vapours, the island grew out from the sea, showing here and there its naked members of basaltic rock through the rents of heavy foliage. Later, in the great spilling of all the riches of sunset, Malata stood out green and rosy before turning into a violet shadow in the autumnal light of the expiring day. Then came the night. In the faint airs the schooner crept on past a sturdy squat headland, and it was pitch dark when her headsails ran down, she turned short on her heel, and her anchor bit into the sandy bottom on the edge of the outer reef; for it was too dangerous then to attempt entering the little bay full of shoals. After the last solemn flutter of the mainsail the murmuring voices of the Moorsom party lingered, very frail, in the black stillness.

They were sitting aft, on chairs, and nobody made a move. Early in the day, when it had become evident that the wind was failing, Renouard, basing his advice on the shortcomings of his bachelor establishment, had urged on the ladies the advisability of not going ashore in the middle of the night. Now he approached them in a constrained manner (it was astonishing the constraint that had reigned between him and his guests all through the passage) and renewed his arguments. No one

The Planter of Malata

ashore would dream of his bringing any visitors with him. Nobody would even think of coming off. There was only one old canoe on the plantation. And landing in the schooner's boats would be awkward in the dark. There was the risk of getting aground on some shallow patches. It would be best to spend the rest of the night on board.

There was really no opposition. The professor smoking a pipe, and very comfortable in an ulster buttoned over his tropical clothes, was the first to speak from his long chair.

"Most excellent advice."

Next to him Miss Moorsom assented by a long silence. Then in a voice as of one coming out of a dream—

"And so this is Malata," she said. "I have often wondered . . ."

A shiver passed through Renouard. She had wondered! What about? Malata was himself. He and Malata were one. And she had wondered! She had. . . .

The professor's sister leaned over towards Renouard. Through all these days at sea the man's—the found man's—existence had not been alluded to on board the schooner. That reticence was part of the general constraint lying upon them all. She, herself, certainly had not been exactly elated by this finding—poor Arthur, without money, without prospects. But she felt moved by the sentiment and romance of the situation.

"Isn't it wonderful," she whispered out of her white wrap, "to think of poor Arthur sleeping there, so near to our dear lovely Felicia, and not knowing the immense joy in store for him tomorrow."

There was such artificiality in the wax-flower lady that nothing in this speech touched Renouard. It was but the simple anxiety of his heart that he was voicing when he muttered gloomily—

"No one in the world knows what tomorrow may hold in store."

The Planter of Malata

The mature lady had a recoil as though he had said something impolite. What a harsh thing to say—instead of finding something nice and appropriate. On board, where she never saw him in evening clothes, Renouard's resemblance to a duke's son was not so apparent to her. Nothing but his—ah—bohemianism remained. She rose with a sort of ostentation.

"It's late—and since we are going to sleep on board tonight . . ."she said. "But it does seem so cruel."

The professor started up eagerly, knocking the ashes out of his pipe. "Infinitely more sensible, my dear Emma."

Renouard waited behind Miss Moorsom's chair.

She got up slowly, moved one step forward, and paused looking at the shore. The blackness of the island blotted out the stars with its vague mass like a low thundercloud brooding over the waters and ready to burst into flame and crashes.

"And so—this is Malata," she repeated dreamily, moving towards the cabin door. The clear cloak hanging from her shoulders, the ivory face—for the night had put out nothing of her but the gleams of her hair—made her resemble a shining dream-woman uttering words of wistful inquiry. She disappeared without a sign, leaving Renouard penetrated to the very marrow by the sounds that came from her body like a mysterious resonance of an exquisite instrument.

He stood stock still. What was this accidental touch which had evoked the strange accent of her voice? He dared not answer that question. But he had to answer the question of what was to be done now. Had the moment of confession come? The thought was enough to make one's blood run cold.

It was as if those people had a premonition of something. In the taciturn days of the passage he had noticed their reserve even amongst themselves. The professor smoked his pipe moodily in retired spots. Renouard had caught Miss Moorsom's eyes resting on himself more than once, with a peculiar and grave expression. He fancied that she avoided all opportunities of conversation. The maiden lady seemed to nurse a grievance. And now what had he to do?

The lights on the deck had gone out one after the other. The schooner slept.

About an hour after Miss Moorsom had gone below without a sign or a word for him, Renouard got out of his hammock slung in the waist under the midship awning—for he had given up all the accommodation below to his guests. He got out with a sudden swift movement, flung off his sleeping jacket, rolled his pyjamas up his thighs, and stole forward, unseen by the one Kanaka of the anchor-watch. His white torso, naked like a stripped athlete's, glimmered, ghostly, in the deep shadows of the deck. Unnoticed he got out of the ship over the knight-heads, ran along the back rope, and seizing the dolphin-striker firmly with both hands, lowered himself into the sea without a splash.

He swam away, noiseless like a fish, and then struck boldly for the land, sustained, embraced, by the tepid water. The gentle, voluptuous heave of its breast swung him up and down slightly; sometimes a wavelet murmured in his ears; from time to time, lowering his feet, he felt for the bottom on a shallow patch to rest and correct his direction. He landed at the lower end of the bungalow garden, into the dead stillness of the island. There were no lights. The plantation seemed to sleep, as profoundly as the schooner. On the path a small shell cracked under his naked heel.

The faithful half-caste foreman going his rounds cocked his ears at the sharp sound. He gave one enormous start of fear at the sight of the swift white figure flying at him out of the night. He crouched in terror, and then sprang up and clicked his tongue in amazed recognition.

"Tse! Tse! The master!"

"Be quiet, Luiz, and listen to what I say."

Yes, it was the master, the strong master who was never known to raise his voice, the man blindly obeyed and never questioned. He talked low and rapidly in the quiet night, as if every minute were precious. On learning that three guests were coming to stay Luiz clicked his tongue rapidly. These clicks were the uniform, stenographic symbols of his emotions, and he could give them an infinite variety of meaning. He listened to the rest in a deep silence hardly affected by the low, "Yes, master," whenever Renouard paused.

"You understand?" the latter insisted. "No preparations are to be made till we land in the morning. And you are to say that Mr. Walter has gone off in a trading schooner on a round of the islands."

"Yes, master."

"No mistakes—mind!"

"No, master."

Renouard walked back towards the sea. Luiz, following him, proposed to call out half a dozen boys and man the canoe.

"Imbecile!"

"Tse! Tse! Tse!"

"Don't you understand that you haven't seen me?"

"Yes, master. But what a long swim. Suppose you drown."

"Then you can say of me and of Mr. Walter what you like. The dead don't mind."

Renouard entered the sea and heard a faint Tse! Tse! Tse! of concern from the half-caste, who had already lost sight of the master's dark head on the overshadowed water.

Renouard set his direction by a big star that, dipping on the horizon, seemed to look curiously in his face. On this swim back he felt the mournful fatigue of all that length of the traversed road, which brought him no nearer to his desire. It was as if his love had sapped the invisible supports of his strength. There came a moment when it seemed to him that he must have swum beyond the confines of life. He had a sensation of eternity close at hand, demanding no effort—offering its peace. It was easy to swim like this beyond the confines of life looking at a star. But the thought: "They will think I dared not face them and committed suicide," caused a revolt of his mind which carried him on. He returned on board, as he had left, unheard and unseen. He lay in his hammock utterly exhausted and with a confused feeling that he had been beyond the confines of life, somewhere near a star, and that it was very quiet there.

IX

Sheltered by the squat headland from the first morning sparkle of the sea the little bay breathed a delicious freshness. The party from the schooner landed at the bottom of the garden. They exchanged insignificant words in studiously casual tones. The professor's sister put up a long-handled eye-glass as if to scan the novel surroundings, but in reality searching for poor Arthur anxiously. Having never seen him otherwise than in his town clothes she had no idea what he would look like. It had been left to the professor to help his ladies out of the boat because Renouard, as if intent on giving directions, had stepped forward at once to meet the half-caste Luiz hurrying down the path. In the distance, in front of the dazzlingly sunlit bungalow, a row of dark-faced houseboys unequal in stature and varied in complexion preserved the immobility of a guard of honour.

Luiz had taken off his soft felt hat before coming within earshot. Renouard bent his head to his rapid talk of domestic arrangements he meant to make for the visitors; another bed in the master's room for the ladies and a cot for the gentleman to be hung in the room opposite where—where Mr. Walter—here he gave a scared look all round—Mr. Walter—had died.

"Very good," assented Renouard in an even undertone. "And remember what you have to say of him."

"Yes, master. Only"—he wriggled slightly and put one

The Planter of Malata

bare foot on the other for a moment in apologetic embarrassment—"only I—I—don't like to say it."

Renouard looked at him without anger, without any sort of expression. "Frightened of the dead? Eh? Well—all right. I will say it myself—I suppose once for all...." Immediately he raised his voice very much.

"Send the boys down to bring up the luggage."

"Yes, master."

Renouard turned to his distinguished guests who, like a personally conducted party of tourists, had stopped and were looking about them.

"I am sorry," he began with an impassive face. "My man has just told me that Mr. Walter..." he managed to smile, but didn't correct himself... "has gone in a trading schooner on a short tour of the islands, to the westward."

This communication was received in profound silence.

Renouard forgot himself in the thought: "It's done!" But the sight of the string of boys marching up to the house with suit-cases and dressing-bags rescued him from that appalling abstraction.

"All I can do is to beg you to make yourselves at home... with what patience you may."

This was so obviously the only thing to do that everybody moved on at once. The professor walked alongside Renouard, behind the two ladies.

"Rather unexpected—this absence."

"Not exactly," muttered Renouard. "A trip has to be made every year to engage labour."

"I see... And he... How vexingly elusive the poor fellow has become! I'll begin to think that some wicked fairy is favouring this love tale with unpleasant attentions."

Renouard noticed that the party did not seem weighed down by this new disappointment. On the contrary they moved with a freer step. The professor's sister dropped her eye-glass to the end of its chain. Miss Moorsom took the lead.

201

The Planter of Malata

The professor, his lips unsealed, lingered in the open: but Renouard did not listen to that man's talk. He looked after that man's daughter—if indeed that creature of irresistible seductions were a daughter of mortals. The very intensity of his desire, as if his soul were streaming after her through his eyes, defeated his object of keeping hold of her as long as possible with, at least, one of his senses. Her moving outlines dissolved into a misty-coloured shimmer of a woman made of flame and shadows, crossing the threshold of his house.

The days which followed were not exactly such as Renouard had feared—yet they were not better than his fears. They were accursed in all the moods they brought him. But the general aspect of things was quiet. The professor smoked innumerable pipes with the air of a worker on his holiday, always in movement and looking at things with that mysteriously sagacious aspect of men who are admittedly wiser than the rest of the world. His white head of hair—whiter than anything within the horizon except the broken water on the reefs—was glimpsed in every part of the plantation always on the move under the white parasol. And once he climbed the headland and appeared suddenly to those below, a white speck elevated in the blue, with a diminutive but statuesque effect.

Felicia Moorsom remained near the house. Sometimes she could be seen with a despairing expression scribbling rapidly in her lock-up diary. But only for a moment. At the sound of Renouard's footsteps she would turn towards him her beautiful face, adorable in that calm which was like a wilful, like a cruel ignoring of her tremendous power. Whenever she sat on the verandah, on a chair more specially reserved for her use, Renouard would stroll up and sit on the steps near her, mostly silent, and often not trusting himself to turn his glance on her. She, very still with her eyes half-closed, looked down on his head—so that to a beholder (such as Professor Moorsom, for instance) she would appear to be turning over in her mind

The Planter of Malata

profound thoughts about that man sitting at her feet, his shoulders bowed a little, his hands listless—as if vanquished. And, indeed, the moral poison of falsehood has such a decomposing power that Renouard felt his old personality turn to dead dust. Often, in the evening, when they sat outside conversing languidly in the dark, he felt that he must rest his forehead on her feet and burst into tears.

The professor's sister suffered from some little strain caused by the unstability of her own feelings towards Renouard. She could not tell whether she really did dislike him or not. At times he appeared to her most fascinating; and, though he generally ended by saying something shockingly crude, she could not resist her inclination to talk with him—at least not always. One day when her niece had left them alone on the verandah she leaned forward in her chair —speckless, resplendent, and, in her way, almost as striking a personality as her niece, who did not resemble her in the least. "Dear Felicia has inherited her hair and the greatest part of her appearance from her mother," the maiden lady used to tell people.

She leaned forward then, confidentially.

"Oh! Mr. Renouard! Haven't you something comforting to say?"

He looked up, as surprised as if a voice from heaven had spoken with this perfect society intonation, and by the puzzled profundity of his blue eyes fluttered the wax-flower of refined womanhood. She continued. "For—I can speak to you openly on this tiresome subject—only think what a terrible strain this hope deferred must be for Felicia's heart—for her nerves."

"Why speak to me about it," he muttered feeling half choked suddenly.

"Why! As a friend—a well-wisher—the kindest of hosts. I am afraid we are really eating you out of house and home." She laughed a little. "Ah! When, when will this sus-

203

The Planter of Malata

pense be relieved! That poor lost Arthur! I confess that I am almost afraid of the great moment. It will be like seeing a ghost."

"Have you ever seen a ghost?" asked Renouard, in a dull voice.

She shifted her hands a little. Her pose was perfect in its ease and middle-aged grace.

"Not actually. Only in a photograph. But we have many friends who had the experience of apparitions."

"Ah! They see ghosts in London," mumbled Renouard, not looking at her.

"Frequently—in a certain very interesting set. But all sorts of people do. We have a friend, a very famous author—his ghost is a girl. One of my brother's intimates is a very great man of science. He is friendly with a ghost . . . Of a girl too," she added in a voice as if struck for the first time by the coincidence. "It is the photograph of that apparition which I have seen. Very sweet. Most interesting. A little cloudy naturally. . . . Mr. Renouard! I hope you are not a sceptic. It's so consoling to think . . ."

"Those plantation boys of mine see ghosts too," said Renouard grimly.

The sister of the philosopher sat up stiffly. What crudeness! It was always so with this strange young man.

"Mr. Renouard! How can you compare the superstitious fancies of your horrible savages with the manifestations . . ."

Words failed her. She broke off with a very faint primly angry smile. She was perhaps the more offended with him because of that flutter at the beginning of the conversation. And in a moment with perfect tact and dignity she got up from her chair and left him alone.

Renouard didn't even look up. It was not the displeasure of the lady which deprived him of his sleep that night. He was beginning to forget what simple, honest sleep was like. His hammock from the ship had been hung for him on a side verandah, and he spent his nights in it on his back, his hands folded on his chest, in a sort of half-conscious, oppressed stupor. In the morning he watched with unseeing eyes the headland come out of a shapeless inkblot against the thin light of the false dawn, pass through all the stages of daybreak to the deep purple of its outlined mass nimbed gloriously with the gold of the rising sun. He listened to the vague sounds of waking within the house; and suddenly he became aware of Luiz standing by the hammock—obviously troubled.

"What's the matter?"

"Tse! Tse! Tse!"

"Well, what now? Trouble with the boys?"

"No, master. The gentleman when I take him his bath water he speak to me. He ask me—he ask—when, when, I think Mr. Walter, he come back."

The half-caste's teeth chattered slightly. Renouard got out of the hammock.

"And he is here all the time—eh?"

Luiz nodded a scared affirmative, but at once protested, "I no see him. I never. Not I! The ignorant wild boys say they see . . . Something! Ough!"

He clapped his teeth on another short rattle, and stood there, shrunk, blighted, like a man in a freezing blast.

"And what did you say to the gentleman?"

"I say I don't know—and I clear out. I—I don't like to speak of him."

"All right. We shall try to lay that poor ghost," said Renouard gloomily, going off to a small hut near by to dress. He was saying to himself: "This fellow will end by giving me away. The last thing that I . . . No! That mustn't be." And feeling his hand being forced he discovered the whole extent of his cowardice.

X

That morning wandering about his plantation, more like a

frightened soul than its creator and master, he dodged the white parasol bobbing up here and there like a buoy adrift on a sea of dark green plants. The crop promised to be magnificent, and the fashionable philosopher of the age took other than a merely scientific interest in the experiment. His investments were judicious, but he had always some little money lying by, for experiments.

After lunch, being left alone with Renouard, he talked a little of cultivation and such matters. Then suddenly:

"By the way, is it true what my sister tells me, that your plantation boys have been disturbed by a ghost?"

Renouard, who since the ladies had left the table was not keeping such a strict watch on himself, came out of his abstraction with a start and a stiff smile.

"My foreman had some trouble with them during my absence They funk working in a certain field on the slope of the hill."

"A ghost here!" exclaimed the amused professor. "Then our whole conception of the psychology of ghosts must be revised. This island has been uninhabited probably since the dawn of ages. How did a ghost come here? By air or water? And why did it leave its native haunts? Was it from misanthropy? Was he expelled from some community of spirits?"

Renouard essayed to respond in the same tone. The words died on his lips. Was it a man or a woman ghost, the professor inquired.

"I don't know." Renouard made an effort to appear at ease. He had, he said, a couple of Tahitian amongst his boys— a ghost-ridden race. They had started the scare. They had probably brought their ghost with them.

"Let us investigate the matter, Renouard," proposed the professor half in earnest. "We may make some interesting discoveries as to the state of primitive minds, at any rate."

This was too much. Renouard jumped up and leaving the room went out and walked about in front of the house. He would allow no one to force his hand. Presently the professor joined him outside. He carried his parasol, but had neither his book nor his pipe with him. Amiably serious he laid his hand on his "dear young friend's" arm.

"We are all of us a little strung up," he said. "For my part I have been like sister Anne in the story. But I cannot see anything coming. Anything that would be the least good for anybody—I mean."

Renouard had recovered sufficiently to murmur coldly his regret of this waste of time. For that was what, he supposed, the professor had in his mind.

"Time," mused Professor Moorsom. "I don't know that time can be wasted. But I will tell you, my dear friend, what this is: it's an awful waste of life. I mean for all of us. Even for my sister, who has got a headache and is gone to lie down."

He shook gently Renouard's arm. "Yes, for all of us! One may meditate on life endlessly, one may even have a poor opinion of it—but the fact remains that we have only one life to live. And it is short. Think of that, my young friend."

He released Renouard's arm and stepped out of the shade opening his parasol. It was clear that there was something more in his mind than mere anxiety about the date of his lectures for fashionable audiences. What did the man mean by his confounded platitudes? To Renouard, scared by Luiz in the morning (for he felt that nothing could be more fatal than to have his deception unveiled otherwise than by personal confession), this talk sounded like encouragement or a warning from that man who seemed to him to be very brazen and very subtle. It was like being bullied by the dead and cajoled by the living into a throw of dice for a supreme stake.

Renouard went away to some distance from the house and threw himself down in the shade of a tree. He lay there perfectly still with his forehead resting on his folded arms, light-headed and thinking. It seemed to him that he must be on fire, then that he had fallen into a cool whirlpool, a

The Planter of Malata

smooth funnel of water swirling about with nauseating rapidity. And then (it must have been a reminiscence of his boyhood) he was walking on the dangerous thin ice of a river, unable to turn back.... Suddenly it parted from shore to shore with a loud crack like the report of a gun.

With one leap he found himself on his feet. All was peace, stillness, sunshine. He walked away from there slowly. Had he been a gambler he would have perhaps been supported in a measure by the mere excitement. But he was not a gambler. He had always disdained that artificial manner of challenging the fates. The bungalow came into view, bright and pretty, and all about everything was peace, stillness, sunshine....

While he was plodding towards it he had a disagreeable sense of the dead man's company at his elbow. The ghost! He seemed to be everywhere but in his grave. Could one ever shake him off? he wondered. At that moment Miss Moorsom came out on the verandah; and at once, as if by a mystery of radiating waves, she roused a great tumult in his heart, shook earth and sky together—but he plodded on. Then, like a grave song-note in the storm, her voice came to him ominously.

"Ah! Mr. Renouard...." He came up and smiled, but she was very serious. "I can't keep still any longer. Is there time to walk up this headland and back before dark?"

The shadows were lying lengthened on the ground; all was stillness and peace. "No," said Renouard, feeling suddenly as steady as a rock. "But I can show you a view from the central hill which your father has not seen. A view of reefs and of broken water without end, and of great wheeling clouds of sea-birds."

She came down the verandah steps at once and they moved off. "You go first," he proposed, "and I'll direct you. To the left."

She was wearing a short nankin skirt, a muslin blouse; he could see through the thin stuff the skin of her shoulders, of her arms. The noble delicacy of her neck caused him a sort of transport. "The path begins where these three palms are. The only palms on the island."

"I see."

She never turned her head. After a while she observed: "This path looks as if it had been made recently."

"Quite recently," he assented very low.

They went on climbing steadily without exchanging another word; and when they stood on the top she gazed a long time before her. The low evening mist veiled the further limit of the reefs. Above the enormous and melancholy confusion, as of a fleet of wrecked islands, the restless myriads of sea-birds rolled and unrolled dark ribbons on the sky, gathered in clouds, soared and stooped like a play of shadows, for they were too far for them to hear their cries.

Renouard broke the silence in low tones.

"They'll be settling for the night presently." She made no sound. Round them all was peace and declining sunshine. Near by, the topmost pinnacle of Malata, resembling the top of a buried tower, rose a rock, weather-worn, grey, weary of watching the monotonous centuries of the Pacific. Renouard leaned his shoulders against it. Felicia Moorsom faced him suddenly, her splendid black eyes full on his face as though she had made up her mind at last to destroy his wits once and for all. Dazzled, he lowered his eyelids slowly.

"Mr. Renouard! There is something strange in all this. Tell me where he is?"

He answered deliberately.

"On the other side of this rock. I buried him there myself."

She pressed her hands to her breast, struggled for her breath for a moment, then: "Ohhh!... You buried him!... What sort of man are you?... You dared not tell!... He is another of your victims?... You dared not confess that evening.... You must have killed him. What could he have done to you?... You fastened on him some atrocious quarrel and..."

The Planter of Malata

Her vengeful aspect, her poignant cries left him as unmoved as the weary rock against which he leaned. He only raised his eyelids to look at her and lowered them slowly. Nothing more. It silenced her. And, as if ashamed, she made a gesture with her hand, putting away from her that thought. He spoke quietly ironic at first.

"Ha! the legendary Renouard of sensitive idiots—the ruthless adventurer—the ogre with a future. That was a parrot cry, Miss Moorsom. I don't think that the greatest fool of them all ever dared hint such a stupid thing of me that I killed men for nothing. No, I had noticed this man in a hotel. He had come from up-country I was told, and was doing nothing. I saw him sitting there lonely in a corner like a sick crow, and I went over one evening to talk to him. Just on impulse. He wasn't impressive. He was pitiful. My worst enemy could have told you he wasn't good enough to be one of Renouard's victims. It didn't take me long to judge that he was drugging himself. Not drinking. Drugs."

"Ah! It's now that you are trying to murder him," she cried.

"Really. Always the Renouard of shopkeepers' legend. Listen! I would never have been jealous of him. And yet I am jealous of the air you breathe, of the soil you tread on, of the world that sees you—moving free—not mine. But never mind. I rather liked him. For a certain reason I proposed he should come to be my assistant here. He said he believed this would save him. It did not save him from death. It came to him as it were from nothing—just a fall. A mere slip and tumble of ten feet into a ravine. But it seems he had been hurt before up-country—by a horse. He ailed and ailed. No, he was not a steel-tipped man. And his poor soul seemed to have been damaged, too. It gave way very soon."

"This is tragic!" Felicia Moorsom whispered with feeling. Renouard's lips twitched, but his level voice continued mercilessly.

"That's the story. He rallied a little one night and said he

The Planter of Malata

wanted to tell me something. I, being a gentleman, he said, he could confide in me. I told him that he was mistaken. That there was a good deal of a plebeian in me, that he couldn't know. He seemed disappointed. He muttered something about his innocence and something that sounded like a curse on some woman, then turned to the wall—and just grew cold."

"On a woman," cried Miss Moorsom indignantly. "What woman?"

"I wonder!" said Renouard, raising his eyes and noting the crimson of her ear-lobes against the live whiteness of her complexion, the sombre, as if secret, night-splendour of her eyes under the writhing flames of her hair. "Some woman who wouldn't believe in that poor innocence of his. . . . Yes. You probably. And now you will not believe in me—not even in me who must in truth be what I am—even to death. No! You won't. And yet, Felicia, a woman like you and a man like me do not often come together on this earth."

The flame of her glorious head scorched his face. He flung his hat far away, and his suddenly lowered eyelids brought out startlingly his resemblance to antique bronze, the profile of Pallas, still, austere, bowed a little in the shadow of the rock. "Oh! If you could only understand the truth that is in me!" he added.

She waited, as if too astounded to speak, till he looked up again, and then, with unnatural force as if defending herself from some unspoken aspersion, "It's I who stand for truth here! Believe in you! In you, who by a heartless falsehood—and nothing else, nothing else, do you hear?—have brought me here, deceived, cheated, as in some abominable farce!" She sat down on a boulder, rested her chin in her hands, in the pose of simple grief—mourning for herself.

"It only wanted this. Why! Oh! Why is it that ugliness, ridicule, and baseness must fall across my path?"

On that height, alone with the sky, they spoke to each other as if the earth had fallen away from under their feet.

The Planter of Malata

"Are you grieving for your dignity? He was a mediocre soul and could have given you but an unworthy existence."

She did not even smile at those words, but, superb, as if lifting a corner of the veil, she turned on him slowly.

"And do you imagine I would have devoted myself to him for such a purpose! Don't you know that reparation was due to him from me? A sacred debt—a fine duty. To redeem him would not have been in my power—I know it. But he was blameless and it was for me to come forward. Don't you see that in the eyes of the world nothing could have rehabilitated him so completely as his marriage with me? No word of evil could be whispered of him after I had given him my hand. As to giving myself up to anything less than the shaping of a man's destiny—if I thought I could do it I would abhor myself...." She spoke with authority in her deep, fascinating, unemotional voice. Renouard meditated, gloomy, as if over some sinister riddle of a beautiful sphinx met on the wild road of his life.

"Yes. Your father was right. You are one of these aristocrats..."

She drew herself up haughtily.

"What do you say? My father!... I am aristocrat."

"Oh! I don't mean that you are like the men and women of the time of armours, castles, and great deeds. Oh, no! They stood on the naked soil, had traditions to be faithful to, had their feet on this earth of passions and death which is not a hothouse. They would have been too plebeian for you since they had to lead, to suffer with, to understand the commonest humanity. No, you are merely of the topmost layer, disdainful and superior, the mere pure froth and bubble on the inscrutable depths which some day will toss you out of existence. But you are you! You are you! You are the eternal love itself—only, O Divinity, it isn't your body, it is your soul that is made of foam."

She listened as if in a dream. He had succeeded so well in

The Planter of Malata

his effort to drive back the flood of his passion that his life itself seemed to run with it out of his body. At that moment he felt as one dead speaking. But the headlong wave returning with tenfold force flung him on her suddenly, with open arms and blazing eyes. She found herself like a feather in his grasp, helpless, unable to struggle, with her feet off the ground. But this contact with her, maddening like too much felicity, destroyed its own end. Fire ran through his veins, turned his passion to ashes, burnt him out and left him empty, without force—almost without desire. He let her go before she could cry out. And she was so used to the forms of repression enveloping, softening the crude impulses of old humanity that she no longer believed in their existence as if it were an exploded legend. She did not recognize what had happened to her. She came safe out of his arms, without a struggle, not even having felt afraid.

"What's the meaning of this?" she said, outraged but calm in a scornful way.

He got down on his knees in silence, bent low to her very feet, while she looked down at him, a little surprised, without animosity, as if merely curious to see what he would do. Then, while he remained bowed to the ground pressing the hem of her skirt to his lips, she made a slight movement. He got up.

"No," he said. "Were you ever so much mine what could I do with you without your consent? No. You don't conquer a wraith, cold mist, stuff of dreams, illusion. It must come to you and cling to your breast. And then! Oh! And then!"

All ecstasy, all expression went out of his face.

"Mr. Renouard," she said, "though you can have no claim on my consideration after having decoyed me here for the vile purpose, apparently, of gloating over me as your possible prey, I will tell you that I am not perhaps the extraordinary being you think I am. You may believe me. Here I stand for truth itself."

"What's that to me what you are?" he answered. "At a sign

213

The Planter of Malata

from you I would climb up to the seventh heaven to bring you down to earth for my own—and if I saw you steeped to the lips in vice, in crime, in mud, I would go after you, take you to my arms—wear you for an incomparable jewel on my breast. And that's love—true love—the gift and the curse of the gods. There is no other."

The truth vibrating in his voice made her recoil slightly, for she was not fit to hear it—not even a little—not even one single time in her life. It was revolting to her; and in her trouble, perhaps prompted by the suggestion of his name or to soften the harshness of expression, for she was obscurely moved, she spoke to him in French.

"*Assez! J'ai horreur de tout cela,*" she said.

He was white to his very lips, but he was trembling no more. The dice had been cast, and not even violence could alter the throw. She passed by him unbendingly, and he followed her down the path. After a time she heard him saying:

"And your dream is to influence a human destiny?"

"Yes!" she answered curtly, unabashed, with a woman's complete assurance.

"Then you may rest content. You have done it."

She shrugged her shoulders slightly. But just before reaching the end of the path she relented, stopped, and went back to him.

"I don't suppose you are very anxious for people to know how near you came to absolute turpitude. You may rest easy on that point. I shall speak to my father, of course, and we will agree to say that he has died—nothing more."

"Yes," said Renouard in a lifeless voice. "He is dead. His very ghost shall be done with presently."

She went on, but he remained standing stock still in the dusk. She had already reached the three palms when she heard behind her a loud peal of laughter, cynical and joyless, such as is heard in smoking-rooms at the end of a scandalous story. It made her feel positively faint for a moment.

214

The Planter of Malata

XI

Slowly a complete darkness enveloped Geoffrey Renouard. His resolution had failed him. Instead of following Felicia into the house, he had stopped under the three palms, and leaning against a smooth trunk had abandoned himself to a sense of an immense deception and the feeling of extreme fatigue. This walk up the hill and down again was like the supreme effort of an explorer trying to penetrate the interior of an unknown country, the secret of which is too well defended by its cruel and barren nature. Decoyed by a mirage, he had gone too far —so far that there was no going back. His strength was at an end. For the first time in his life he had to give up, and with a sort of despairing self-possession he tried to understand the cause of the defeat. He did not ascribe it to that absurd dead man.

The hesitating shadow of Luiz approached him unnoticed till it spoke timidly. Renouard started.

"Eh? What? Dinner waiting? You must say I beg to be excused. I can't come. But I shall see them tomorrow morning, at the landing place. Take your orders from the professor as to the sailing of the schooner. Go now."

Luiz, dumbfounded, retreated into the darkness. Renouard did not move, but hours afterwards, like the bitter fruit of his immobility, the words: "I had nothing to offer to her vanity," came from his lips in the silence of the island. And it was then only that he stirred, only to wear the night out in restless tramping up and down the various paths of the plantation. Luiz, whose sleep was made light by the consciousness of some impending change, heard footsteps passing by his hut, the firm tread of the master; and turning on his mats emitted a faint Tse! Tse! Tse! of deep concern.

Lights had been burning in the bungalow almost all through the night; and with the first sign of day began the bustle of

The Planter of Malata

departure. House-boys walked processionally carrying suitcases and dressing-bags down to the schooner's boat, which came to the landing-place at the bottom of the garden. Just as the rising sun threw its golden nimbus around the purple shape of the headland, the Planter of Malata was perceived pacing bareheaded the curve of the little bay. He exchanged a few words with the sailing-master of the schooner, then remained by the boat, standing very upright, his eyes on the ground, waiting.

He had not long to wait. Into the cool, over-shadowed garden the professor descended first, and came jauntily down the path in a lively cracking of small shells. With his closed parasol hooked on his forearm, and a book in his hand, he resembled a banal tourist more than was permissible to a man of his unique distinction. He waved the disengaged arm from a distance, but at close quarters, arrested before Renouard's immobility, he made no offer to shake hands. He seemed to appraise the aspect of the man with a sharp glance, and made up his mind.

"We are going back by Suez," he began almost boisterously. "I have been looking up the sailing lists. If the zephyrs of your Pacific are only moderately propitious I think we are sure to catch the mail boat due in Marseilles on the 18th of March. This will suit me excellently. . . ." He lowered his tone. "My dear young friend, I'm deeply grateful to you."

Renouard's set lips moved.

"Why are you grateful to me?"

"Ah! Why? In the first place you might have made us miss the next boat, mightn't you? . . . I don't thank you for your hospitality. You can't be angry with me for saying that I am truly thankful to escape from it. But I am grateful to you for what you have done, and—for being what you are."

It was difficult to define the flavour of that speech, but Renouard received it with an austerely equivocal smile. The professor stepping into the boat opened his parasol and sat

The Planter of Malata

down in the stern-sheets waiting for the ladies. No sound of human voice broke the fresh silence of the morning while they walked the broad path, Miss Moorsom a little in advance of her aunt.

When she came abreast of him Renouard raised his head.

"Good-bye, Mr. Renouard," she said in a low voice, meaning to pass on; but there was such a look of entreaty in the blue gleam of his sunken eyes that after an imperceptible hesitation she laid her hand, which was ungloved, in his extended palm.

"Will you condescend to remember me?" he asked while an emotion with which she was angry made her pale cheeks flush and her black eyes sparkle.

"This is a strange request for you to make," she said, exaggerating the coldness of her tone.

"Is it? Impudent perhaps. Yet I am not so guilty as you think; and bear in mind that to me you can never make reparation."

"Reparation? To you! It is you who can offer me no reparation for the offence against my feelings—and my person; for what reparation can be adequate for your odious and ridiculous plot so scornful in its implication, so humiliating to my pride. No! I don't want to remember you."

Unexpectedly, with a tightening grip, he pulled her nearer to him, and looking into her eyes with fearless despair—

"You'll have to.... I shall haunt you," he said firmly.

Her hand was wrenched out of his grasp before he had time to release it. Felicia Moorsom stepped into the boat, sat down by the side of her father, and breathed tenderly on her crushed fingers.

The professor gave her a sidelong look—nothing more. But the professor's sister, yet on shore, had put up her long-handled double eye-glass to look at the scene. She dropped it with a faint rattle.

The Planter of Malata

"I've never in my life heard anything so crude said to a lady," she murmured, passing before Renouard with a perfectly erect head. When, a moment afterwards, softening suddenly, she turned to throw a goodbye to that young man, she saw only his back in the distance moving towards the bungalow. She watched him go in—amazed—before she too left the soil of Malata.

Nobody disturbed Renouard in that room where he had shut himself in to breathe the evanescent perfume of her who for him was no more, till late in the afternoon when the half-caste was heard on the other side of the door.

He wanted the master to know that the trader *Janet* was just entering the cove.

Renouard's strong voice on his side of the door gave him most unexpected instructions. He was to pay off the boys with the cash in the office and arrange with the captain of the *Janet* to take every worker away from Malata, returning them to their respective homes. An order on the Dunster firm would be given to him in payment.

And again the silence of the bungalow remained unbroken till, next morning, the half-caste came to report that everything was done. The plantation boys were embarking now.

Through a crack in the door a hand thrust at him a piece of paper, and the door slammed to so sharply that Luiz stepped back. Then approaching cringingly the keyhole, in a propitiatory tone he asked:

"Do I go too, master?"

"Yes. You too. Everybody."

"Master stop here alone?"

Silence. And the half-caste's eyes grew wide with wonder. But he also, like those "ignorant savages," the plantation boys, was only too glad to leave an island haunted by the ghost of a white man. He backed away noiselessly from the mysterious silence in the closed room, and only in the very doorway of the bungalow allowed himself to give vent to his feelings by a deprecatory and pained—

"Tse! Tse! Tse!"

XII

The Moorsoms did manage to catch the homeward mail boat all right, but had only twenty-four hours in town. Thus the sentimental Willie could not see very much of them. This did not prevent him afterwards from relating at great length, with manly tears in his eyes, how poor Miss Moorsom—the fashionable and clever beauty—found her betrothed in Malata only to see him die in her arms. Most people were deeply touched by the sad story. It was the talk of a good many days.

But the all-knowing Editor, Renouard's only friend and crony, wanted to know more than the rest of the world. From professional incontinence, perhaps, he thirsted for a full cup of harrowing detail. And when he noticed Renouard's schooner lying in port day after day he sought the sailing master to learn the reason. The man told him that such were his instructions. He had been ordered to lie there a month before returning to Malata. And the month was nearly up. "I will ask you to give me a passage," said the Editor.

He landed in the morning at the bottom of the garden and found peace, stillness, sunshine reigning everywhere, the doors and windows of the bungalow standing wide open, no sight of a human being anywhere, the plants growing rank and tall on the deserted fields. For hours the Editor and the schooner's crew, excited by the mystery, roamed over the island shouting Renouard's name; and at last set themselves in grim silence to explore systematically the uncleared bush and the deeper ravines in search of his corpse. What had happened? Had he been murdered by the boys? Or had he simply, capricious and secretive, abandoned his plantation taking the people with him. It was impossible to tell what had

The Planter of Malata

happened. At last, towards the decline of the day, the Editor and the sailing master discovered a track of sandals crossing a strip of sandy beach on the north shore of the bay. Following this track fearfully, they passed round the spur of the headland, and there on a large stone found the sandals, Renouard's white jacket, and the Malay sarong of chequered pattern which the Planter of Malata was well known to wear when going to bathe. These things made a little heap, and the sailor remarked, after gazing at it in silence—

"Birds have been hovering over this for many a day."

"He's gone bathing and got drowned," cried the Editor in dismay.

"I doubt it, sir. If he had been drowned anywhere within a mile from the shore the body would have been washed out on the reefs. And our boats have found nothing so far."

Nothing was ever found—and Renouard's disappearance remained in the main inexplicable. For to whom could it have occurred that a man would set out calmly to swim beyond the confines of life—with a steady stroke—his eyes fixed on a star!

Next evening, from the receding schooner, the Editor looked back for the last time at the deserted island. A black cloud hung listlessly over the high rock on the middle hill; and under the mysterious silence of that shadow Malata lay mournful, with an air of anguish in the wild sunset, as if remembering the heart that was broken there.

Commentary on 'The Planter of Malata'

Writing to a friend about *Within the Tides*, the collection from which this tale comes, Conrad said: 'I cherish a particular feeling for that volume as a deliberate attempt on four different methods of telling a story—an essay in craftsmanship which of course the public won't notice.' But this tale is narrated directly by an omniscient observer, the simplest technique of all, and we are unlikely to take as much notice of the technique as of the story's extreme romanticism, its reworking of a familiar Conrad theme (the dangers of isolation), and of the portrayal of the two main characters.

Conrad was working on *Victory* at the time when he wrote this tale and this perhaps accounts for the similarities between Geoffrey Renouard and Axel Heyst; both have chosen to live in isolation and detachment from normal human intercourse and as a result both find themselves unable to come to terms with life when faced with a crisis and commit suicide. Martin Decoud in *Nostromo* shares many of the same characteristics and the same fate but his love for the virtuous and high-principled Antonia Avellanos is much easier to understand than Renouard's passion for Felicia. The dangers of isolation are spelt out to Renouard by the Editor in the third section. When Renouard says he does not see why he should make a long stay on the mainland, the Editor replies: 'For your mental health, my boy.... To get used to human faces

Commentary on 'The Planter of Malata'

so that they don't hit you in the eye so hard when you walk about the streets. To get friendly with your kind.' Ironically Renouard has already been hit very hard in the eye by Miss Moorsom. This man who was 'ready enough for arduous enterprises' and who 'doesn't count the cost' but who was 'inclined to evade the small complications of existence' finds himself unable to cope with a major complication—falling in love. We may well feel that Conrad's greatest success in this story is the carefully controlled contrast between Renouard's silent, smouldering passion and the shallow social niceties of the Dunsters' dinner parties and the platitudinous chatter of the Editor.

There is irony enough in the spectacle of this self-confident empiricist becoming the helpless victim of a paralysing love, but Conrad reserves his finest irony for the revelation that Felicia is a frigid and selfish girl with a closer affinity to Diana than to Venus or Minerva. Her true motive for wanting to rescue and marry Arthur is revealed to us in remarks made to the unheeding Renouard by Professor Moorsom. Having characterized his daughter as the director of the department of sentiment in his household, he goes on to describe her as having 'moved, breathed, existed, and even triumphed in the mere smother and froth of life—the brilliant froth . . . a sort of superior debauchery . . . meaning nothing, leading nowhere.' He suspects that she is 'merely deceiving her own heart by this dangerous trifling with romantic images.' And it is abundantly clear to us that her concern is less for the wronged man than for her own reputation and self-respect. Her egocentric determination to shape a man's destiny is purely selfish and she stands fully revealed at last in her curt response to Renouard's passionate declaration of love. '*Assez! J'ai horreur de tout cela*' (Stop it! I loathe all that sort of thing).

There is no need to stress the irony of such words issuing from the lips of one described as 'Venus' and even 'the eternal

Commentary on 'The Planter of Malata'

love itself', but one may be left with the impression that this contradictory element in Felicia's character is due to the lack of a clear purpose on the author's part—or two irreconcilable purposes; she can hardly be both a Divinity and a shallow and purposeless society girl. Conrad does not really succeed in making the passion convincing despite the whole wealth of classical allusion brought in to reinforce Felicia's awe-inspiring beauty in Renouard's eyes, or the latter's 'daemonic' dream of her marble head crumbling into dust in his hands. Perhaps Conrad's ambivalent attitude towards Felicia is due in part to memories of his own early rejection by Doña Rita. It is certainly true that he seemed to find romantic love an uncongenial subject and was seldom very successful in portraying it. The decline of his later fiction is usually attributed to his giving more and more space to this essential ingredient for popular success at the expense of the detailed analysis of the psychological or moral aspects of masculine self-knowledge which he handled with so much more subtlety.

One can certainly detect an element of self-defence in his Author's Note to *Within the Tides*: 'Indeed the task of the translator of passions into speech may be pronounced "too difficult"'. The difficulty is not overcome by the melodramatic excesses of much of the phraseology: Felicia's mere presence makes Renouard feel 'fire in his breast, a humming in his ears, and a complete disorder in his mind', or he notes 'the crimson of her ear-lobes against the live whiteness of her complexion, the sombre, as if secret, night splendour of her eyes under the writhing flames of her hair'. But Conrad's portrayal of Mrs. Travers in *The Rescue* showed that he could make a better job of the frigid woman who lives in a dream world of false emotions. Despite these weaknesses, the character of Renouard is powerfully conveyed, and as we leave him setting out 'calmly to swim beyond the confines of life', we might ponder upon his kinship with those other victims of loneliness, Carlier and Kayerts. We might also ask

Commentary on 'The Planter of Malata'

ourselves why their fates differed from the survivors: Karain, returning triumphant to his people with his infallible charm, and Leggatt, 'a free man, a proud swimmer striking out for a new destiny.'

SUGGESTIONS FOR FURTHER READING
Victory
The Rescue
Nostromo
Freya of the Seven Isles
A Reader's Guide to Joseph Conrad by Frederick R. Karl. Chapter 8, 'Late Conrad', is particularly relevant
Joseph Conrad's Fiction by John A. Palmer—see Chapter 6, 'Knights and Damsels'
Conrad's Short Fiction by Lawrence Graver—see Chapter 5, 'Last Tales'

224